ROGUE Angel™

Alex Archer

TRIBAL WAYS

A GOLD EAGLE BOOK FROM

WORLDWIDE®

TORONTO • NEW YORK • LONDON
AMSTERDAM • PARIS • SYDNEY • HAMBURG
STOCKHOLM • ATHENS • TOKYO • MILAN
MADRID • WARSAW • BUDAPEST • AUCKLAND

First edition July 2010

ISBN-13: 978-0-373-62144-6

TRIBAL WAYS

Special thanks and acknowledgment to
Victor Milán for his contribution to this work.

Printed in U.S.A.

THe
LEGEND

...THE ENGLISH COMMANDER TOOK
JOAN'S SWORD AND RAISED IT HIGH.

The broadsword, plain and unadorned,
gleamed in the firelight. He put the tip against
the ground and his foot at the center of the blade.
The broadsword shattered, fragments falling
into the mud. The crowd surged forward,
peasant and soldier, and snatched the shards
from the trampled mud. The commander tossed
the hilt deep into the crowd.
Smoke almost obscured Joan, but she continued
praying till the end, until finally the flames climbed
her body and she sagged against the restraints.

Joan of Arc died that fateful day in France,
but her legend and sword are reborn....

PROLOGUE

Standing in the open door of the RV with a mug of coffee steaming in his hand Paul Stavriakos cursed the freezing wind and wondered why he'd ever moved to the Great Plains.

"Either go or stay, but shut the damn door," Allison York called from the bed. "That wind is freezing."

Paul sighed and stepped down to the grass, still dry and tan from winter. He shut the door behind him. The wind howled around him.

Dawn was still a drizzle of red along the horizon. Clouds hid the stars overhead.

The land was all tilted planes. It was flat, in a way, but flat that tipped this way and that in big plates furred in yellow-brown grass. There wasn't much relief; but it was deceptive land, with more hollows and heights than first struck the eye.

"Not enough to cut the damn wind, though," he muttered to himself.

Lights appeared in the trailer that Donny Luttrell shared with TiJean Watts. The battered Toyota pickup with the camper shell belonging to Dr. Ted Watkins from the State Archaeological Division was rocking on its suspension more than the wind's buffeting would account for. Paul hoped he was pulling on his jeans. The muffled swearing coming from inside seemed to support that thesis.

"Ever wonder why those old Indians picked a miserable spot like this to make their camp?"

Paul turned. Eric James was swinging off the back of his old buckskin gelding. He wore a sheepskin coat and a battered felt cowboy hat. The hair hanging in thick braids to either side of his head was gray as slate. The wide face between, the color of Oklahoma clay, had a tough and weathered quality but was barely lined. A full-blooded Comanche and full-time rancher, he owned the land where they stood.

He returned to his saddle for a moment, then turned back to Paul. He held white bags with a colorful logo in each hand.

"Brought doughnuts for you kids," he said. "Hope you make decent coffee. Wasn't carrying *that* in my saddlebags."

Paul smiled. It felt as if ice was cracking off his face. The digging season seemed to start earlier each year. The ground wasn't fully frozen. That was about all you could say for it.

Then again, he thought, it's getting harder and harder

to beat the protestors out here. Digging in colder and worse weather was one way of keeping them at bay as long as possible. Even so, they'd be out there with their signs and their shouting as soon as the day warmed up.

The trailer door opened. TiJean started down the steps wearing jeans and a T-shirt. He let out a yelp and popped back inside like a startled prairie dog. The door banged behind him. A second-generation Haitian from Miami, he didn't quite get winter. Even if it was supposed to be spring on the Great Plains.

Like an unlovely butterfly from its cocoon Ted emerged from his camper. Unlike their host his face looked as if each of his fifty years had stomped it hard on the way out the door. He was skinny, with long dark-blond hair hanging out from his grimy Sooners ball cap, white stubble sticking out of his long chin and gaunt cheeks. He wore a drab plaid lumberman's jacket. He completed his ensemble with faded blue jeans over pointy-toed cowboy boots.

"Another lovely day in western Oklahoma," he muttered. "Christ."

Paul winced as the older man unwrapped a piece of gum and popped it into his mouth. Ted was trying to quit smoking. Apparently gum was his designated sub-stitute crutch.

Allison started out from the RV. Like the trailer it was owned by their employer, the University of Oklahoma at Norman. Unlike the trailer it was at least relatively modern. Since Paul and Allison were the assistant pro-fessor and graduate student on the dig, they claimed it by right of rank. Allison had a red wool knit cap pulled down over her long, straight blond hair and a white Hudson's Bay blanket with big bold stripes of blue, yellow, green and red wrapped around her slim frame. Gray sweatpants showed below the bottom of the blanket above fleece-lined moccasins.

"Hey, Ally," Paul called softly. "Could you make more coffee?"

He didn't speak loudly, partly out of consideration for Allison, but mainly to keep his own head from cracking open. They probably shouldn't have drunk quite so much last night, he thought. Indeed, they shouldn't have been drinking inside the RV at all, since it was contrary to university policy.

Not that it's the only rule we're breaking, he thought. And what the hey? We have proud archaeologist traditions to uphold.

Allison scowled. The spanking of the cold wind was making her cheeks red and her blue eyes water. "Why me?"

"Because you're still mostly inside where it's warm," he said, "and we have the only coffeemaker that works."

"Chauvinist," she said. "Did your girlfriend who's coming to visit make you coffee?" She turned and went back inside, banging the door.

"She's not my girlfriend," he shouted at the door. "She's just an old friend."

Actually, Annja Creed was a young friend. She was a year or two younger than Paul. They'd met on a dig four years ago. Sparks had flown; the fire they kindled flamed up and flamed out. The end.

Now she was a semifamous cable-TV personality and globe-trotting archaeologist, coming out at his request to touch bases and look the dig over. Inviting her hadn't even been his idea. It had been at the department's request, in the probably unrealistic expectation that the resident expert on *Chasing History's Monsters* might bring some good publicity their way.

"Women," Donny said. He had emerged from the trailer to stretch and yawn, like an outsize nearsighted cherub with his dark curly hair and beard, his thick-lensed glasses and his belly sticking out between his green-and-white University of North Dakota T-shirt and sweatpants. He was a cold-weather guy and liked to show off his indifference to low temperatures. He wore sandals on otherwise bare feet. "You can't live with them, you can't—"

"We Numunu have an old tradition," Eric said, interrupting him, using the Comanche word for his people. "We kill anybody says a cliché. Scalp 'em, too."

Paul tried not to wince. Native Americans on campus usually believed, or at least said, all the right things. Outside the university those he met almost to a man and woman defiantly called themselves Indians and expressed contempt for political correctness in any form. You just had to get used to it. And for what it was worth Eric seemed genuinely friendly.

For one thing he let them dig his land—invited them to, when he accidentally unearthed the paleo-Indian site—in the face of rising rumblings of opposition from some of his people. For another he brought doughnuts. Even if they were bad for you.

Paul looked to Eric. "Really nice of you to be okay with us diggin' up your ancestors, dude."

"Not *my* ancestors," their host said. "We didn't live here then. Either we or the Kiowa ran off the people whose ancestors these were around three hundred years ago."

He shook his head. "Well, one good thing about this damn cold wind—it'll keep the professional Indians inside by their space heaters for a while. As much money as I give to the Nation every year the loafs-about-the-fort got nothing better to do than send me death threats and try to trespass so they can picket me on my own land."

"Are you crazy, man?" TiJean's voice, muffled by the layers of clothing he had donned before venturing forth again, rose perilously near to cracking. He was a freshman, only nominally out of adolescence. "Why don't you got nothin' on your *feet?*"

He was staring in horror at his roomie's feet.

"Jesus, TiJean," Donny said. "What, are you dressed to scale Everest?"

"For Sweden," Ted added. The Floridian undergrad wore a blue-and-yellow parka with the fur-clad hood over his head.

Allison emerged from the RV bearing a tray with a pot of coffee and an assortment of chipped and colorful mugs. "All right, you big, strong, helpless men. The woman comes to the rescue."

"Ah," Ted croaked. "The stuff of life itself!"

Allison held the tray while the rest crowded around. "Best leave some for me," she said ominously, "if you don't want to wind up wearing it. Whoa, does anybody hear a hissing?"

"Wow! Doughnuts!" Donny exclaimed, his eyes belatedly lighting on the two paper bags Eric had left on the grass.

"Yeah," Paul said after a beat. "I do. Strange."

Midway to the doughnuts Donny froze. "Don't tell me there's a snake?"

TiJean crowed laughter. "Who's a wimp now, Eskimo Boy? Afraid of a little bitty old snake."

"Whoever heard a snake hiss that continuously?" Allison asked.

"Or that loud, to hear it over this wind," Paul said.

"Wait," Donny said. "Did you guys see a shadow move? Off there to the left—"

"Shadow?" Paul said, feeling an inexplicable chill that had nothing to do with the wind.

"Yeah," Allison said. "I thought I saw something out of the corner of my eye. Like a dog or something."

"Shit," Donny said, "that'd be a big dog."

They were all turning and staring around. Paul felt a little woozy. Maybe he was turning too fast, getting dizzy.

"We should all chill," he said. Then he noticed that Eric James had drawn the slab-sided .45 automatic he wore on his hip and was holding it two-handed with its muzzle tipped toward the unfriendly sky. His face was the consistency of stone.

"This is starting to freak me out—" Donny began.

Allison's scream, sharp as glass, made Paul spin toward her. As he did something hot splashed across his face.

For a moment he thought she'd thrown scalding coffee on him.

Then the darkness hit him.

1

It was all over the flat-screen TVs hung from the rafters and tuned to CNN when Annja entered the airport terminal. Five dead and one gravely injured in an inexplicable attack on an archaeological dig in western Oklahoma.

It's so tragic about those other poor people, she thought as she headed to the baggage claim. Does it make me a bad person that I feel glad that Paul's the one who survived?

She hadn't been coming to rekindle any old embers. It had been good with Paul while it lasted. And when it was done, it was over. He was still a sweet guy, if a little bit of a player, and a good archaeologist on the tenure track at the university.

Now she just hoped he was still on any track at all.

She collected her single black bag. And I thought I

was due for a little relaxation here, she thought as she walked briskly through the crowds toward the car rental desk.

Because of the severity of his injuries, Paul had been taken by helicopter from the site west of Lawton to the trauma unit in Norman, right outside Oklahoma City.

Finding the trauma center wasn't hard. Once inside amid the bright lights and muted sounds and quietly purposeful traffic of the hospital, things got a little dicier. The staff initially tried to keep Annja from seeing Paul in intensive care.

It seemed to be a well-run facility, so Annja didn't even try playing her journalist-cum-TV-personality card. It was never her first choice in any event. But Paul's family had yet to arrive, given that the crime had actually occurred while she was in transit from New York to Houston. His next of kin, it seemed, would only arrive late that evening. Though the nurses wouldn't say so, Annja got the sickening impression they didn't expect him to live long enough to see them.

In the meantime, Paul was asking incessantly for Annja Creed so his doctors and the police officer in charge of the case agreed to let her in.

Sunlight streamed through the window. The early online weather reports had showed clouds over western Oklahoma, but they'd dissipated by the time her flight touched down.

Paul was all tubes and bandages and taped-on wires. Half his face was obscured by a bandage. But his good brown eye was open. It turned toward her as she walked in the door.

"Annja," he said. His voice was a croak. He tried to sit up.

"Paul." She stopped in the doorway, momentarily overcome.

The nurse who had escorted Annja to the room—a short, wide woman—moved past Annja. Though a head shorter she was heavy enough to push Annja aside as if she were a child. Annja frowned, but held her temper. She's doing her job, she told herself.

"Now, Paul, calm down," the nurse said. She turned and glared back with narrowed blue eyes. "Ms. Creed, I'm afraid you're going to have to cut short your visit, after all."

"No," Paul said. Alarms shrilled as his heart rate spiked. "Please, Roslee. Please! I have to talk to her. I have to tell her."

The nurse gave Annja a speculative scowl. The businesslike amiability with which she had initially greeted Annja was long gone.

"Okay," she said. "He seems to really need to get something off his chest. It may be good for him to have company. I'll give you five minutes. And I do *not* want you stressing my patient. Please tell me you understand."

Annja took no offense at the woman's words or her tone. A good nurse had the same outlook on anyone or anything that might prove detrimental to her patients as a mother grizzly bear toward potential threats to her cubs.

"I understand," Annja said. And she did. Perfectly. Herself a chronic defender of innocence, she could only approve of the nurse's protectiveness.

The nurse looked at her a beat longer. Then she nodded. "All right. Call me if any changes happen. I'll be right outside."

The nurse left. Annja sidestepped to give her plenty of clearance. Then she moved forward and took Paul's unbandaged hand.

"Paul, what happened?"

The torn lips quirked into a painful smile. "Something right up your alley, Annja."

"What's that, Paul?"

Suddenly his fingers clenched hers in a death grip. "A *monster*," he said.

For a mad moment she thought he was making a joke well beyond good taste. But his lone visible eye showed white all around, and a tear rose in the corner of it and rolled down his cheek. His whole body seemed to tense.

"Paul," she said, trying to keep her own voice low and steady. "Please calm down."

"No! There's no time. There's something out there, Annja. Something awful. It killed them."

"What did?"

His fingers dug into her hand. "I told you. That— creature."

"Paul, please. Settle down. You're getting upset and not making any sense."

"Annja! I saw it. It was a wolf, but it wasn't. Sometimes it seemed like a man, sometimes like an animal. And it killed and killed."

"That's just in the movies," Annja said.

"No! It looked like a wolf but didn't move like one."

He shook his head from side to side so violently Annja was afraid he'd pull something loose. "No! No! It was terrible. Oh, God. It killed them. It was so fast. So strong. Not anything natural—"

"Why would a wolf attack such a large group of people?" she asked. It made no sense to her that a solitary member of a pack-hunting species would attack multiple human beings. It totally reversed the whole mathematics of wolf predation.

"It wasn't natural, I tell you. Wasn't an animal!" His eye rolled. "Annja, listen. It wasn't an animal. It wasn't. And it's hunting me!"

He sat up and grabbed her arm with his good hand. Alarms began to shrill.

"It was a skinwalker! A Navajo wolf! I saw his eyes—those glowing—"

The frantic cry ended.

Paul seemed to shrink, then fell back onto the bed. His one visible eye stared at the ceiling.

The keening of the flatline alarms was barely audible through the roaring in Annja's ears.

2

"What's your interest in this poor deceased fella, Ms. Creed?"

Lieutenant Tom Ten Bears of the Oklahoma Highway Patrol sat down behind the plain wooden desk in his office. He had the unmistakable look of an officer who'd spent many years with the force. Not a tall man, he was built strong and low to the ground, short in the legs, wide around the middle, suggesting still both strength and a certain agility.

Annja sat across from him in a not very comfortable wooden chair. It reminded her way too much of being called before the Mother Superior back at Our Lady of Perpetual Sorrow. She suspected the visiting-the-principal effect wasn't entirely accidental.

"We're friends, Lieutenant," she said. "Uh, were friends."

The highway patrol officer's round, pockmarked

face, beneath a salt-and-pepper military cut, was set in lines and contours of grave compassion. He probably gets a lot of practice with that look in his line of work, she realized. It also didn't mean he didn't feel it.

The office walls were wood paneling. An Oklahoma state flag hung behind him, along with a plaque in the arrowhead shape of the OHP patch, certificates of completion from training courses and numerous citations, including a commendation from the Comanche Nation. From his features and body type, which would have been burly and bearlike even if he hadn't been carrying a certain excess above the belt, Annja suspected he was a member of the Nation himself. She gathered they hadn't named this Comanche County for nothing.

"My condolences," he told her. "I know that don't help much. All the times I've offered condolences over the years, I never yet figured out a way that actually does a body any good. I keep trying."

"I appreciate it, Lieutenant. Really."

"It was unusual for them to let you in to see him. But the ICU staff tell me he kept asking for you so insistently they figured it was better for him to let him see you."

"Maybe that was a mistake," she said, faltering.

He shook his head. "No point second-guessing something like that, Ms. Creed. That poor boy was pretty torn up. I don't reckon he could've lasted long regardless of anything you did or didn't do."

"Thanks," Annja said.

She drew in a deep breath and tried to ignore the stinging in her eyes. "I was coming out to visit him," she said. "He was also kind enough to want to consult with me on the dig, even though pre-Columbian North American archaeology is way outside my area of study."

"You're doin' *me* a favor, Ms. Creed, by comin' out here to see me," he said. "I was needing to interview you, anyway."

He put on a pair of heavy-framed reading glasses and moved his mouse around on the pad, peering at a flat-screen monitor set at an angle so as not to intrude between him and a visitor. Aside from an in-box stacked with papers, the only other objects on his desk were a picture of a grinning young and handsome Indian man wearing an Army uniform, a much younger girl, maybe twelve, with pigtails, both built along much more aerodynamic lines than the lieutenant, and another picture of a young man in BDUs and combat gear with a bullet-pocked adobe wall for a backdrop. The soldier held a CAR-4 assault carbine decked out with the usual array of sights and lights. He looked like the same person as the grinning kid in the other photo, only older. Not so much in years, maybe, but still much older, Annja thought.

"So you work for a television show," he said.

"Yes. I'm kind of the resident skeptic—the token voice of reason. I suspect Paul's superiors hoped that by inviting me out they might put their department in the way of some free publicity."

"The anthro department at OU wanted to get on something called Chasing History's Monsters?"

She shrugged. "The hope of getting on TV can have a strange effect on people. Even intelligent, well-educated ones."

He made a face, took off the glasses and looked at

her. "Maybe the monster thing's actually appropriate now. Is that what brings you to see me, Ms. Creed?"

"I want to learn everything I can about what happened to my friend," she said. "Also his colleagues. And the poor man whose property the dig site was on."

"Old Eric," Ten Bears said. "Pretty righteous guy. Did well for himself and his family from leasing natural-gas rights on some of his land out there south of the Wichita Mountains Wildlife Refuge. Always quick to help out a fellow Nation member or crack a joke. Even if he did have lousy taste in 'em."

"He was a friend of yours?"

Ten Bears nodded. "I know a lot of people in our region. Know a whole lot of Indian good old boys like me."

"I'm sorry."

"Thanks. Listen, it was a pretty ugly scene out there, Ms. Creed. I've worked a lot of homicides over the years. I've worked some pretty terrible accident scenes. Never saw anything like that anywhere. I can't really tell you anything the department hasn't already released to the media. Tell the truth, I'm sorta glad."

He sat back, looking at her. He seemed not unfriendly. Not unkind, in fact. From the laugh lines bracketing his eyes and mouth she guessed he was by nature a pretty decent guy. She also knew that a seasoned homicide investigator wouldn't hesitate to feign those emotions when he didn't feel remotely kind or friendly, if it would help advance the case.

"What'd the decedent tell you?" he asked quietly.

"He said he was attacked by what, frankly,

sounded more like a movie monster than anything in the real world."

"You've had some experience investigating monsters, I guess," he said. "What's your take on that?"

"Are you *serious?* I'm sorry, Lieutenant, I'm not trying to be uncooperative. It just sounds like—a strange question for somebody who seems so no-nonsense to be asking."

"I try not to close any possible avenues of inquiry. Especially in a case like this. I'm not giving away any confidential information when I tell you we don't have a whole lot of ideas on this thing. Not ones that make any sense. So, hey, I'll at least give a listen to ones that might not seem to make much sense. I don't believe in werewolves. But if our perp really is a damn werewolf, I want to be there when they pump silver into his veins or whatever they'd use for an execution. Maybe you'd call it putting him to sleep."

A strangled squeak of laughter escaped Annja's lips before she could clap her hand over her mouth. She bent forward in her chair, then straightened.

"Sorry," she said. "I'm…not normally like that."

"*I'm* sorry," Ten Bears said. "Sometimes I've got pretty lousy taste in jokes, too. I can see you're shaken up some. Anybody would be. Nice young woman like you isn't used to having people up and die right in front of her."

She managed to show no reaction to that statement. Unfortunately she *was* used to having people up and die in front of her. Poor Paul wasn't even the first ex-lover and friend Annja Creed had seen die. Although she was sure she would never get used to that.

None of which she wanted to admit to the lead investigator on Comanche County's most lurid multiple-murder case of modern times.

The thought helped her compose herself. "This has hit me hard, I must admit," she said. "I have to ask you to believe me that I'm not going to pieces on you. And I'm determined to find out what happened to those people."

"All right," he said, nodding and drawing it out. His accent was a weird blend of Indian staccato and cowboy drawl, something she wouldn't have thought was possible. "So, not to be boring or anything, what do you make of what Mr. Stavriakos told you?"

"I don't believe in werewolves, either, Lieutenant. Yet I know Paul Stavriakos is—was—a trained scientist, and not what I'd call an impressionable man. Obviously, something terrible and…unusual happened out at the dig site this morning. The suddenness and speed of the attack, the shock of seeing his friends brutally murdered, the terrible emotional impact of having someone attack him in person, the physical injuries he took—none of those things leads to careful observation.

"The thing is, there are no documented reports of wolf attacks on humans in North America. And I have a hard time imagining any North American animal, no matter how hungry or scared or angry or even rabid, attacking a group of six adult humans, much less being able to kill or mortally wound them all. So I'd have to imagine a very strong man, berserk even, probably wearing a wolf skin or even some kind of costume, was responsible for the attack."

She shook her head. "It's hard for me to imagine what happened no matter what."

"I been doing some digging since I got back from interviewing Mr. Stavriakos at the hospital, before you got there," Ten Bears said. "It turns out there are some pretty well-documented wolf attacks on people. Just a lot of people *said* there weren't, and everybody got believing it. But there hasn't been a wolf seen in Comanche County since the 1890s. And again I'm not giving away much when I tell you that's how I got it sized up, too."

"I understand from the news reports that there have been previous attacks under similar circumstances," Annja said.

"Yeah. Two in New Mexico. One out near the Continental Divide between Gallup and Grants, one between Santa Fe and Albuquerque. All of them on archaeological digs, all of them nasty. Mr. Stavriakos's passing brings the death toll to fifteen. In all three attacks at least one witness survived. They all gave similar details—including that their attacker was either a great big wolf or something that looked like a man-wolf hybrid, like the wolfman from the movie."

He paused, frowning. "Along with what you said, the whole notion it's a single animal with one helluva range, much less three separate animals that suddenly and simultaneously developed a serious taste for archaeologists, strikes me as a lot more far-fetched than it's being a werewolf. We got evidence from all three attacks that tells us there was just the one perpetrator. To me he's obviously got to be a crazy man in some kind of murder suit, like that old Zodiac killer gone Hollywood."

He shifted in his swivel chair and sighed. "Public's gonna be crawling straight up our…trouser legs on this one. I don't even blame 'em. All we can do is try to keep calm, do good police work, let the forensics people do their thing, try to identify this killer and wrap him up before he can do this again. And barring that, hope that next time he tries, some good-old boy archaeologist will pull an octagonal-barrel Winchester lever action out the rifle rack of his pickup truck and let some badly needed sunlight into this bad boy's skull. If you'll pardon my speaking what you might call frankly."

"Nothing I disagree with, Lieutenant," she said. "One thing. Paul seemed very specific that the attacker was a skinwalker. A Navajo wolf—he called it that, too. Beyond the fact that there are legends of skinwalkers, I don't know anything about that, or what might make Paul so positive that was what attacked him. Do you know anything about skinwalker myths?"

"Not much more than you. They're a Navajo thing, just like he said. Not something us *Numunu*—Comanches—would get up to. Nor the Kiowa, either. Not even Plains Apache, far as I know. They still speak an Apache language, but they picked up Plains Indian culture since they joined up with the Comanche and the Kiowa a couple of centuries back."

"I want to see the site, Lieutenant."

He looked at her with frank appraisal. "Is this a personal thing? Or are you gonna go for journalistic status, try the power of the press routine?"

"Whatever it takes," she said. "I want the killer caught. It *is* personal. Of course it is. I've consulted with investigative agencies before—I know enough to keep out of the way of real forensic investigators. And as an archaeologist I certainly know how to avoid contaminating or disturbing a site. Also I may be able to infer something from the dig site that someone who isn't a trained and experienced archaeologist would miss."

His black eyes gazed at her for the space of several breaths. "I'm not proud, Ms. Creed," he said. "Leastwise, not prouder than I am eager to save a whole bunch more poor folks from getting torn up like that. I could use any information I can get. So let's go ahead and call you a consultant on this one. You need a contract?"

She shook her head. "Nor do I need any fees. Let me use your name, and back me up if I need it. I promise I won't embarrass you."

He nodded. "Good enough. And thanks for not asking for any money—things are pretty tight, budgetarily speaking, even for a sensational case like this. I've worked with archaeologists before. Heck, I worked with Ted Watkins, the archaeologist who got killed out there this morning. So I know you understand about not trampling through a crime scene like a herd of buffalo. I wish half the law enforcement people who've been up through there already had half the sense about that kind of thing as you people do. I'll give you the little speech, anyway. Stay out of the way of any cop types, whether they're troopers, county mounties or, heaven help us, the Feds. If you encounter the suspect do not try to detain or interact with him, for God's sake. Otherwise, knock yourself out. And I'll put out the word you're helping me on a discreet kinda basis."

"Thank you, Lieutenant."

"I'm not sure it's a thanking matter, ma'am."

They both stood. He was a good three inches shorter than her. Annja nodded at the beefy revolver holstered at his right hip. It was matte silver metal with contoured wooden grips. They looked well-worn.

"I couldn't help noticing you carry a double-action revolver, Lieutenant," she said. "Looking at the other troopers I thought the Oklahoma Highway Patrol issued Glock 22s."

He looked as if her query surprised him. It clearly didn't displease him.

"Smith & Wesson 657," he said with unmistakable pride. "It's a .41 Magnum, N-frame, stainless. Custom Hogue grips. Got me a special exemption from the department to carry it. Helps I'm a Comanche and all, plus I've been with the patrol since old Quanah Parker was a lance corporal. I got nothing against the Glocks— they're pretty good guns, even if I can't help feeling like they're flimsy for being half made out of plastic and all. And there's nothing wrong with .40 caliber. I just like the authority the .41 Mag gives you, without it having so much recoil it takes all day to haul it back down on target every time you shoot, like a .44 Magnum does. And maybe some of that cowboy wheel-gun mystique."

He slapped the weapon affectionately. "This pup got me all the way through the fast drive to Kuwait City in '91. Not much call to use it then, although it was a power of comfort to me. Been out of the holster a time or two since, though. And never once let me down."

"Kuwait City, 1991? Wait, you were Force RECON?"

"That's right, ma'am. You wouldn't be former military yourself, would you? Or from a service family? You seem to know a fair amount about the forces."

"I have a lot of friends in the military. But—you're a Marine." She already knew better than to say *ex*-Marine.

"*Semper fi,* ma'am!"

"The young man in the photos on your desk is Army."

Ten Bears' thin-lipped mouth tightened ever so slightly, and his eyes narrowed just a hair. "Boy always did know how to piss me off," he muttered. "Even if he did make Ranger."

"Well, thank you, Lieutenant. I'll let you know if I find anything that I think you might be able to use."

"You look like a woman who knows how to take care of herself," he said.

"I like to think I can."

"Well, this isn't the time or the place to show how tough and independent you are."

"What do you mean? Why?"

"There's a mass murderer on the loose," he said. "You didn't forget already?"

"No," she said slowly. "I didn't."

"I'm just joshing you," he said. "About the forgetting part. Not about the murderer. I don't think this fella plays well with others."

"I'll try to stay away from him."

"You be sure to do that. Let us professionals handle him. We do a bad enough job without any help."

She wasn't sure quite how to take that. He seemed

like a man who, for all his cockeyed banter, took his job very seriously. She also didn't think his tongue was more than halfway in his cheek, and wondered just who wasn't doing their job quite so well.

She also knew better than to ask. Lieutenant Ten Bears clearly thought of himself as a stand-up cop. He'd never bad-mouth a fellow officer to an outsider. But he might not be above dropping some sidewise comments about his comrades who didn't measure up.

"One more thing before you go," he told her as she started for the door of his small office. "We got us some young South Plains braves here in western Oklahoma who don't much like white-eyes. And they play rough. Tempers are extrashort right now since some of them don't like it that we got us a great big new casino the Nation's opening up in a few days."

He laughed at her expression. "Don't worry," he said. "They can't fire me for calling them *braves*. Any more than they can make us Indians call ourselves *Native Americans*. That fight we won, anyway. Maybe it's a trend."

Annja had to laugh. She found herself liking the lieutenant.

As she left she thought, I don't believe in werewolves. But there are plenty of things I don't believe in that have a nasty habit of turning up, anyway.

3

The site was a bust.

The sun was setting when Annja got there. The only people present in the mellow dusk light slanting beneath gray clouds were some gloved techs moving gingerly around inside the yellow-tape perimeter whipped constantly by the wind, and a pair of Comanche County deputies in cowboy hats. Both were lean young men, one with hair cut so painfully short it suggested a recent military discharge, the other with gleaming black braids hanging over the dark brown shoulders of his jacket. They both gave her a rock-hard look.

She told the deputies Lieutenant Ten Bears had sent her. Having seen more than her share of interdepartmental rivalry in law enforcement she wasn't sure how they'd respond. But they both instantly broke into smiles. When she showed them her ID they readily allowed her access.

"I've seen you on TV, Ms. Creed," the braided deputy said. He looked marginally older than his partner, and was clearly senior. "I know you'll be careful. Not like some people we've had out here. And on a totally unrelated subject, the FBI just left." He frowned. "I reckon we're mainly out here to keep them federal boys takin' over altogether."

"I was surprised they didn't offer to tip us on the way out," his partner said. He reminded her slightly of the young man in the pictures on Ten Bears' desk, only not so handsome.

Annja nodded, keeping her expression neutral. Like most local law-enforcement types, their regard for the self-billed world's leading investigative agency tended to vary proportionally to their first-hand experience with them.

For her part Annja tried to keep on good terms with people. Especially the ones with guns and implied or explicit permission to use them.

She smiled and nodded in response to the deputies' conversation, which wasn't hard since they seemed to be pleasant and earnest young men. She was surprised and flattered when the junior deputy asked shyly for her autograph. He seemed way too impressed when she signed his notebook with a little note of thanks for his help.

Inside the tape the techs nodded brusquely toward her and went about their business. They kept studiously clear of the dig itself, marked off and gridded by string stretched between stakes. If she wasn't supposed to be there, they clearly reasoned, the county boys would never have let her step over the tape. The evidence team

had jobs to do and not much daylight left to do them.
She guessed nobody wanted to be out there with a generator going and stand lights shining as the temperature
dropped and the prairie wind came up.

She walked around with her arms crossed in front of
her. The wind was indeed picking up as the sun fell
toward the rumpled horizon in the west.

The geographic region lay in the Red Beds Plains,
which ran all the way from Kansas down across the Red
River into Texas. Unlike the true Great Plains farther
north, this land was wide but rolling, dotted with small
stands of trees. There weren't any signs of cultivation
in view. This particular part of the Red Beds was walled
off to the north by the rough granite ramparts, built on
a foundation of Cambrian sandstone beds, of the Wichita
Mountains. Annja's maps showed none of them got as
high as twenty-five hundred feet, and the general elevation of the landscape was around a thousand. To Annja
they were really just rugged hills by the standards of the
ranges not far to the west in New Mexico and Colorado.
Much less the Andes and the Himalayas, which she also
knew firsthand. But the locals seemed adamant about
their "mountain" status, so she felt disinclined to argue.

There really wasn't much to see but some nasty dark
splashes, now pretty dried out, on the short grass and the
rocks. Where it was bare the red soil had sucked the blood
down without much trace she could see, although the
techs were taking samples and the spots where blood
spatter had been found were marked with little plastic
tabs. As were the places where the bodies had been found.

The dig team had been housed in a small RV, a trailer

and a small camper pickup. If there was any sign the attacker had entered any of them Annja hadn't been told. She decided to keep clear of them. She wasn't looking for criminal evidence, and part of being a trained professional at site preservation meant minimizing the risk of messing anything up.

She searched for tactical evidence. How had the attack happened? How had the killer come so swiftly on the six people, whose attention, the transcript of Ten Bears' interview with Paul indicated, had been innocently focused on coffee and doughnuts?

Some blurred tracks in the dirt suggested the killer had gotten close by using the trailer for concealment, before launching a blitz assault. If the tracks had given the investigators any clues as to the true nature of the monster—and whatever or whoever it was, there was no doubt it was a monster—they hadn't shared them with her. She didn't expect they would.

Following a few quiet words from Ten Bears the troopers at the Troop G HQ had also permitted Annja to see photos of the attack scene taken before the bodies were removed. They seemed surprised at how calmly she studied them.

They had affected her. But she was long past the point of breaking down from seeing butchery, no matter how horrific. Especially not mere images.

Now she tried to retrace the killer's steps. He had worked incredibly fast, ripping or slashing open state archaeologist Dr. Watkins's throat, then those of the two undergrads, Watts and Luttrell. Next it attacked Allison York, eviscerating her at a single blow.

All this occurred while Paul had his head turned, and apparently without his becoming aware of it. That was according to what he had told the trooper who rode with him in the helicopter when he was airlifted to Norman.

The killer then struck Paul. The landowner, Eric James, apparently tried to jump the killer when he was attacking Annja's friend. The killer then knocked the Comanche man away, leaped on him and savaged him before turning back to further maul his other victims.

Even with the deadly advantages of surprise and shock, it had been a breathtakingly effective assault. Annja tried to envision what weapons the killer used. Did he carry knives, or wear Freddy Krueger-style knife gloves? Did he actually bite his victims? The highway patrol had declined to divulge to Annja any such particulars. She understood. She had no need to know, and those were the very kinds of things investigators always tried to hold back, on the theory that they could trap the killer, or authenticate any confession, on the basis that he knew details about the crime no one else had access to except detectives.

Also it spared the victims' families reading about or, worse, seeing on TV too many titillatingly horrific details about their loved ones' terrible last moments.

Annja couldn't see the murderer in her mind. Just a blur, blood, people falling. In her mental movie there was no soundtrack. She felt grateful for that.

Having gotten what little she could from the murder scene Annja raised her face to the wind and looked around. The site was along an ancient dry streambed that ran from northwest to southeast. The trailer was parked on the north of the dig team's camp, forming an upside-down U with the camper on the west side and the RV on the east. There was a pretty short line of approach to the humpback trailer from the natural cover provided by the northerly rise and some rocks and tall weeds.

The wind sighed and whispered, promising secrets it never delivered. Annja nodded politely to the evidence techs, then climbed carefully back over the flapping yellow tape and made her way up the little slope to the north.

She found another area marked off by yellow tape fluttering between plastic pickets. Tracks, blurred and indistinct. She realized they'd no doubt been broken down from having impressions taken.

She walked around, trying to survey with an attacker's eye. It wasn't an entirely unfamiliar operation to her.

The approach and setup to the attack had been dead easy. The dig camp had been sited with no remote notion that defense could conceivably be necessary in a normal, orderly, law-abiding universe. The victims had not bothered keeping a lookout. Not even their genial host, secure in the midst of his own domain— unlike his ancestors of a century before, who had found themselves chivvied constantly from one ever-shrink- ing sanctuary to the next. The fact he'd carried his own Marlin lever-action carbine in a saddle scabbard on his horse, which had bolted back to the barn after the attacker spooked it, suggested nothing of paranoia or even wariness to Annja. It was just a Western thing. He did it because he could, and because it came naturally to him.

She began to walk around the camp, periodically coming across more recovered tracks. Using the brushy, rocky terrain, the killer had circled around and around. Scoping his target. That part, at least, had been painfully simple.

He'd stalked them like a cougar hunting sheep. Waited, in the strange, almost submarine predawn light, until he was sure all his prey had come out of their shelters and clumped into a nice compact group. Then he'd slipped down to his final line of departure, crept to the rear of the trailer and attacked.

He'd probably rehearsed the whole event in his mind, crouching there by the trailer. Savored it like a hungry man's anticipation of a juicy steak. Reveled in the sense of power—of knowing something those poor, hapless people didn't know. They were about to die.

She shuddered. "You're not a profiler," she reminded herself in a soft voice.

But Annja had stalked human prey before. And killed. They were all violent men, sometimes women. Not victims but victimizers.

They were always wary, those whose lives she took. And always armed.

By contrast the wolfman was picking easy prey. Like any standard-issue serial killer who picked prostitutes to murder because they'd voluntarily get in the car with him.

And isn't that what any successful predator does? she reminded herself. She shivered. Such moments of identification as this, with a being who epitomized the very evil she lived to fight against, chilled her worse than the rapidly cooling prairie wind.

She shook her head. A strand of her long chestnut hair had worked its way loose from her ponytail. The wind whipped it ticklingly across her face. The same wind teased her with little voices that hinted at meaning but never revealed it.

The western sky was changing from blood to mauve. The sun was long gone. It was time to emulate it. She went back to her rental car, waved to the deputies and drove away.

"DAMN!"

Annja slammed a palm on the steering wheel. The rented car's motor was jerking and coughing. Jouncing along the no-name dirt track, severely rutted before even the spring rains came in earnest, wasn't making the car any happier.

The day's final remnants were a line of hot-iron-red glow along the western hills. Overhead the sky shaded from indigo to star-shot black. Some clouds, their bottoms showing just a faint yellowish glow of artifact light, were sweeping in from the east, piling up darkly as if to show bad intentions.

"Don't do this to me," she told the car. "I don't want to hike up to the highway in freezing rain."

The country was getting seriously hilly, preparatory to becoming the Wichitas. Highway 62, which ran from Lawton straight as a leveling laser west and formed the southern boundary of a spur of the military reservation

that stuck out under the wildlife refuge, still lay, as
closely as she could reckon, three miles north. And it
was cold. Despite the heater she could feel the chill
beating off the car windows like a negative furnace.

For the dozenth time she hauled out her phone. Still
no bars. Her GPS was frozen.

Ahead to her considerable relief she saw artificial
lights—a red-and-yellow oasis in a sea of dark. They
weren't bright lights, but then again this definitely
wasn't the big city. It wasn't even the town of Cache,
whose glow was faintly visible a few miles north, with
its booming population of twenty-four hundred.

The flickering red neon sign read Bad Medicine
Bar & Grill.

Below the battered sign stood a rectangular shack
with a slanted tin roof, fronted by a wooden porch under
a swaybacked roof of planks. The yellow light came
through frosted front windows. The joint looked as if it
had been built during the boom of interstate construction
after World War II, possibly as an ersatz Indian trading
post to attract the tourists. That struck Annja as optimism
insane even by the standards of fifties-boom thinking.

As her rental lumped and bucked closer she saw
there were no actual cars in the parking lot. There was
a pickup truck and a minivan, not too unexpected in this
part of the world, and another pickup hunched in the
shadows out back. Dominating the dirt-and-gravel lot
were at least a score of motorcycles shining in the light
of the sign. The long low-slung beasts had heavily
modified frames with burly V-twin engines. With pride
of place in the middle of the pack sat the least visibly

modified bike of the lot: a big Indian motorcycle with the trademark metal fairings over the tires. It looked to Annja's none-too-expert eye like an original, not one of the never-too-successful attempts to revive the design, or at least the brand.

She went inside. She felt little trepidation. While a single woman had to tread warily in the borderlands, in the U.S. as well as everywhere in the world, she didn't feel much concern. She had no problem with outlaw bikers, which in her experience had meant they had no trouble with her. She tended to take people on their own terms, and that seemed to work.

Of course, part of her intrinsic self-confidence sprang from the proven fact that if you *did* have a problem with Annja Creed, then you had a very bad problem, indeed.

The first things to hit her were heat and the slam of heavy-metal music blasting from a jukebox. Annja pushed on inside and let the door swing closed behind her.

After the darkness of the Plains night the bar's dimly lit interior was still pretty dim. She paused just inside the door a moment to get her bearings. As the place resolved out of gloom she noticed it followed through with the outside's deliberately rustic look, with a wood ceiling and exposed rafters bolstered in placed by square columns so rough-cut they looked as if you'd get splinters if you brushed up on one. It had the usual split-backed vinyl barroom chairs, tables to match the architecture, a bar with a long fly-specked mirror behind it. Bare bulbs cast a faint yellowish glow from lamps hung from the ceiling. Most of the illumination seemed to emanate from the jukebox beside her, which pulsated with polychromatic lights. Glancing down she saw the floor was actual wood planks. With sawdust on it, no less, like the Old West saloon the joint was obviously trying hard to emulate.

Her mental tracking system had already located the bar's occupants. A few bellied up to the bar on foot or rickety-looking wood stools; the rest clustered around tables, or kibitzed while a short, wide man with a black bandanna tied around his head lined up a shot on the pool table in the far corner. Everyone in view but the bartender was dressed in the standard dark-hued biker drag; she could tell that much at a flash impression. She realized the truck and van outside were probably support vehicles for the club. Any joking and talking had stopped when she entered.

Time to break the ice, she thought.

"That's a nice Indian out front," she said.

Then she stopped dead.

There were nothing but Indians inside the bar.

And they looked anything but nice.

4

Everyone was staring at Annja, with nothing resembling a smile or eye twinkle in sight. She was quite aware she may have just said the wrong thing.

It was the classic situation where any attempt at explanation could only make things worse.

"Right, then," she said. "Sorry to intrude. My car broke down. My cell phone isn't getting a signal."

She held the offending object up by her face and waved it. "I'll just borrow the phone, make a quick call and get out of your...way."

She was deliberately playing typical airhead tourist, in hopes they'd think her an idiot too innocuous to be worth bothering with. Not a great plan. But no really great options jumped up to present themselves, either.

She stepped up to the bar, noting that the two burly men next to her had colors on the backs of their old-school bad-biker denim jackets that showed an Indian warrior bestriding an Indian motorcycle—it looked suspiciously like the bike parked out front—shooting a bow. The legend on the back of the nearer biker read Iron Horse People MC, Comanche Nation. The other was similar, but substituted Kiowa for Comanche.

The bartender was a white guy, skinny as an alley cat, with craggy features and wild white hair. He looked white, anyway. Annja knew of numerous people who'd been born into full membership of their respective tribes who looked no more native. His blue eyes were piercing and unwelcoming when they turned on Annja. He didn't ask her pleasure.

"May I borrow the phone, please?" she asked politely.

He jerked his head. "Pay phone," he said. "Booth in the back."

She raised a surprised eyebrow. In this cell-phone era pay phones were becoming an endangered species.

"It's a dead zone," said the biker who stood farther away from Annja to her right. He was a big bearlike guy with his black hair hanging free to his shoulders in twin braids.

"And we like it that way," said the man next to her.

With a shock Annja noticed, more than a beat late, one of the very sort of details she was normally adept at picking up on quickly—he wore a semiautomatic pistol holstered on his left hip. A SIG-Sauer, she thought. She realized just about everyone in the bar was packing.

She was pretty sure it was a violation of Oklahoma law to carry a firearm into an establishment that served alcohol. She decided not to bring it up.

Annja turned in the direction indicated by the bartender and headed for a niche sunk in a plank wall beside a faded and torn poster for a bullfight, in Madrid in September 1963.

Suddenly she found herself blocked by a figure a good three inches taller than she was. It was a woman, with hair bound back from a long, strikingly beautiful face with high exotic cheekbones and long, narrow eyes. She looked to Annja as if she came from a North Plains nation, Cheyenne maybe. Despite the weather outside, she wore a black tank top under a denim vest. Where lots of bikers sported U.S. flag patches she wore a yellow-and-red Gadsden flag. The one with the snake and the motto Don't Tread on Me.

She had, Annja felt, a somewhat snaky appearance in general. She was smaller in the chest and hips than Annja, and moved with sinuous grace that suggested the serpentine. The metaphor was extended by tattoos that twined from her biceps down her bare brown forearms—rattlesnakes striking with fangs sticking straight out from their gaping jaws like Kiowa lances.

"Excuse me," Annja said, and started to go around.

The woman seemed to flow in front of her again. "The white-eyes made us sign away our ancient right of roaming for reservations. Then they cheated us out of those and turned us out. So we tend to be a bit territorial these days. And you're off your reservation here, white-eyes. This is Indian country," she said.

"Yes, that whole land-grab thing sucked," Annja said as conversationally as she could. "And neither of us was alive back then, so it's probably way too late to debate it, isn't it? Now, if you'll excuse me."

She sidestepped once again. To her relief the woman didn't move to intercept her. Annja noted the 1911-style Springfield Armory .45 that rode in a black Kydex holster on her left hip. A gunfighter's rig for an old-school gunfighter's piece.

Annja made for the pay phone only to see that the bearlike guy had stopped playing pool and had slipped into the booth. She realized with a start that he didn't have a shirt on beneath his own denim vest, and that his considerable paunch was covered in an intricate blue tattoo.

He showed her a happy grin. "Sorry," he said with patent insincerity, trapping the handset between his shoulder and his ear. "I got to call my broker to see how much money I lost on stocks today. I'm still waitin' on my personal bailout."

He punched a number and pretended to listen. All the while he smiled beatifically at Annja out of his wide, round face.

She found it much scarier than the snake woman.

"You should probably go," he said, as if as an after-thought.

After a moment Annja said, "You're right." She turned and started to walk out.

Discretion, in this case, was the better part of staying alive. Anyway I can hike to the highway much better if both my legs aren't broken, she told herself.

A young biker emerged from a dark oblong opening in the back wall next to the phone booth. He was tall and straight, long-legged and narrow-waisted in his blue jeans, broad-shouldered in his colors. Unlike almost everybody else in the bar, men or women, he wore his long black hair unbound in a straight gleaming fall down his back. He was, undeniably, gorgeous.

From his carriage, from the way the feeling in the room suddenly shifted, he was clearly the boss. His dark-chocolate eyes locked on Annja's. "Who the hell are you?" he asked.

She made a beeline for the door. Away from him.

She felt a strong hand clamp on her right biceps.

"Not so fast," the biker chieftain said, spinning her around. "I got a few questions for—"

Annja used the momentum imparted by his yanking her around to jam her left knee into his groin really hard.

Okay, this is probably not the brightest thing you've ever done in your life, she thought even as she brought her knee up to its inevitable rendezvous with the juncture of those long, lean legs. It didn't diminish in the slightest the sheer fierce satisfaction she felt. He had laid hands on her. Even in the lion's den boundaries must be drawn, and rigorously enforced. Perhaps even more so. And Annja had not had a good day.

Clearly her victim didn't remotely expect any such response to trying to turn the interloper around. The breath burst out of him and he doubled over, then collapsed to the floor.

Despite herself, Annja was impressed by her results.

Unfortunately the entire bar full of rough Indian outlaw bikers were too. And after a beat or two of goggling at their pack leader lying there helpless on the sawdust-covered planks—was that even in code?—they got pissed.

"She dropped Johnny!" a voice cried. "Get her!"

A heavy weight landed on Annja's shoulders, staggering her. She reached back to grab a handful of coarse hair, then jackknifed forward, pulling hard. A figure flew over her back to slam on the planks in a cloud of sawdust. Annja saw it was a woman.

Hands clutched at Annja from several directions. A hand grabbed her jacket. Somebody yanked her hair. She slapped the hands away, lashing out with quick jabs and backfists. All the time she waded through the crowd toward the door.

As if materializing from the gloom itself the snake woman blocked Annja's path. She grabbed a handful of Annja's blouse through her open jacket and cocked her left fist back for a punch.

As she did she rocked her weight back. Annja grabbed the woman's left wrist and stepped quickly forward with her right foot, stepping out so that her hip brushed the woman's right hip. Her left hand shot up and around to grab the denim vest up near the slim neck. At the same time Annja pressed her elbow into her opponent's upper arm, effectively fouling the blow.

Annja twisted hard counterclockwise, putting her hips and all the strength of her own long legs into it. The other woman was wiry-strong, but Annja was strong, too; and she'd been practicing her grappling techniques. With her own weight already going backward the taller woman was easily toppled over Annja's outthrust hip and slammed flat on her back onto the pool table. Her head hit with a crack and the air rushed out of her.

For a moment the way cleared. Annja started to move

for the door but the short, wide guy who'd occupied the phone booth now stood in her way.

A flash decision faced Annja. She had an ace in her sleeve, but it wasn't one she cared to turn up in public. And also there were all those guns. If this confrontation turned lethal she'd be able to hope for nothing better than an honor guard to take into the afterlife with her.

Besides, even though these people were attacking her, Annja knew *she* was the intruder. And they hadn't used weapons yet. Should the need arise, she knew she could summon her sword from the otherwhere. But she did not want to have to explain the sudden appearance of the weapon to a bar full of people.

But she was going to have to even the odds somehow. And that entailed a certain risk.

She grabbed a discarded pool cue that lay on the pool table near the moaning, disoriented snake woman and snapped it right over the wide guy's cannonball head. He thumped to his knees, grabbed his head with both hands and howled.

She raced past him. Holding two feet of cue in a wide grip she used it as a riot baton or a pitchfork, prodding and levering bodies out of her path.

"Stop her!" Annja heard the leader call out. To her satisfaction she noticed his voice was still pretty choked.

But she was fast and very determined. She sent tables and chairs spinning to the sawdust in her wake, with a clatter of heavy glass and yeasty slog of beer arcing through the thick air. In a few steps she reached the door.

Tossing the broken cue aside she yanked the door

open. She stepped into the teeth of a now-icy wind, hauling the door closed behind her.

If the pursuit didn't develop too quickly she'd try to start the balky car and get as far as she could. If that didn't pan out she'd run off into the hills. Outlaw bikers weren't famous for their cross-country running abilities. And their motorcycles, heavy and low-slung as a lot of them were themselves, were optimized for high-speed cruising on paved road. The opposite of dirt bikes, they'd quickly bog down in the rolling landscape.

Annja liked her chances of evading the Iron Horse People in the dark. Whatever they might like to pretend, they weren't their ancestors, wild children of the wind, grass, sun and moon. They were products of the same modern cell-phone and flat-screen culture as she was.

She neared her car. And suddenly men stood from behind it. The bar sign's jittery pink glow glistened on faces painted black.

And on the knives and hatchets in their hands.

From the footsteps and angry shouts she understood a bunch more bad guys had crowded in between the vehicles behind her. She'd fled just in time.

Out of the corner of her eye she saw a brighter light stretched across the gravel from the direction of the bar's sagging facade. The front door was opening.

A male voice bellowed, "Dog Soldiers!" Then a lot of shouting erupted inside the bar in a guttural language she didn't understand.

That was the most fortuitous diversion she could ever have hoped for. She had a flare of hope that the sudden discovery of the Dog Soldiers, whoever they were, and the consternation that caused among the Iron Horse People, would cleanly cover her getaway.

She heard handgun shots popping from the parking lot. The deep hard-edged boom of a shotgun answered from inside the bar.

Annja never broke stride. She had her plan and she followed through. She ran straight to the back of the bar, cut around behind it and then, when she was sure she was out of everybody's sight, beelined right up a low ridge nearby and was gone with the wind.

5

Even though Annja's GPS built into her phone stayed
AWOL, she was not lost.

She could see the bright yellow glow of Lawton to
the east. The clouds actually made that a better beacon
by providing a handy surface for the lights to reflect off.
As long as Annja kept that glow, the largest in the
vicinity in any direction, on her right, she knew she was
heading north toward the graded-earth country road and
eventually the highway.

She wondered whether the two groups of crazy
outlaws back at the bar might sort things out enough to
give chase to her. It was so frigid in the wind and rain
that it felt as if her bones would break. She knew the
bikers might be the least of her problems.

Every time the chill grew intolerable she picked up
the pace a notch.

Even though she reckoned later she hadn't been

hiking even twenty minutes—after what seemed an eternity—she reached the county road. She walked on, hoping to eventually get a signal on her cell phone.

Approaching from the right, a quarter mile off, she spotted a pair of headlights.

Coming out of the east made it unlikely the car was chasing her from the bar. There was always the frightening possibility that it might contain reinforcements for either set of her enemies.

That concern died away as she saw the Lawton skyglow refract through the light-bar atop the car as it neared her. It slowed as if to come to a stop beside her.

Even before it did, Annja recognized, illuminated by the multicolored lights of the onboard computer and dashboard, the indefatigably cheerful face of Lieutenant Tom Ten Bears.

"Little cold out to be hitchhiking, ain't it, Ms. Creed?" Ten Bears asked.

"Yes," she said, hugging herself tightly against the biting cold. She wasn't really in the mood for a lot of ironic repartee.

"Hop on in and get warm, why don'tcha?" he asked.

She could think of any number of reasons why she wouldn't, actually. None of them was as compelling as either getting out of the cold or putting the symbolic bulk of the Oklahoma Highway Patrol between her and the bikers and midnight ambushers. She wasn't naive enough to believe a lone trooper in a cruiser would necessarily deter them. But along with his .41 Smith & Wesson, Ten Bears had a radio.

She settled into the passenger's seat. Beaming

between his uniform collar and his peaked cap, Ten Bears put the cruiser back in gear and drove off along the county road at a just-over-walking pace.

She regarded him through narrowed, suspicious eyes. "Small world, huh?"

"Small world," he agreed. "Welcome to Indian country, Ms. Creed. Not much goes on here that folks don't see. What they see, they like to talk about. Especially when you're a white-eyes from outside. And most especially a real nice-looking lady white-eyes, if you get my drift."

Annja knew full well that the coming of any stranger would spark gossip in a tight-knit community. While Annja didn't think of herself as particularly beautiful, she knew that her tall, lean-muscled, leggy form tended to attract added attention that, say, a dumpy fifty-year-old bearded archaeologist would not.

"I heard some things got me kind of concerned," the lieutenant said. "I checked your motel but you weren't there. Them Comanche County deputies told me you'd left the dig site right around sundown. So I wondered if you hadn't broken down along the way. Or something."

Or something, she thought. But carefully did not say.

"The breakdown scenario. My rental car died on me. I just managed to ditch it in the parking lot of the Bad Medicine Bar."

"Hoo," Ten Bears said. "Tell me you didn't go inside?"

"No cell-phone coverage out there," she said. "I didn't think I had much choice." She shrugged. "The reception I got didn't exactly make me feel welcome. So I left."

He laughed at that. "Them boys rowdy you up some?" he asked.

"Let's say I got out of there before things got really out of hand," she said with a grin.

"You're a big TV star and all. Anything happened to you, it'd reflect poorly on the department and the Comanche Nation. Also you seem like a nice lady, if a bit idealistic," he said.

"Thanks. I think."

"See, there's something going on in Indian country. Mostly western Oklahoma and northern Texas. Something not so good. We got some people here, young people, who are kind of on the radical side."

He glanced at her. "You met some of them tonight. Iron Horse People Motorcycle Club."

"I see." She tried to keep her tone neutral.

"They got a rival bunch," he said, "call themselves the Dog Society. Both sets want to live in the good old days, you know? Ride around whooping and hollering and shooting buffalo. They don't much like the government. Okay, nobody does. They are also not too fond of the white-eyes."

He drove a moment in silence. To their right the land began to pitch up into rough granite hills. Ten Bears didn't seem to be in a hurry to get anywhere. That he was heading away from Lawton didn't particularly alarm Annja. She had fairly well-honed survival instincts. She didn't sense anything sketchy from Ten Bears, just concern.

She knew he wasn't telling her everything. Police never told outsiders everything about a live investigation. It didn't mean much.

"Most of all they don't like each other," he continued. "There's trouble between 'em. Regular trouble. Lots of bad blood. And it's getting worse."

"I don't ever see anything about this on the news," Annja said.

"I hope you don't, Ms. Creed." He looked at her. "I hope you won't be going public with it."

"Not much danger of that," she said with a little smile. "I'm an archaeologist, not a reporter."

"Nation's trying to keep it all quiet. So's the state. The Comanche Nation's got this new casino opening up in a few days, you know. Your young bloods, the radical-traditional types, aren't happy about that. It's Indian business and white-eyes don't much care. Anyway, if word of the problem does get out, what with the whole continuing terror hysteria and all, it's just going to bring more grief to Indians without calming the passions that are causing the problems."

"I understand," she said.

"Most people here are good folks. Indians, whites, blacks, Asians, whatever. But there are strong undercurrents of racism and anger. And plenty of areas where white-eyes aren't in the majority. And not real popular. You know?"

"I got the impression."

He chuckled softly.

"So why don't I give you a ride back to the motel," Ten Bears said amiably. "I'll talk to the car rental company. You can call them in the morning to retrieve your broke-down ride and get a new one. Better still, why not just fly on back to New York City, get yourself some nice arugula?"

"I'm not a big arugula fan, Lieutenant. I'm more the unabashed carnivore. I promise I won't interfere with your investigation. I'll do my best to keep from turning up on the news for any reason whatever. But I lost a good friend today. I'm not ready to pack it in and head home."

She turned away from him and wiped moisture from her cheek. The ghostly fun-house-mirror image of her face looked back at her with exaggerated eyes. Snow-flakes beat against the windows like suicidal moths bent on flame.

Ten Bears sighed theatrically. "I figured you'd take that line. Well, it was worth a try. Listen. The whole skinwalker angle is tough for a cop to approach. Even a native cop—we're supposed to be close to the spirits and the earth and all that. But us Indians don't like to give our brother officers too many excuses to roll their eyes when they think we're not looking, you know? You want to give me a real leg up catching the party or parties who murdered your friend, I'd certainly be willing to look at any evidence you might turn up on that aspect of the case."

"Thanks, Lieutenant."

"Don't thank me. I should probably lock you up or something. But if I could make a small suggestion, you might want to take a closer look at the earlier attacks. As in, firsthand. They took place in what would seem more like skinwalker country, anyway."

"Conveniently distancing myself from Comanche territory?"

"Exactly! I knew you were a smart lady."

I'm not too unhappy about making myself scarce for a while, either, come to think of it, she thought.

"If you want to pick up on some of the cultural backdrop, both on South Plains Indians and the Navajo," he said, "there's somebody I know you might want to talk to, since you'll be down Albuquerque way, anyway…."

THAT NIGHT THERE was no mention at all, on TV or online, about anything at all happening at a lonely bar in the sticks of western Oklahoma. Nor was there any the next morning.

In between Annja slept like one dead.

6

To Annja's complete surprise, the car rental agency not only failed to give her a molecule of grief when she called them the next morning to report her mishap, but they insisted she have a replacement without her even asking. They'd come pick her up.

She suspected the jovial and heavy hand of one Lieutenant Tom Ten Bears, OHP. She could imagine him calling the agency to talk over what she had told him and in that self-effacing, aw-shucks, good-old-boy way of his, making it quite clear, in case they didn't get it up front, what it would mean to them if they were difficult with her.

So almost before she knew it, Annja found herself driving north up I-44 behind the wheel of a shiny new rental car. Then she turned west on Interstate 40 and headed to New Mexico.

The land flattened out as Annja drove through the Texas panhandle. As she entered New Mexico, the terrain gradually became vast wide swoops of tawny land. The occasional lone peak, most likely a volcanic extrusion, showed in the distance. The vegetation ran mostly to short grass, dotted with scrub.

Once, she saw a herd of pronghorn antelope grazing away off to her right.

As she neared her destination the land rose and grew more broken, mounting to what Annja, with all respect to the Wichita Range, considered something closer to real mountains, with ridges and slopes densely furred with straight-boled pines. These, she knew, were the Sandias.

The mountains rose left and right of the highway, then fell steeply in sheer granite walls to foothills that became high desert, sloping gently down to a line of trees that marked the course of the Rio Grande. Before her and to each side stretched the gray and chrome encrustation of an urban concentration—Albuquerque. She stopped there for lunch before continuing west into the desert.

Past the Acoma Reservation and the triangular bulk of Mount Taylor lay the small town of Grants. Following her GPS, confirmed by reference to a Google Earth map she'd summoned in her motel room in Lawton the previous night, a few miles west of Grants Annja turned left down a none-too-obvious dirt road. It wound quickly upward between steep, scrub-covered hills into the Zuni Mountains with their forests of ponderosa pine, along the Continental Divide.

The first attack had taken place at a dig in the Cíbola National Forest, working what was believed to be the remnants of an encampment of Warm Springs Chiricahua Apache led by the great guerrilla master Victorio during his war with the U.S. during the 1870s. The excavation had been protested by Native American groups even though the Mescalero tribe—which incorporated most of the survivors of the various Chiricahua groups except the Mexican Chiricahua, who were still in Mexico—offered no objection. It lay in a steep-sided draw. It had been discovered by a USDA team checking the results of reseeding by air after the area was burned over in a 2004 fire.

The attack had occurred the previous autumn. No signs remained of the dig or the murders. The excavation had been canceled after the incident. Wind and weather had smoothed out the disturbed earth.

Annja found no great mystery as to how the attacker could have struck from ambush there, either. The site lay along one side of a dry streambed, with the tree line beginning barely twenty yards away on one side and a rock outcropping looming twelve feet right above where, from the files, she knew the actual excavation had taken place. It would have taken a very athletic man to have dropped that distance without injuring himself. Then again it also took a very athletic man to kill three able-bodied adults—two men and one woman—and fatally wound a third man.

The sun was falling behind the divide as Annja drove back east. Although she still felt mostly numb about Paul's death, in between wracking bouts of grief, she'd had a stressful couple of days. Not to denigrate the sheer physical toll long travel and combat took. She pulled off the highway just east of the river and spent the night in the Hotel Albuquerque on Rio Grande Boulevard, just north of Old Town.

AFTER EATING BREAKFAST the next morning at Little Anita's near the hotel, she walked a few blocks south to the Old Town Plaza. It was a pleasant morning, still crisply cool, although warmer than out on the Plains near Lawton, with the sun just beginning to sting where it touched exposed skin. She sat on a cast-iron bench across from the old cathedral, beneath elm branches starting to turn green, while she used her computer to check her e-mail and confirm some information for her day's quest. Then she made a few calls on her cell phone and hiked back to the hotel for her car.

The second attack had taken place in early March on land owned by San Ildefonso Pueblo between Santa Fe and Albuquerque. The pueblo itself had invited a state team in to excavate what was believed to have been a temporary settlement by Pueblo Indians sometime predating the great Pueblo Uprising that threw the Spanish out in 1680. Despite that fact, and the fact that both State of New Mexico archaeologists and pueblo experts had confirmed the absence of human remains, the site had once again drawn protestors. There had been an ugly confrontation when pueblo police removed them for trespassing, although there was no record of injuries, nor charges filed.

Apparently there was some sentiment, in the Southwest at least, that any kind of archaeological excavation of potential Indian sites was profane.

Although this massacre was just a few weeks old Annja didn't learn anything new there, either. As in the other two cases a cautious approach could easily have gotten the killer in range for a final rush without being seen. Especially since nobody would really have been looking.

She got back to Albuquerque about two o'clock and spent the rest of the afternoon as she waited for her next appointment going through local and national news accounts of the murders online at a coffee shop on a fairly rustic-looking section of Rio Grande Boulevard a few miles north of her hotel.

The common threads among the murders, aside from the obvious gross similarities, were that they took place on dig sites that were protested by obscure groups. These had no apparent connection between themselves, other than professed radical pro-Native American sympathies. It wasn't even clear how many of the protestors were actually Indians themselves.

She sat on the outdoor patio beneath a cottonwood beginning to leaf, drinking tea and pondering a few questions. Was the fact that all three attack sites had been protested significant or purely coincidental? If significant, what was the connection? Even the FBI, notoriously eager to discover terrorist conspiracies even where they weren't, had either actively cleared the protestors of involvement or at least failed to list them as persons of interest.

Plus, frankly, people who'd go out and picket an archaeological dig struck Annja, who'd encountered a few in her time, as precisely the sort who would *not* be inclined to carry out impossibly violent blitz attacks ending in multiple murders. Nor, for the most, capable.

The light took on a late-afternoon yellowness. The sun had gotten tangled in the branches of the massive old cottonwoods across the boulevard. Time to go, she told herself, and folded her computer shut.

7

The western sky blazed in orange like burning forests when the silver Prius pulled up to the curb by the park and stopped. A tall woman got out of the driver's side. A skinny young girl in jeans, T-shirt and a yellow Windbreaker, with her black hair in pigtails, got out of the passenger's side. A big floppy yellow Lab pup, an adolescent probably, spilled out after her.

"You must be Dr. Watson," Annja said, rising from the picnic table a short way down a grassy slope from the street as the woman walked toward her. She was handsome if a bit heavy in face and hip, and the hair hanging unbound around the shoulders of her mauve cable-knit sweater was black with silver threads. She wore a long dark-blue denim skirt over dark purple suede boots with silver medallions on them.

"Yes," the woman said. "And you're Annja Creed?"

Annja agreed she was. "And I'm Sallie," the girl announced. "It's short for Salamander!"

"No, it isn't, Alessandra," her mother said. "Don't be untruthful."

Annja laughed. Something about the girl's appearance tweaked her subconscious. She couldn't pin down exactly what.

The dog sniffed Annja's legs. She hunkered down to stroke its head. "What's his name?" she asked Sallie.

"It's a she," Sallie said. "Her name's Eowyn. She's kind of silly."

"Young Labrador retrievers act that way," her mother said. "Why don't you and she go play?"

The girl was looking intently at Annja. "You're on TV, aren't you?" she said.

Her mother looked stern. Annja said, "Yes."

"Oh. I like your show."

"Thanks," Annja said.

Sallie reached in a pocket of her jacket and produced a pale-green tennis ball, which she launched down the hill. The dog bounded in pursuit. Sallie ran after her, romping through the shadows of big elm trees lengthening across the hills of Roosevelt Park, which was located roughly halfway between the University of New Mexico campus, where Watson worked, and downtown.

"Thanks for taking the time to meet with me, Dr. Watson," Annja said.

"Susan, please. I'm certainly willing to do anything I can to get to the bottom of these terrible crimes. And I thank you for being willing to meet with me under such unusual circumstances. I don't really have any time free at school this week, and I don't want to leave Sallie at day care longer than necessary."

She leaned forward and fixed Annja with a disconcertingly probing look. Even without the low boot heels she had to stand six feet clear. Annja did not envy any student of Dr. Watson's who failed to measure up to her expectations.

"So, is your interest in skinwalkers personal or professional?" Watson asked.

If she wanted to keep things up front Annja could match that. "Both," she said. "I lost a close personal friend in the last attack." She felt a nasty twinge as she said it.

"Also the authorities in Oklahoma have asked me unofficially to consult on certain anthropological aspects of the case."

"You're an archaeologist by training, aren't you?"

"Yes. Of course, my training included extensive education in social and physical anthropology, as well as subjects like geology."

"Oh, yes." Watson herself was a professor of cultural anthropology at the University of New Mexico, specializing in the study of Southwestern native cultures. "So what can I do for you?"

"My specialty's the European Renaissance. It's a little far afield from the South Plains and the Rio Grande Valley. And to be perfectly honest, while we studied Native American history and cultures, my memory isn't as sharp as it could be."

"I understand," Watson said with a grin. "I forgot all my geology pretty much the instant I turned in my last exam."

"So if you could fill me in a bit on the cultural background of the Southwest and Plains cultures, and any hint you can provide me as to why something out of Navajo folk belief would be operating in the Comanche country of western Oklahoma would definitely be appreciated."

"Well, to start with, the Indian cultures of North America didn't live in vacuums, much less isolation from one another," Watson said.

Annja was only mildly surprised at a tenured professor using such a politically incorrect term as *Indian*; very few Native Americans she'd ever met showed anything but the most strident contempt for the phrase *Native American*. Tom Ten Bears hadn't had much use for it, either.

"Even before the Europeans' arrival, my own people, the Kiowas, were especially famed for their roles as raiders and traders. Rather as the Vikings were in Europe and even the Mediterranean. So were the Comanches, especially after the two nations allied in the late eighteenth century. Comanche relics have turned up in the Cahokia Mounds. Kiowa tradition recalls trading voyages to the country of the Maya—who were themselves noted for the long journeys of their own traders, who also served as proselytizers for their religion."

"Really?"

Watson nodded. "So the South Plains people were common visitors to New Mexico. What's now northeastern New Mexico was part of their customary range. In fact, the Kiowa-Comanche alliance got its start in the 1790s on what's now the site of Las Vegas, New Mexico—you did know there was one, didn't you?"

"Oh, yes. In the mountains east of Santa Fe," Annja said.

"That's it. You'd be surprised how many people have only heard of the one in Nevada. Or maybe you wouldn't. At any rate, the relationship between the Pueblos and the South Plains people was especially problematic. Sometimes the Plains folk came to the Pueblos to trade, sometimes to pillage and kill. It was the usual antagonism between settled groups and nomads."

"I'm familiar with that," Annja said. "So where do the Navajos come in?"

"Originally as rivals," Watson said with a smile. "As an Apachean subgroup of the Athabascan peoples they and their fellow Apacheans also raided the prosperous and populous riparian communities. That often brought them into conflict with the South Plains people. Usually the Apache came off second best."

Annja noted a half-hidden grin at that. That was something she'd noticed in her dealings with people of Plains Indian extraction—no matter how vocally they tried, as many did, to disavow violence and war, they remained at core warrior cultures. And thoroughly proud of their histories.

"It wasn't perfectly straightforward, of course," Watson said.

"Are human interactions ever?"

Watson laughed. "Not that I've noticed." She shook her head, seemed to go introspective for a moment. "Anyway, one thing that happened was that the Jicarilla band of Apaches early on settled in northern New Mexico, and entered into alliance with the Taoseños.

They provided security for the great annual Taos trade fairs."

"Really? I didn't know that."

"Yes. So there was always considerable contact between the people of the Southwest and of the South Plains. A famous hide painting exists of a battle—at about the time of the American Revolution—between Spanish troops with Apache mercenaries and French ones alongside Comanche allies."

"Who won?"

"The French and Comanche. I'm tempted to add *of course*. Anyway, the contacts, if anything, grew stronger with the conclusion of the wars of Indian subjugation. After the final surrender of the Chiricahua Apaches to the U.S. Army in the 1880s they were eventually shipped to Fort Sill in Oklahoma."

"Which is the heart of Comanche territory."

"Yes. About half the Nation still lives around Sill and Lawton. Of course, by the time the Chiricahua gave up their relatives the Navajo had long since come to terms with the inevitable and settled down to become sheep-herders. Meanwhile, the Chiricahua had extensive exposure to Comanche culture on the reservation."

"I didn't think there were any reservations in Oklahoma," Annja said.

"There aren't anymore. It was the usual story. The free peoples of the Plains kept being restricted to smaller and smaller chunks of less and less desirable real estate. Then as soon as they got settled in, somebody would discover something on the land they'd been ceded—gold in the Black Hills, say—and they'd be pushed off again.

"In Oklahoma the Kiowa and Comanche were both forcibly settled onto reservations, which were then whittled away to nothing. The last Kiowa were forced out for white settlement in 1901, the Comanche in 1906."

"That's sad," Annja said.

"Yes. It is. Don't worry—I know you didn't do it."

Annja laughed. "So what can you tell me about the Dog Society?"

"Originally a Cheyenne warrior society. One of six, actually."

"Why would Comanche radicals be calling themselves after a Cheyenne group?"

Watson shrugged. "You'd have to ask them. However, the Cheyennes spent a lot of time in the South Plains, and had much contact with the Kiowas and Comanche. They still do. Also, the Dog Soldiers were known for their extreme aggression. They were eventually outlawed and cast out of the Cheyenne tribe after one of their members murdered a fellow tribesman, and formed their own band. That could be part of the attraction for violent radicals, that aggressive association."

"I see. What I still don't understand, I'm afraid, is how and why someone evidently caught up in Navajo witchcraft would wind up committing murders in Oklahoma."

"Again, I have no good explanation to give you. Such an individual would be very…twisted, by the standards of any human culture. Navajos—Athabascans—still take witchcraft with the utmost seriousness. It's the blackest evil to them. People accused of witchcraft still have a tendency to turn up dead.

"The Navajo wolf, or skinwalker, is basically the

worst kind of witch. You can only gain that kind of power through extensive contact with the dead—something most of the Southwest Indians are very leery of, and which the Athabascans in particular dread. Also, the shape-changing power can only be won through committing one or more ritual murders."

"Wow," Annja said.

"That's not a life-way I'm terribly conversant with. Modern Navajos don't like to talk about it for two reasons. The acculturated ones dislike associating their people with what seems to them a potentially pernicious superstition. The traditionalists dislike talking about religious beliefs to outsiders because to talk about witches invites their attentions, which traditional Navajos believe can be literally deadly."

Watson shook her head. "Really, I'd say even a lot of the most modern Navajos feel at least a certain thrill of dread about skinwalkers. Just as atheists raised amid Christian society sometimes harbor secret fears of hell."

"I'm familiar with that phenomenon," Annja said.

"Now, there is someone who might be able to expand on what little I can tell you about the Navajo wolf phenomenon. I can put you in touch with Dr. Yves Michel of the World Health Organization. He's spent the past couple of years among the native peoples of Arizona and New Mexico, studying Southwest Indian health issues on behalf of the U.N. Particularly mental health issues—he's a psychiatrist as well as holding a doctorate in cultural anthropology. A very erudite man. Although I have to caution you—he can be difficult."

"Thanks for the warning."

"He does, however, like to talk about his areas of interest. In particular, he's made an intensive study of the skinwalker belief complex. While he has yet to publish any papers, he's passed drafts around to many friends and colleagues that I understand have created quite a stir."

"Wait—I think I've heard of him."

In fact, Annja was pretty sure she'd seen his work on skinwalkers discussed on alt.archaeology, a Web site she frequently visited that was devoted to discussions of fringe archaeology. While she considered herself a stout skeptic, she also felt she owed it to her discipline to maintain an open mind; hence, her continuing attention to the outer limits of archaeological research. It was entirely possible that among the piles of printouts stacked on the sofa or coffee table of her Brooklyn loft apartment was actually a copy of Dr. Michel's draft paper. She spent so little time there these days she couldn't keep track of everything.

Dr. Watson took out one of her own business cards and wrote Dr. Michel's phone number and e-mail address on the back of it. As she did so Sallie came racing back with Eowyn loping behind her. The girl plopped herself on the cold cement bench near her mother. The Lab lay down beside her, panting and grinning.

Annja found herself studying the girl. Sallie noticed and, like any bright child instinctively mistrusting adult scrutiny, said, "What? Do I have a booger?"

"Sallie!" her mother said sharply. She passed the card to Annja. "Sorry."

"No, I'm sorry. It's rude to stare. You just look familiar somehow."

"Wait till I'm famous," Sallie said. "I'm going to be a superheroine."

Watson sighed exaggeratedly. "We Plains people tend to have active imaginations. A cultural thing, I think."

She reached out to tousle the girl's hair. Sallie endured it a moment, then leaped up and went dashing off once more with Eowyn in happy pursuit.

"I guess you wonder why a middle-aged woman has such a young daughter," Watson said. "She was the outcome of an attempt to save a marriage."

She sighed. "And like most such attempts, it didn't work. I try not to talk about that where she can hear. I hate keeping things from her. But it's a terrible responsibility to lay on a child. She's a wonderful child."

Light began to dawn on Annja. "She wouldn't have an older brother, would she?"

"Yes. His name's John. He's fourteen years older than she is. They love each other, but there are limits to how close they can be across that kind of gap."

"I think I know why she looks familiar. Please forgive my asking a highly personal question, but you wouldn't happen to have been married to Lieutenant Ten Bears, would you?"

"Yes," Watson said.

Annja sagged as if she'd been sandbagged. "So that's why he recommended I talk to you."

Watson laughed again. She had a hearty laugh. "I'd like to think a degree of respect for my competence influenced him. We do respect each other, even if we're miles apart in most of our viewpoints on things. I'm a leftist, if not an entirely respectable one—he's a right-winger, a total gung-ho patriot. I guess what you'd expect from a war hero and lifelong cop. We still feel…affection for each other, too. The divorce was amicable. Of course, you couldn't say that for the last few years of our marriage."

"Wait—your son's name is John? *Johnny?*"

"Why, yes," Watson said. "He served with the Army Rangers in Iraq and Afghanistan. When he came home he was changed."

"And now he's leader of the Iron Horse People Motorcycle Club?"

"He's a community activist," Watson said, "who prefers to think of himself as an outlaw biker. Not that I altogether approve of what he's trying to achieve. Sometimes he seems way too much like the militia crazies of the nineties, who're starting to make such a comeback now. But I'm much calmer about his activities than my ex-husband is."

A dog barking vigorously broke the thread of conversation. Annja and Watson looked across the large park. The sun had set. The air grew chilly, with only a bloodred band on the horizon and reddish undertints on a few clouds. The evening filled the hollows of the park like velvet.

Down in the bottom of the depression between the slope the picnic table stood on and a hill, Sallie was digging her heels in to restrain Eowyn, apparently newly leashed. The adolescent Lab barked furiously toward the top of the far hill. The yellow pup didn't sound floppy-friendly now. Even a hundred feet away

Annja could see the hackles standing up on her neck. She was in serious guardian mode, with only Sallie's determination keeping her from launching a preemptive attack on something she perceived as immediately dangerous.

Following the line of the dog's fury Annja felt the hair at her own nape rise. Silhouetted on the hillcrest was the broad head and pointed ears of what appeared to be a wolf. Otherwise, it was indistinct, a black shadow against the twilight.

"Why is Eowyn so mad at that Malamute, or whatever it is?" Watson asked, rising. "She's usually so friendly with everybody. Dogs as well as humans."

Annja was up and running down the slope.

As she came up to Sallie the girl finished reeling in the leash, grabbed the bristling Eowyn's collar and sat down with her legs braced. "You're not going anywhere, girl," she said through clenched teeth. "What's gotten into you?"

The wolflike head vanished as Annja started uphill toward it. She wasn't sure what she intended. If the animal attacked her, and she had to use her sword to defend herself, she would have many, many questions to answer that she frankly never wanted to face.

When she reached the top of the hill she saw no sign of the creature.

She spotted a doglike shadow flitting between a couple of the houses across the street on the park's other side. She got an eerie sensation down her spine again as it turned and looked directly at her. Then it vanished.

Annja stood and watched for half a minute, her heart

pounding in her chest far more than the brief exertion—even at a mile's altitude—would account for. She didn't see the animal again. Deciding she was not going to go tramping around through people's yards hunting for what would almost certainly turn out to be somebody's stray husky, she turned and walked back down toward where Watson had joined her daughter, kneeling beside Eowyn. Both stroked the animal and spoke soothingly to her.

Why did I get so worked up about a dog? Annja asked herself. I shouldn't let myself be so suggestible.

It was fatigue, she decided. Physical and emotional. Had to be.

The tall Plains woman stood. Eowyn had settled down. She wagged her tail and grinned at Annja, inviting her to admire her heroism. Annja bent down and petted her head and told her she was a good watchdog.

"Was it just a dog, then?" Watson asked. Her tone sounded strained.

Annja looked at her sharply. "Why? What else would it be?"

Watson turned her eyes away from Annja's. She seemed shaken.

"Thank you for your willingness to protect my daughter," she said. "We'd better go now."

8

"It's a great honor to meet you, Dr. Michel," Annja said in French, shaking hands with the psychiatrist.

His face was pinched. "Please," he said in thickly accented English. "Americans should not try to speak French. It is almost a form of cultural imperialism, to butcher the language so."

Annja tightened her lips. His tone as well as his words cut like a slap to the face. Especially since she was proud of her French. Justly so—she'd spoken it all her life, so far as she could remember, had minored in Romance languages in college and, most to the point, passed among the French themselves for a native speaker on more than one occasion.

She forced herself to draw a deep breath to calm herself. *I think I see what Dr. Watson meant about him being difficult,* she thought.

She wasn't exactly unaccustomed to arrogance from

the French, although they could also be a lovely, charming people. This man definitely pushed the envelope of rudeness, though.

He was short, a head shorter than Annja, dressed in a white shirt with the sleeves rolled up, khaki pants, hiking boots. He had broad shoulders and a marathoner runner's build. Despite the fact his close-cropped hair was steely, and his résumé, which Annja had looked up online the night before, said he was in his early fifties, his narrow features were quite youthful, relatively unmarked. Surprisingly so given a tan of apparent long-standing. He wasn't what she would call a handsome man, but his appearance and manner suggested a kestrel; and that dark tan made his eyes, of a blue so pale as to be almost silver, look striking almost to the point of eeriness.

At least I lucked out when it came to tracking him down, she reminded herself. He was currently working in Sandia Pueblo. It formed basically the northern boundary of Albuquerque, stretching from the river to the foothills of the Sandia Mountains, and north to within a few miles of the town of Bernalillo. For whatever reason, Dr. Michel had chosen to meet Annja late in the afternoon at a scenic lookout spot in the foothills, along the road past the exits that led to the pueblo's immense and relatively recent casino and the Bien Mur Indian Center.

The Sandias' flat gray faces rose almost a mile above the river valley. They looked anything but watermelon-like, though that was what the name meant in Spanish. While various explanations for the name existed, Annja tended to believe that the Spaniards thought the north mountain looked like a big slice of watermelon. At sunset, at certain times of year, the westward-facing cliffs turned a startling red. Annja had seen that herself.

When she arrived at the appointed spot, a little before the agreed-upon time as was her cautious custom, she'd found the doctor already waiting for her, leaning with arms folded against a vehicle that was apparently his mobile living quarters. It looked to Annja like the front end of a Toyota pickup mated to a body, like a panel van customized into an RV. She wondered if the U.N. had shelled out to build it or if he'd found it somewhere used. It bore the markings of many miles.

"What can you tell me about the skinwalker phenomenon, Dr. Michel," Annja asked in English. What with one thing or another she figured the best course was to get this interview over with as quickly as possible.

He nodded briskly. "First you must have a basic understanding of the Navajo witch. He, or she, is a follower of the Witchcraft Way. The Athabascans of the Southwest fear ghosts more than anything. Not unnaturally, they associate ghosts with corpses, of whom they consequently feel a peculiarly poignant terror. They likewise fear owls, whom they suspect to be ghosts—and also of serving as spies and servitors to witches. The basic reason for this fear is that contamination by ghosts or the dead can cause a wasting ghost sickness or corpse sickness, which can bring about decline, decrepitude, even eventual death, to the victim. And make no mistake—people have died of ghost sickness. They die of it today—they will into the future, unless the white man succeeds in finally murdering the native culture. Or the entire planet. It is a phenomenon like 'pointing the bone' in Haiti."

"A psychosomatic effect?" Annja asked.

He sneered. His fine, mobile features, the cheeks and chin lightly stubbled in silver, lent themselves well to it, she had to admit.

"Does it comfort you to think so? The symptoms in such cases are real. And so, as I say, are the deaths. Call that psychosomatic, if you like.

"The most dangerous medium of the ghost sickness is corpse powder—human bodies dried and ground. The corpse powder is the very core of the witch's power. Far from shunning contact with death or the dead, he revels in it. It is his route to his chosen supernatural power, what the Westerners used to call *medicine*. It is the source of magic and effective personality. Corpse powder's most potent and coveted form is that obtained from the bodies of young children."

Annja set her lips against what she felt trying to rise from her stomach. She wasn't squeamish. Nobody who'd spent time on protracted digs around the world and survived was. And she'd seen and encountered things in the gross and horrific departments since inheriting her sword that went far beyond what she'd found on her plate as an academic archaeologist.

But if he's trying to spook me, she thought grimly, he's succeeding. She was dead set on not giving him the satisfaction of letting him know that.

"Now, you may look down on all this in dismissal from your lofty perch as a Western-trained, so-called scientist. Let me assure you this matter is deadly serious. These people, who are as human as you or me, take it with literal deadly seriousness.

"There exists today a small community, which I will not name, whose population consists entirely of Navajos believed to be witches and their descendants. They went into exile rather than face punishment. The tribe allowed them to do so, rather than face the white-eyes' retribution for punishing them according to the ancient ways. I have gone among these exiled witches, spoken to them. When they and other Navajos encounter one another, each pretends not to recognize the other. Otherwise, there would be blood."

"Do they still practice witchcraft?" Annja couldn't help herself asking.

"Some say they do. Some say they do not. Who is to say who lies and who tells the truth?"

"Wouldn't they be natural suspects as the source for our killer?"

"They have learned to survive by keeping their heads down—to fly under the white-eyes' radar, as you might say. They chose to accept permanent partition from their clans, from their sacred earth, which are as much a part of them as their bones and flesh and blood. If they made that sacrifice, would they jeopardize the safety they bought at such terrible cost?"

"Dr. Michel," she said through clenched teeth, "fifteen people, including a very dear friend of mine, have died at the hands of one or more apparent Navajo wolves. I think the last thing you need to worry about is whether I take the phenomenon seriously."

He smiled thinly. "*Bon.* Now, the most terrible form

of witch is the skinwalker. It is the most extreme and difficult path of the Witchcraft Way. It requires rituals even more horrific and forbidden than the less esoteric witchcraft. Needless to say, murder, blood and corpse powder figure prominently in its attainment."

"Of course," Annja said. By this point she felt need for a bit of flippancy to save her sanity, and damn the risks of this uptight man's overly sharpened tongue.

If she hadn't seen the photographs of the victims, if her friend hadn't virtually died in her arms, she would not be reacting so strongly to Michel's catalog of horrors, no matter how much relish he recited them with. She was vulnerable. He seemed to sense that, and enjoy taking advantage.

"The skinwalker is said to have many fearful gifts," Michel went on. "The power to read thoughts. The ability to imitate the voice of any person or animal, sometimes impersonating loved ones to lure victims to their doom. Some stories even credit them with being able to steal another's body by gazing deeply into their eyes. And, of course, they have the power to assume animal form— predominantly, though not restricted to, that of a wolf. Hence, the common appellation *Navajo wolf.* Some others assert that they assume a sort of hybrid human-animal form. In these altered shapes, or skins, they are said to possess strength, speed and resistance to damage far in excess of either human or animal."

"I see," Annja said. "That would be a pretty formidable package."

He shrugged. "Most likely, of course, you are dealing with a mere poseur—an imitator, a copy cat, you might say. If you are dealing with a real skinwalker, you are in very grave trouble, indeed."

"Define *real* in this context, Dr. Michel, please."

He laughed. "A skeptic, eh? Very well. When I say a real skinwalker, I mean a person who has undergone the grueling, horrific and largely illegal rituals prescribed for becoming a Navajo wolf. Such an individual would likely possess above-average intelligence and almost superhuman determination.

"Indeed, as you would know had you read my paper, which I have circulated on a limited basis in preliminary form, I theorize that the witch, particularly the skinwalker, constitutes a peculiarly Navajo life-way for what we would term a sociopath. Such people, in other cultures, are known for high intelligence, resourcefulness and a complete lack of conventional inhibitions. They can behave quite obsessively in pursuit of their goals. Including developing their skills to an extraordinarily high level."

"I have read your paper, Doctor," Annja said. She'd found a copy online last night. "I wanted to get what insight I could from you in person."

If the fact she'd read his paper mollified the French psychiatrist, he hid it well. "If a true skinwalker is responsible for these killings, I blame the corruption of Western influence—unremitting violence in popular culture and everyday life. And, of course, materialist, consumerist capitalism, which corrupts all it touches."

Consumerism? she thought. His twists of logic were starting to make Annja's head swim the way his stories turned her stomach.

"In line with that understanding," Michel said, "I have formed an alternative hypothesis. While traditional Navajo wolves renounce humanity—meaning, to them, the Navajo people—as part of their power quest, and actively embrace evil, I have come to suspect that certain other aspirants to the Witchcraft Way undertake to, in effect, sacrifice themselves for the good of the People. That being, of course, what the Navajo call themselves. To make themselves night stalkers and superhuman killers precisely in order to protect the People, they embrace the appurtenances of evil in order to derive the power to do good.

"In this they make themselves the opposite of sociopaths, although their actions are almost impossible to discern from each other. Whereas the sociopathic serial murderer kills without conscience, because he lacks empathy, this other being becomes a killer on a mission, who kills because his conscience drives him to do so. He averts his empathy from his victims because he is driven by empathy for those whom he believes he serves. Once many psychologists used the term *psychopath* for such a one, the conscience-driven killer as opposed to the conscienceless sociopath. The terms have long been conflated in the public awareness, such as it is, and in any event thoroughly obfuscated by the official professional jargon."

"Thank you, Dr. Michel," Annja said, before he could plunge any deeper into what seemed likely to be another of his numerous wells of disregard. "Have you thought of approaching the authorities with your expertise on the subject? Your theories might prove helpful toward solving these crimes."

"You must understand, Ms. Creed," he said, "fascinating as I naturally find this case, my interest remains purely scientific. As for whether they apprehend the killer or not I give not a fig." He made a dismissive flick of his fingertips.

"So far as I am concerned archaeologists are nothing more than despoilers of native peoples and violators of their tombs. The more the skinwalker kills of them, the better."

With maximum effort Annja controlled herself. "I'm an archaeologist, Dr. Michel."

He shrugged. "So? It is on your soul, not mine. Good day to you, Ms. Creed. I shall not talk to you again. I have important work to do."

STILL STEAMING OVER her encounter with the arrogant French psychiatrist Annja drove back the way she had come. At Tramway Road she turned south toward I-40. She intended to return to Lawton straightaway. She had decided she'd been away from Comanche country long enough for things to settle down sufficiently.

It was after dark when she stopped at a rest area near the Texas border. The wind blew down the Plains with little to hinder it. It buffeted her rental car and chilled her right through as soon as she stepped out. Though unheated, the restroom seemed a sanctuary of warmth and calm.

When she finished her business she opened the stall door to find two men with their faces painted black awaiting her. The one on her left wore an indigo hoodie and what looked like sweatpants; the one on her right a black Windbreaker and pants. Both wore black athletic shoes. The bareheaded one had his dense black hair slicked back.

They showed no weapons. She was not naive enough to assume that meant they didn't have them. Most likely, they didn't feel a need to display them.

Annja had decided that the attack in the Bad Medicine parking lot resulted from an extreme case of being in the wrong place at the wrong time. The fact these two weren't awaiting her with gun or blade in hand seemed to reinforce that. But unlike the Bad Medicine, was clearly personal—targeted at her directly.

Reading the intent in her eyes, they fell back a step. Sadly, they talked themselves out of doing the sensible thing, which was simply to walk away and leave Annja Creed alone.

"Dog Soldiers, I'm guessing," she said, stepping back into the stall. It gave her, she reckoned, maximum choice of engagement ground should they attack. If she thought mobility might serve her best she had the larger restroom to move about in. If she wanted to ensure they could only come at her one at a time she could retreat fully back into the stall and accept the restrictions on her own scope of movement.

And if at any time the opportunity presented itself, she'd bolt out the door and be gone with the ice-nasty Plains wind that beat and boomed outside.

"You shouldn't think so much," the man on her left said. "You should just leave."

"Indian people don't want you here," the other said.

She frowned. Tom Ten Bears spoke with a blend of

rolling Okie drawl and Indian staccato. Strange as that sounded when she tried to describe it to herself, in his actual speech it came out perfectly naturally. These men were both speaking deep in their throats in an exaggerated stereotype of a Native American accent.

"You should turn aroun', drive back to Albuquerque," the first man said. "Get on a plane and fly away home. You don't belong here, stickin' your long nose in where it don't belong."

The bad grammar sounded as forced as their accents. By their builds and the general shapes of their faces, which was all she could make out for the paint and the not-very-good illumination, she figured they really were Indians, probably Comanche. But they seemed to be playing a role, and rather too hard at that.

"Thanks for the advice," she said. "I'll give it the consideration it deserves. Now, if you'll excuse me—" She started to walk between them.

The man on the left said, "Not so fast," and grabbed her upper arm.

She spun smartly into him. Her left arm came up and struck his forearm on the underside, knocking his grip loose before he'd had a chance to clamp it down. The palm-heel strike she followed up with flattened his nose with a satisfying crunch of cartilage breaking.

He emitted a squeal and dropped to his knees, clutching his face, which was pouring blood. Having your nose broken for the first time tended to affect you that way, Annja had observed.

His partner had already started grabbing for her right shoulder; if the object lesson provided by his buddy made an impression it came too late for him. She wheeled back into him. Her right forearm struck his left, again breaking his hold on her. She let her hand flop onto his arm. Then, putting her hips into it, she snapped right, yanking his trapped arm straight, back into the open stall, and locking out the elbow. She put her upraised left forearm against the locked-out joint and drove with her hips.

Annja knew very well how much pressure it took to break an elbow, and exactly how it felt to apply it.

The Dog Soldier did not choose to find out for himself what it took to give his elbow a whole new dimension of play. He had no choice but to allow himself to be swung face-first into the stout floor-to-ceiling upright that anchored the stall's front.

His face cracked against metal. He groaned and slumped. Annja gave him a Phoenix-eye fist, first knuckle extended, in the right kidney, just to get his mind right. He dropped with a painful thunk to his knees.

The other guy was game. On his knees, still trying futilely to staunch the blood from his broken nose with one hand, he groped for Annja with the other hand as she turned to go. She gave him a side kick that drove his other hand into his broken nose and snapped his head back against the other metal upright. He collapsed like an empty grain sack.

"Good evening, gentlemen," she said. "No need to get up. The pleasure was all mine."

9

"Mind if I sit down?"

Annja Creed's blood froze. It was a warm, charismatic baritone voice, absolutely dripping testosterone-fueled charisma.

It also belong to Johnny Ten Bears, chieftain of the outlaw Iron Horse People Motorcycle Club.

Chiding herself for being unobservant she looked up. He loomed above her, smiling in a nonthreatening way all over his darkly handsome face, with his black hair hanging again unbound over his colors.

She kept herself from flicking her eyes left and right like a frightened rabbit to look for other threats. Instead, she softened and widened the focus of her eyes. It showed her only the blurry shapes of the diners who had been there a moment before. When she was eating in peace, alone.

"Do I have a choice?" she asked.

He laughed softly. "We always have a choice," he said.

He sat down across from her. "It just doesn't always make a difference."

A mere quarter mile from her motel on the southwest outskirts of Lawton—not even a decent warm-up for long-legged Annja Creed—the Oklahoma Rose Café served a great breakfast.

Annja regarded the outlaw biker lord across the Formica tabletop. Outside the sun was bright, if not too far up the sky; the sky itself was pale blue and brushed over with thin tufts of cloud. The wind buffeted the picture window to Annja's right, and despite all that glorious sunshine she felt the chill beating from it like heat from a well-stoked woodstove. The diner itself was nice and toasty, though, and filled with the smells of good cooking.

"How're you walking these days?" she asked.

"Gingerly," he admitted.

"Good."

He laughed.

Annja's server turned up. The tall, good-looking black woman in early middle age had light skin and straight auburn hair wound up on her head in something that irresistibly reminded Annja of soft-swirl ice cream. "Johnny Ten Bears!" she exclaimed. "What do you think you doin', showin' your face around here? This a respectable establishment."

"Yeah, well, I'm the exception to the rule, Ruth. Coffee, please," he said with a wink and a big grin.

Ruth went away shaking her head.

"Don't even *try* turning that charm on me," Annja told him.

"Wouldn't think of it, Ms. Creed."

"You know my name?"

He shrugged. "Turned out Billy White Bird, my head wrench, is a big fan. He recognized you. About an hour after you busted a pool stick on his pumpkin head and blew out of the Bad Medicine."

"Really."

He leaned forward and clasped his hands on the tabletop before him. It was a gesture of such schoolboy earnestness she almost laughed aloud. He had good hands, she couldn't help noticing—big, strong, showing the calluses and scars of hard work despite his relatively few years. Only a few more than hers.

"You and my people kinda got off on the wrong foot," he said. "I apologize for that. Personally, and on behalf of my club."

"Whatever," she said. She went back to eating. "Your family's just full of coincidences, isn't it?"

He raised a brow.

"I mean, you turning up like this," she said.

"You're watched every moment you're in Indian country," he said, and he wasn't grinning. "Not all eyes are friendly. And, uh—what was that about my family?"

"The way your dad turned up in his cruiser on the county road north of the Bad Medicine the other night. To pick an example totally at random."

He shrugged. "He's wired into the Nation, too. Not much happens in Troop G territory he doesn't find out about."

"I got that impression."

"We wondered where you'd got to. Nasty night out."

"Yes, it was."

"I'd like to try my best to correct some misunder-standings you may have picked up along the way. The Iron Horse People Motorcycle Club is not your enemy."

"You put on a good act," she said.

He shook his head. "Anyway. First, you blundered into a place we feel very territorial about. Second, you perfectly fit the profile of the sort of person who should not be wandering into random road houses in western Oklahoma—and I don't mean just Indian bars or outlaw biker bars. Or both. Or, well, at first glance you *seemed* to fit the profile. I guess you showed how wrong that was. Turned out, unlike your normal tenderfoot tourist, you know how to handle yourself."

She smiled thinly. "I like to think so."

"Plus, my father may have fueled some fires here I'd like to tamp down. We *are* Indian secessionists. We're up front about that. It's our whole reason for being. What we aren't is racist."

"Oh, really."

"Please, Ms. Creed. Hear me out. Yes, we picked on you because you were white meat—and would've been meat for real if you went through the wrong door in Comanche County. You still could turn out that way, no matter how tough you are. Our reflex first thought was that you needed a good scare to keep you from making a mistake that could seriously cost you."

"Why would I believe that?"

"To start with," he said, "we let you get out alive."

She froze with a forkful of eggs partway to her mouth. "All right," she said. "Point taken."

"Our grievance is with the Great White Father," Johnny said. "*And* his hirelings, whatever color they are. We want nothing to do with Washington. Take nothing from it—give nothing to it. That's what we're about. Self-determination above everything else."

"Your mother said you had a lot of ideas in common with the old militia types."

"My mother?"

She grinned. Despite the all-knowing-native act he could be caught by surprise, after all. "I met her in Albuquerque. Your father sent me to her for a cultural background briefing. He didn't tell me she was associated with the ubiquitous Ten Bears clan, either."

"Okay, so my dad and I aren't always as dissimilar as we'd maybe both like to believe. How is she?"

"Fine. So's your sister."

His grin showed nothing but genuine pleasure. "Thanks. We don't always keep in touch."

The smile faded. "Please. Hear what I tell you. It's not just that there are some people, whether Indians or shit kickers, in these parts who're inclined to prey on lone young women. Especially ones as pretty as you are. Just fact, ma'am. No familiarity implied.

"It's that this is a very dangerous time and place for any outsiders—especially inquisitive white-eyes. There's a war going on. One that's the more nasty for being underground."

Annja frowned. "Your father told me there was bad blood between you and—"

"And the Dog Society. You saw some of them the other night."

"Maybe."

"Please don't play coy with me, Ms. Creed. This isn't bad blood—it's war. I've seen war. I know what it looks and feels and smells like."

"I know." He spoke like someone who *did* know war. Those who only experienced it at second hand seldom understood about the smell.

"I'm talking about midnight disappearances. Decomposed bodies found in washes. A body count nobody talks about. And it keeps on rising."

She couldn't doubt the truth of what he said. She was surprised, though, by how much Johnny's ever-helpful father hadn't told her.

"The Dog Society were originally Cheyenne," Johnny said. "A lot of them live around here, too."

"I know the history part," Annja said. "Your mother filled me in. It's current events I'm not too clear on."

"Well, okay. The Dog Soldiers, twenty-first-century edition. A few actual Cheyennes belong, as well as some Kiowa. Most of them are young Comanches. They *are* racists, who don't like white-eyes worth spit. They're hard-core traditionalists, or what they like to imagine Numunu traditions are, anyway. They really believe, and I can't emphasize this enough, that as the American empire weakens, the time approaches when they can throw off the white-eyes' yoke and rule."

"Really?" she asked. "And that differs from your philosophy, how?"

"Fair question. We—the Iron Horse People—don't want to force anybody to do anything but let us alone. We only want to rule ourselves. Yes, we think the empire's going down, too. We've got eyes. Don't *you* see it?"

She hesitated. "Let's stick with the sales pitch for your philosophy."

"The Dogs are eager to kill anybody whose feet stray from their very narrow path. We fight them, yes. To contain them. To try to keep them hurting too many people. Or setting a wildfire that could consume the whole Comanche Nation."

He sighed. "My father will never believe it," he said, "but we're the good guys."

"You expect *me* to believe it?"

He shrugged. "It's the truth. Like any gift, what you choose to do with it once I give it to you is your business."

Annja nodded.

He sat back, cocked his head and regarded her appraisingly.

Without warning the window exploded inward toward them.

10

With rattlesnake-strike speed Johnny Ten Bears reached over the table, grabbed Annja's wrist as she hoisted another forkful and yanked her from the booth. As she cleared the table he pulled her toward him hard.

Shards of glass cascaded across the red vinyl seats of the booth, over the table and onto the floors. Annja slid past Johnny on the slick floor.

Automatic gunfire snarled outside. Glass and porcelain tinkled as bullets raked the diner's interior, shattering crockery on the counter and beyond. Yellow-and-white chintz curtains flapped as the wind blew through the shot-out windows.

Annja writhed in Johnny's grasp. Ignoring his shout to stop she pushed up to all fours, then ran bent over through more broken glass toward the door. It was exactly the sort of behavior safety experts told you *not* to engage in.

Annja did a lot of things that would make safety experts go faint. She didn't always have much use for their advice, anyway. Given that somebody was spraying and praying—probably from a moving car—a quick glance outside would expose her to little additional risk. A lot less risk, in her estimation, than hunkering down and getting caught helpless if the shooters decided to stop their car, get out and walk inside to finish the job.

Luckily that didn't happen. Instead, when she took a three-second look out the door she saw a junker brown sedan screaming around a corner with the long black barrels and distinctive ribbed foregrips of M-16s sticking out the windows. She glanced around to see if there were follow-up vehicles, or gunmen approaching on foot. She saw nothing threatening.

When Annja turned around she saw Johnny going quickly from customer to customer, making sure no one was badly hurt. She started doing the same. The diners had all gotten onto the floor and laid low with no apparent panic. They were picking themselves up now.

Ruth's soft-serve hairdo popped up from behind the counter. "What the hell," she demanded, "was *that?*"

"Dog Soldiers' social call," Johnny said.

The bullets had missed everyone. An elderly woman and a trucker had suffered cuts on their faces. They seemed pretty calm, considering.

"Why would somebody want to go and do something like that?" the old woman said as Ruth came up to examine the gash in her cheek. "What's the world coming to?"

Annja turned to frown at Johnny.

"The Dog Society plays for keeps," he said.

"Are you sure those were Dog Soldiers?" Annja asked.

Johnny shook his head and laughed in disbelief. "Do you think I'm dumb enough to sit there waiting for my own people to take a shot at you from a moving car, just to prove some point? You can't be sure of hitting what you aim at, blasting full rock and roll from a moving vehicle. So you can't be sure of missing, either, can you?"

"You're right," she said. "So, more coincidence."

"Not really," he said. "Somebody saw me and dropped a dime. Remember what I told you about life in Indian country."

He raised his head and frowned in concentration, as if sniffing the air. Annja heard the faint whine of sirens begin to rise.

"This place is about to get even less healthy for me," he said, "so I'm gone. Think about what I told you."

"I will," she said.

He tossed a few bills on an interior table and left, moving with purpose but no haste. She stood and watched as he forked his big red-and-buff bike, fired it up and blasted away.

Sirens were screaming on the wind, which blew unimpeded into the shot-up diner. Annja surveyed the scene. Ruth had mustered the kitchen staff, who were all unharmed, to see to the customers. They seemed to have the situation well in hand, with no serious injuries suffered. Annja found a safe chair and sat to await the arrival of the law.

To her surprise the first to arrive on the scene weren't Lawton cops or Comanche County officers, nor even the highway patrol, but a pair of gleaming gray sedans full of trim young Indian men in business suits with short haircuts. Some of them drew handguns and moved out of sight, evidently to check the rear exits to the building. Three entered the diner.

The obvious leader was a man in his late twenties, who was built like a power lifter. He stood a moment with hands on hips, pooching out the tails of his suit coat, frowning over the scene. Then he approached Annja.

"You're Annja Creed?" he said, flipping open a leather case to display a shield that read Comanche Nation Law Enforcement.

"Yes."

"I'm pleased to meet you. I'm George Abell, chief inspector of the Comanche Nation's new special investigative unit."

He seemed young for such a prestigious assignment. It never did any good that Annja had seen to point that sort of thing out to people. It always annoyed her mightily when someone said something like that to *her*. So she made no comment beyond politely acknowledging the introduction.

"What happened here?" he asked. His two companions drew handguns and went back to check the kitchens and the back rooms.

She told him. Since the other people in the diner would tell the investigators about her companion she told him the truth. Most of it, anyway; she saw no point in mentioning the Bad Medicine. After all, he was concerned with what just happened *here*.

Abell started frowning at mention of Johnny Ten Bears. His frown only dug itself deeper into his round, slightly coarse face as she gave him an edited account of their conversation.

"You're a very lucky woman, Ms. Creed," he said when she'd finished. "John Ten Bears is a dangerous man."

"I'm sure he is, Chief Inspector," she said. "But wasn't it the Dog Society that shot at me?"

He scowled even deeper and put his hands behind his hips, elbowing out the tails of his dark suit coat. His men came out of the back shaking their heads—nobody hiding there. He nodded briskly to them and they began moving among the witnesses, asking questions of their own.

"The Dog Society are basically radical activists," he said. "Sometimes they let their zeal for social justice run away with them. While I won't rule out that some Dog hotheads might've been responsible for the shooting, since Johnny Ten Bears is a bitter and brutal enemy, I think most likely our shooters were disaffected Iron Horses. They're a gang of violent criminals, Ms. Creed. There's nothing they're not capable of."

Except stabbing or shooting me when they had their chance, and I even gave them a halfway decent excuse, Annja thought. Interesting. Then again Abell wouldn't be the first cop with a hatred for bikers.

The chief inspector spoke like a college-educated man—closer to an academic than a stereotypical Midwestern law-enforcement man, or even Lieutenant Tom Ten Bears, who wouldn't settle for being anybody's stereotype. He was surface pleasant, at least, slick in a way that belied his powerful appearance.

He lost points when, smilingly, he said, "I really urge you to go home to New York and leave the investigation to professionals, Ms. Creed."

"I'm a journalist," she reminded him, "as well as an archaeologist. I've done consulting work for law enforcement before. I won't interfere in your investigation."

"You misunderstand me," he said, shaking his head and smiling. "I only have your safety at heart. It might not be going too far to suggest you may be a marked woman. Ten Bears is a criminal. Probably even a terrorist. He's also a punk. He's always been a punk and a wannabe."

Annja shied back from him, ever so slightly.

"Please forgive my vehemence," Abell said. "I've known John since we were kids. It makes me angry that he'd put you and these other innocent people at risk from such potentially deadly violence."

"I was afraid I'd find you here," a voice said from the door.

Both Annja and Abell turned, the latter frowning again.

"Lieutenant Ten Bears," Annja said.

The stocky highway patrol officer had stepped aside to clear the way for emergency crews bustling in to examine the wounded. He stood with his thumbs hooked in the front of his belt. He didn't look as cheerful as usual.

"Morning, Annja," he said. "Mr. Abell."

Abell nodded shortly. "Lieutenant."

The air temperature dropped a few degrees from where the nasty Plains wind had already pushed it. She could practically see the testosterone swimming in midair, like dust motes. Departmental rivalry in action, she thought. No doubt complicated by the fact of Johnny Ten Bears.

Ruth rushed up. "Tom! That crazy son of yours was in here. He brings trouble with him wherever he goes."

"Tell me something I don't know, Ruth. Everybody okay?"

"Aside from a few nicks and scratches. Nothing they won't get over. I sure hope Mrs. Kubica's insurance covers this mess, though." She scrubbed her hands in her apron, shaking her head. "Lucky thing those so-and-sos couldn't shoot for diddly."

"Amen," the lieutenant said. Other troopers came in with evidence techs and began taking statements. "Ms. Creed, I'd like you to come back to the barracks and give me a statement."

Abell opened his mouth.

"Of course, Lieutenant," she said. Turning to Abell she extended a hand. He gave it a firm if perfunctory shake.

"I appreciate your solicitude, Mr. Abell. Goodbye."

"I'll want a copy of any statements the witnesses make," Abell called as the lieutenant and Annja left.

"Send the request through channels, George," the elder Ten Bears said. "You know the drill."

Once safely enclosed in the car and prowling away down the road from the shot-up diner, Annja said, "Thanks for rescuing me—again."

"All part of the service, Ms. Creed. That Georgie's always been way too full of himself. Is a bit of a bully— loves to throw his weight around. And had a lot to do it with, too."

He shook his crew-cut head. "You can get serviceable cops out of beginnings like that. A good one, I don't know about. Guess we ought to give the youngster a chance to grow up some."

Annja bit down hard on the urge to ask if George Abell had bullied Johnny when they were kids. Instead, on the drive to the Troop G barracks on the east edge of Lawton, she gave the lieutenant a summary of current events. A considerably fuller one than she'd given Abell, extending to the previous couple of days.

At the station she gave a videotaped statement and then filled out the usual reams of forms. When that was done she went back to Ten Bears' office, as he'd requested.

He was peering over the tops of his reading glasses at his computer monitor, as if whatever he saw there smelled bad. He waved her to a seat.

"You report that little restroom encounter to the New Mexico authorities?" he asked.

"No," she said quietly.

He sighed, took off the glasses and swiveled to face her. "Your little playmates in there committed multiple crimes. Including a little thing we call felony battery."

"Outside your jurisdiction," she said.

"Well, I *am* sworn to uphold the law. And I've always gotten along pretty good with those New Mexico State Patrol boys and girls."

She shrugged. "Well, I am reporting it. To you."

"I'm guessing you don't want to pursue this?"

She shook her head emphatically. "I've already had my face splashed all over the news too much because of my involvement with poor Paul."

He raised an eyebrow at her.

"Okay," she said, "I'm a television personality. That doesn't mean I'm a celebrity, or want to be one. I don't live for face time. I work for Chasing History's Monsters because it's fun, it pays well and I feel as if it gives me a chance, if not always a fair one, to shine the light of science and reason into some dark, superstitious places. In terms of the show, though, I'm just a minor and occasional talking head. That suits me fine."

For far more reasons than I hope you'll ever get wind of, she thought.

He chuckled and nodded. "Fair enough."

She leaned back in her chair then, and gave him an intent look. "So, Lieutenant, why didn't you tell me you were related to Dr. Watson? To say nothing of Johnny?"

"Didn't see it was any of your business."

His tone remained light and bantering; he gave off none of the challenge that usually accompanied that class of statement. From her limited acquaintance of the man she guessed he was capable of both perfect sincerity and total fraud. Whatever served his ends, as a law-enforcement officer or, probably, a Comanche.

"Anyway, I reckoned you'd find all that out. And you did."

He studied her a moment. Outside, the day began to show signs of fading.

"So what'd you make of Johnny?" he asked.

"He's obviously an intelligent man," she said. "He certainly seems sincere in his convictions."

"So he gave you that Great White Father crazy talk

of his. I don't know where I went wrong with that boy. I tried to raise him with his head on face-frontwards."

"Does it ever occur to you, Lieutenant," she said, "that you might have?"

He frowned at her. Then he laughed. "You're a sharp one, Ms. Creed. I see I better look sharp to make sure you don't slip one past this poor old lawman."

"Nothing could be further from my intentions," she said. "Anyway, horsecrap. Nobody ever slips anything past you, Lieutenant. Do they?"

"Well, come to think of it…mebbe not all that often, at that," he said.

"I haven't learned much about what happened to Paul, or what's going on in Comanche County, nor what they might have to do with each other," she said. "But I have a better idea how things stand."

"I'd say so, given all the bullets cracklin' past your ears and all. Now that you've seen for yourself what the stakes are around here, are you sure you want to stick with it?"

"Yes." She started to rise, then hesitated. "You don't believe it was Johnny's own people who shot up the Oklahoma Rose, do you?"

After a moment he said, "No. I don't put much past them, don't get me wrong. But the Dog Society won't be mistaken for the Ladies' Aid anytime soon, either. As you found out back in New Mexico. If I weren't an upholder of the law, sworn in all right and proper, I'd be tempted to opine they deserve each other."

Given her experiences Annja would be much less tempted by that opinion. She almost hated to admit it, but she saw Johnny's point about his club's perspective. It was possible neither she nor her inadvertent hosts had handled things very well that night in the Bad Medicine.

"I'll be in touch, Lieutenant," she said, standing to go.

"One more thing, Ms. Creed. Don't go thinking you know my son. Don't make the mistake of assuming you understand anything about him at all. Even if he can charm a chunk of dead dog out an old snapping turtle's mouth."

She frowned. "I totally don't believe that's an authentic Oklahoma aphorism," she said. "I think you just made it up in hopes of making me throw up."

"Don't want you upchucking on the paperwork, Ms. Creed—all respect, it messes it up so it won't hardly feed through the copy machine. Other than that, you are purely correct."

THROUGH GATHERING TWILIGHT, she ran.

It soothed her. She needed to decompress and process. Even if she couldn't fully give in to her feelings quite yet.

Mourning Paul properly would have to wait until he was avenged. Or until it became apparent it was beyond her ability to do so.

She was on a back road through low rolling hills, on her way back to the motel, which she guessed was a mile away yet. The wind had died at last. With the exertion she was comfortable in her T-shirt and sweatpants in spite of the fact the temperature had dropped noticeably when the sun dipped behind the Wichitas ten minutes or so earlier.

She was jogging, taking a break from running flat

out, when an eerie feeling prickled the skin at the back of her neck and made her belly muscles go taut.

Not slowing her pace she looked around.

She saw a shadow, a black silhouette on a rise not a hundred feet to the west.

It was shaped like a huge wolf.

11

Annja slowed to a stop. She looked hard at the creature. "If you're really the one who killed Paul," she called out, "come try me on for size."

She didn't really believe it. It was surely a human, deranged or evil or both, who had murdered Paul and all those other innocent people. Not an animal like this one. However spooky.

Maybe she couldn't quite disbelieve it, either. But if it did attack her—unusual behavior for a lone wolf or even a feral dog—that would prove it probably was involved with Paul's cruel death.

And Paul would be avenged.

Instead, the creature whirled and disappeared. She thought about pursuing but decided it probably wasn't a good idea. At best it would be as futile as her chasing after the shadowy creature in Roosevelt Park in Albuquerque. They were both almost certainly just random big scary-looking dogs, anyway.

She realized then what had caused the animal to bolt. A dark-colored sedan was driving toward her along the road with its halogen headlights weird actinic eyes in the twilight. It was moving more slowly than the road's surface, rutted by spring rains, seemed to mandate. She stood by the ditch, frowning slightly, as the vehicle slowed to a stop beside her.

The window rolled down. A suit-jacket sleeve and a white shirt cuff came out with a pale hand sprouting from them like a lily. The hand displayed a photo ID with a big gold government seal.

"FBI, Ms. Creed," a male voice said from behind the hand, the cuff and the badge. "I need to ask you to get in the car, please. We need to talk."

THE FEDERAL COURTHOUSE in Lawton was a big yellow-brick cube standing apart from other buildings in the downtown area. It was the sort of mountain-solid late-nineteenth or early-twentieth-century building they didn't build anymore, and consequently the kind of building with a weather-darkened brass plaque stuck on its aboveground cement foundation.

Special Agent in Charge Lamont Young was a big, blond, bland man in a pale gray suit. Annja didn't know, and he didn't volunteer, whether he was in charge of the local Lawton office or of some task force sent from somewhere larger, presumably Oklahoma City. He interviewed her in a room with yellow-painted walls and white trim that smelled of old paint and the steam heat from an old-fashioned radiator under one lone window that was turning the place to a sauna. He perched his broad rump on the edge of a green metal desk and talked in vague terms about a "potentially unstable situation" and "risk factors," with his hands clasped between his knees.

Then he got down to asking questions. They were general. What do you do? What are you doing here? What was your relationship to the deceased? She sat in an uncompromising and uncomfortable wooden chair, gave simple, direct answers and hoped they'd wrap it up soon.

Then he asked, "How do you know John Jacob Ten Bears?"

"Johnny? I met him in a bar. I didn't encourage his acquaintance."

That's putting it mildly, she thought, restraining a smile.

"Do you frequent this bar, Ms. Creed?"

"I've been in Lawton for three days. I'm not sure that gives me an opportunity to 'frequent' anything."

He pursed his lips. "You have spent only a single night in the Lawton area, Ms. Creed."

"I've had kind of a rough time, Special Agent Young. Lots of travel, a close friend being killed. Being shot at. I may be a little fuzzy as to details right now."

He nodded judiciously.

"Are you investigating Johnny?" she asked.

"I'm afraid I can't answer that."

"Is he a person of interest, then?"

"I can't answer that, either."

"Then what difference does it make what I know about him? Anyway, everything is in the statements I gave to Lieutenant Ten Bears. Including my account of what happened in the Oklahoma Rose." About which he'd as yet asked nothing.

"Presumably you know he is John Ten Bears' father?"

"Yes. Do you feel that prejudices the lieutenant's ability to conduct an investigation?"

"Let us say the potential for a conflict of interest is there."

She laughed. "If you'd actually sit down and talk to either man, you'd find out how mistaken that is. If anything, Lieutenant Ten Bears will go harder on his son than he would some random person."

"Perhaps you believe that."

She reminded herself getting annoyed with a federal agent was a waste of time at best. "Look, just what are you investigating here? The serial killings? The Iron Horse People? Some kind of events locally that might connect them?"

"Why would you suspect we're investigating local events?"

"I got shot at this morning. With fully automatic weapons, which are extremely uncommon on the streets in this country, as well as intensely illegal. They were American made, not Kalashnikovs—M-16s. There's obviously some pretty serious game being played around here. I'd have to be a fool not to notice that."

"Have you any special knowledge of what you're calling a 'game'?"

"No. I'm interested in who killed Paul, and is butchering my professional peers. Lieutenant Ten Bears has asked me to consult, on an unofficial basis, from my knowledge not just of archaeology but of the profession of archaeology. I've done contract consulting with law enforcement before. I know the rules."

"Are you aware that the penalties for obstructing a federal investigation are quite severe?"

"Yes. I'd pretty much gathered that."

"It would be advisable for you to leave the area, Ms. Creed. You can only put yourself in the way of unpleasant complications by staying."

"So I'm not under suspicion of anything, then?"

"Why do you say that?"

"Isn't it usual procedure to tell a suspect not to leave the area?"

"I see… You are not a suspect, Ms. Creed. I have the discretion to tell you that."

"Good. Do you have the discretion to let me go?"

"Are you agreeing to leave Oklahoma?"

"No."

"You aren't being very cooperative, young lady."

"You haven't actually asked my cooperation on anything. You've threatened me. You suggested I go away. Not much scope for cooperation there. Now, may I please leave? I'm tired and hungry and want to take a shower."

"Yes."

She got up.

"Ms. Creed?" His voice stopped her at the door.

"Yes."

"You're making a mistake if you stay."

"That wouldn't be the first one. Good evening, Special Agent Young."

THE STARS WERE OUT above the Plains in force when Annja pulled into the gravel lot of the Bad Medicine. The glow of the neon sign did little to push them back as she parked facing the dirt road. She looked to confirm the presence of a certain distinctive red-and-cream Indian bike before she turned off the engine.

The clouds were gone but the wind bit deep as she got out of her car. She wondered how freaked the rental company would be if they checked the car's GPS records and found she'd driven back to the place where she'd left the last one. Which presumably had been turned into a sieve by gunplay by the time they sweet-talked a wrecker into coming out to such dubious precincts to tow it away.

"Take it up with Lieutenant Ten Bears," she suggested aloud to the hypothetical outraged rental agent.

The expected blast of warmth and noise hit her like a blowtorch when she opened the door. Once again all conversation stopped as if a switch had been turned. She could see twenty or so Iron Horses gathered there.

Every face turned as one to peer at her.

Somebody said something and jumped to his feet. She was relieved to see most of the expressions were confused. Somewhat.

But then a familiar lanky figure unfolded from a table in the far corner. "It's all right," Johnny Ten Bears said, his baritone voice ringing out.

"Come on in," Johnny said, walking up to Annja with his rolling gait. "Folks, this is Annja Creed. We met her the other night under kinda unfortunate circumstances. I talked to her today, right before that little shooting scrape you-all heard about, and we agreed to bury the hatchet. She's good people.

"And she's with me," he added.

Not knowing quite how to respond to the sheer force of masculinity the half Kiowa, half Comanche biker lord seemed to radiate, she shook his strong well-shaped hand. It made her feel lame.

"Understand I can't order anybody around," he said, smiling and leaning his head close to hers so his hair fell to either side of his face like shining black curtains. "These aren't the sort of people who take kindly to taking orders. I just try to…set an example."

"All right," Annja said. "Can we talk?"

"Figured you might want to do that." He straightened. "Come on and meet the tribe. This bear-shaped buck is Billy White Bird, my right-hand man and the best wrench in western Oklahoma and the greater panhandle area."

"Sorry we got off on the wrong foot the other night," Annja said as the grinning man enfolded her hand in one paw. "I see your face is healing up nicely."

"Superficial cut," he said. "Head wounds bleed like crazy. Anyway, I always heal fast. And I apologize for my behavior. Sometimes I let a joke get outta hand." She noticed that he still wore his colors over bare skin, and got another glimpse of the intricate blue tattoo over his paunch.

"Wondering why I wander around half-nekkid?" he asked, and shrugged. "Don't like to get too hot. Ed keeps it like a furnace in here during the cold months. And an icebox when it's warm."

He followed them as Johnny escorted Annja through

the crowd, introducing random people. "This is Ricky, Angel, Mose, Quahadi—"

Ricky was blade-lean and had a gold hoop in his right ear. Angel looked almost comically like her name, with a soft oval face that probably looked years younger than she was. She wore a fringed black jacket over her colors. She also carried a dark-blue Taurus .357 with what looked like grips custom cut down to fit her small hands. Beyond that Annja lost track.

As they navigated back toward Johnny's table, Annja met Eagle Eye, Satanta, Loco and Lonny Blackhands.

And, of course, Snake.

"I believe you two got acquainted the other night," Johnny said.

Her handshake was dry and firm and sinuously strong. Well, it would be, Annja thought. "Pleased to met you," Annja said.

"The pleasure's all yours," Snake said. "Anytime you'd like to renew our…getting acquainted—"

"Now, Snake," Johnny said, putting just a hint of whip-crack to his voice. "Is that a hospitable way to treat our guest?"

"If I were hospitable," the tall woman said, turning back to the bar, "would I be named Snake?"

Everybody got back to what they were doing— talking and drinking—while Johnny took Annja to his table. Billy White Bird followed.

The chairs were old-style wooden saloon chairs. They were at least somewhat more comfortable than the one in Special Agent Young's office.

"So why the interest in us?" Johnny asked. "It doesn't seem likely to be our charming company."

She grinned. "Don't underrate yourselves," she said. "I've had plenty worse receptions."

Billy looked at her close. "Reckon you have at that," he said softly. He took a drink from his mug. When he set it down an unmistakable smell reach Annja's nostrils. He was drinking apple cider, not beer.

In fact, now that she noticed it, she hadn't smelled alcohol at all since coming in here. "You have got to be kidding—" she said, leaning back and straightening in her chair.

"I think she's caught on to our terrible secret," Billy said, eyes twinkling.

Johnny shrugged. "It's no big thing. Some of our people are recovering alcoholics. The rest of us don't tend to drink much. Yeah, the stereotypical Indians and alcohol thing—some people say we've got a genetic predisposition to it, but I don't buy. The scientific evidence seems sketchy at best. Anyway. Booze and bikes don't really mix that well—that's a fact. Nor do guns and booze."

She shook her head. "You people are too much."

"Now she's really catching on," Billy said.

"I thought you were hanging around to investigate the skinwalker killings?" Johnny said.

The media had dubbed the murderer the I-40 Killer, since all his attacks had occurred fairly near the big west-to-east artery that had supplanted the famed Route 66. The police were squatting hard on all details that connected the crimes to anything either supernatural sounding or that would hint at an Indian connection. None too surprisingly the Iron Horses seemed to have contacts of their own.

"So why the interest in us?" Johnny asked again.

"The Dog Society connection, mostly," she said. "Which was brought home to me pretty forcefully this morning."

"Listen," Johnny said, "I am really sorry about that. I had no right to expose you to that kind of danger, not to mention those poor people at the diner. I honestly had no idea the Dogs would fly that far off the handle. I didn't realize just how bad things had gotten."

"Why do you assume you were the target?" she asked softly.

A local cone of silence seemed to descend on their little table. "Say what?" Billy asked.

She shrugged. "I've been attracting a lot of attention lately. That attack on your club house I took for just bad timing on my part. Say, none of your people were hurt in that?"

"Nothing they won't get over," Johnny said.

"Them Dogs were planning some kind of surprise attack, we think," Billy said. "Once the guns started talking, they pulled back pretty smart."

"Good. Anyway, I got a personal warning from them night before last." She sketched out the restroom encounter in eastern New Mexico.

Through her mind flitted the memory of wolf shadows at sunset. Seeming to watch her. She dismissed them as irrelevant. Hallucination, mere coincidence. Certainly nothing real.

When she finished her account Johnny sat back, pulling a long face and nodding.

"You're taking this all pretty calm for a well-groomed college-educated white-eyes chick," Billy said.

She shrugged. "Not the first time I've been shot at. With automatic weapons, for that matter. Not the first time people have tried to jack me up in lonely places, either."

The two bikers exchanged glances. "I get the feeling you let us off kinda easy the other night, lady," Billy said.

"Yeah. Well. No offense, but you didn't really trip my deadly threat detectors. Seemed as if you were just trying to rowdy me up some."

Billy guffawed. He made as if to slap Annja on the back, then pulled his hand away as if suspecting her shoulder was forge-hot. "Hoo-baby! We got us a winner here, Johnny."

"As long as you don't get to thinking you're bullet-proof," he said soberly.

"Believe me, I know better," she said. "Anyway, as to your conflict with the Dog Society here—it just seems there has to be a skinwalker connection. First, it seems unlikely the Dogs have decided to lean on me, however hard, just because I'm nosing around their turf. If they know that much, they know I am fixated on solving the death of my friend. Circumstances have kind of forced me to widen my focus. Second, it also strikes me that if the Dogs were after me that first night outside this place, they'd've come on way stronger than they did in that ladies' room."

"Mebbe they put two and two together after you busted those bad boys up some," Billy said.

"Not impossible. But one common theme of the skinwalker attacks seems to be that the digs he targets are protested by Native groups."

"*Nominally* native," Johnny said.

"Okay. But the Dogs opposed the dig here, didn't they? Even if they weren't the ones picketing it?"

"Actually, they were," Billy said. "They have this kind, gentler public-face auxiliary. Kinda like Sinn Féin to the old Provisional IRA."

"The creature—*killer*—does seem to have struck a bit far afield. Coincidentally in an area where radical violence is already taking place."

Johnny looked at Billy again, then back at her, Leaning forward, he said, "Ms. Creed, you don't know the half of it."

"Annja," she corrected half-reflexively. "What don't I know the half of?"

"We have wind that the Dog Soldiers have cooked up a scheme to provoke a race war between Indians and whites," Johnny said. "We think it's about good to go."

12

"That's insane," Annja said. "Indians are a tiny minority of the population. They'd get squashed."

Johnny canted his head to one side. "Maybe not. The U.S. military is spread thin all over the world. It's been weakened, materially and morally, by too many wars for no strategic benefit to Americans, or even any visible strategic point. The economy is struggling. A case for vulnerability could be made."

"But would some kind of shocking terrorist strike be more likely to cause faith in the U.S. government to break down, or to invite hideous retaliation against Indians? And not just from the government?" Annja said.

"Well," Billy said, shrugging, "that's the question, ain't it?"

"We fear the latter," Johnny said. "The Dogs believe strongly in the former. They even believe other radicals, including white anarchists, will actively join them."

Johnny Ten Bears seemed a highly intelligent man, Annja thought. His manner was certainly calm and rational. "What do you think?"

"I think that the Dog Solders have talked themselves into believing there's a good enough chance of success to go for it," he said.

She shook her head and blew out a long breath. "That's a big leap for me to take," she responded. "As I said, I've been shot at before. By some pretty blatantly bad people. And none of them actually thought they could take down the United States government."

"Well, Comanche County has been just a font of new experiences for you, then," Billy said.

"Just do me one favor," Johnny said, shaking his head. "Once you walk out of here. Keep your head on a swivel."

"Always," she said.

"YEAH, JUST LIKE I thought," Lieutenant Tom Ten Bears said, shaking his head. "FBI has been tramping all over this place like yokels gaping at the world's biggest pig at the county fair. I do believe I see the print of Special Agent in Charge Young over there."

Annja doubted it. Admittedly she hadn't been overly impressed with Young herself. But the Bureau maintained at least certain minimum standards of professionalism.

But *somebody* had trampled the University of Oklahoma dig and multiple-murder scene well and truly. Her vote went to the national and global media, before taking flight once more and swarming like locusts to the next showy catastrophe. At the moment she and the lieutenant had it to themselves. Not even the Comanche County sheriff was sending his deputies out to freeze and watch an isolated crime scene that had been so thoroughly picked over.

The wind blew. The clouds threatened. Annja wondered if spring was always like this.

"Don't report me," the lieutenant said, pulling the collar of his bulky brown jacket higher around his neck, "but I could use some of that global warming they're always talking about on TV. This is more like the ice age."

Annja paused by the RV where Paul had lived the last few days of his life. The RV had its doors sealed with yellow crime-scene tape.

"So I've been reading some of those reports you sent me," she said, taking off a glove and briefly touching the cold metal of the RV's side. "It looks as if people were reporting strange wolflike creatures in the vicinity even before the attacks."

"Yeah. And not just wolves. We got shaggy-man stories, too. Not your usual Sasquatch or skunk-ape guy in gorilla-sort yarns, either. We're talking full-on wolfman stuff. Sent you those, too."

She shook her head. "It's probably just people getting worked up and seeing natural animals."

"Got no wolves in Comanche County."

"Well, big dogs, then. Or even coyotes. Coyotes are everywhere now. You can't really believe there's more to these reports than that?"

He stuck his hands deep in his jacket pockets and chuckled. "I surely do love it when you city folk come out here, and you know so much more about the land

and the weather and the animals than us poor dumb country folk who've only lived among all that our entire lives."

"You don't really think there's anything paranormal going on?" Annja said.

"Not necessarily. I don't discount supernatural stuff all the way, either. I've seen some things that aren't exactly dreamt of in your philosophy, Ms. Creed."

"I'm—wait. Did you just quote Hamlet at me?"

"Naw. You're givin' in to that conspiracy-theory stuff again. I'm just an Indian country hick, too dumb to come in out of the rain."

"All right. You can back off. I already know better than to underestimate you. But seriously? You think there might *not* be a rational explanation?"

"Seriously, I don't think we can—anyhow, anyway—discount the possibility of a killer nutbag dressing himself up in a wolfman suit and skulking around the county. Seems I recently got me a report from this highfalutin outside expert, all college credentialed and all, mentioned skinwalkers're supposed to do that very thing. Even quoted a second expert to the effect that playing skinwalker might just be a perfectly natural thing for a sociopath to do. Of course, how you could call that a *rational* explanation is way past me. Ain't nothing rational about this perp."

"Okay, okay! You just have no mercy, do you?"

"I'd have to turn in my Comanche card if I did, ma'am. We got us a historical reputation to maintain."

Annja laughed aloud. This short, portly cop was proving himself a worthy foe.

"Peace," she said. "We need to be on the same side."

"Amen, sister. Preaching to the choir."

"Okay. Well, thanks for taking the time to meet with me. Can we get in out of the cold now?"

"Thought you'd never ask."

They started walking back to their cars.

"So do you have any actual evidence of any kinds of plots against the opening ceremonies for this new Comanche Star Casino?" she asked.

"Now, Annja, don't go getting yourself wrapped up in that kind of thing. It's pure trouble. And it has nothing to do with the deaths of your friend and his associates."

"I seem to have gotten wrapped up in it, regardless. Anyway, how can you be so sure there *is* no connection." She stopped and squared to face him. "There's something seriously nasty going on here. It started long before the murders, and it seems to be ongoing."

"And it's our business," Ten Bears said. "Got nothing to do with this other thing."

"How can you be sure? Is it just coincidence that the killer struck here, where tensions between Indian and white and Indian and Indian are getting wound so tight?"

"But he hit twice in New Mexico," Ten Bears said. "And while there's always tension where Indians come in contact with white-eyes or Mexicans, they're not having troubles across the state line like we are here in Comanche country. I'd know if they were, believe me. There's an old-boy network for Indian lawmen. Yes, and women, too. We keep in touch."

"But he *did* come here. Which is a lot farther from Navajo country than the Rio Grande Valley."

"You said it yourself—he seems to be drawn to these protests by professional Indians, wannabes and loafs-about-the-fort," Ten Bears said. "Like he's trying to show solidarity with them. Why make it more complicated than that?"

"Because it *is* more complicated," she said. "You feel it, too. I know you do."

"It always is," he said, turning away.

As they were opening the doors of their respective vehicles, he called to her. "Just one more little thing."

"This is where you warn me to steer clear of your son because he's pure trouble, isn't it?" Annja said.

"This is where I warn you to steer clear of Johnny," he said solidly. "He's pure trouble. Especially for a pretty woman such as yourself, if you won't take that as sexual harassment and all."

"I have a pretty high harassment threshold, Lieutenant."

"Somehow that doesn't surprise me."

"I'm not going to get romantically entangled with your son, if that's what you're thinking."

He raised an eyebrow. "You sure about that? He can be a pretty charming cuss when he sets his mind to it. Gets it from his old man."

He slapped himself on the belly. "Built the way I am, I *had* to be charming. Or I'd never have got the chance to pass my genes along, as the kids say nowadays."

Given how slick the fat old bastard was, she thought it was a pretty plausible theory.

"Of course I'm sure!" she snapped. "Why shouldn't I be sure?"

"If you say so."

"I do. But he may have information that could help lead to Paul's killer," she said. "I want that information."

"I'm not sure that's the right tree you're barking up," he said. "One way or another, you want to be careful what might come dropping down on your head from the branches.

"I know you're not the usual college-professor type, Annja. But there's trouble you can get into here in Comanche country I can't pull you out of. You may find trouble even *you* can't pull yourself out of."

She looked at him for a moment. Then she smiled. "Thanks," she said. "I mean that. Thank you for caring."

"It's my job," he said. "Not like you're gonna listen to me."

"No," she agreed. "But thanks, anyway."

WHEN SHE GOT BACK to the motel her phone was blinking a red light at her.

"Who'd be calling me here?" she asked the room, which was all done up neat and trim and nice smelling, with the bedspread taut as a drumhead.

"Well, one way to find out." She laid her backpack on that immaculate spread and sat down on the edge of the bed by the phone, still wearing her coat. She picked up the handset, consulted the little chart printed on the phone and punched in the code to retrieve the message.

A strange male voice said, "Ms. Creed? You don't know me but we need to talk. I know what certain people are up to, okay? Johnny said I need to talk to you."

"WHOA," ANNJA SAID, gazing around as she walked through gates that had not been closed for a long time by the looks of them.

"I didn't know there were any old drive-in movie theaters still standing."

She was talking to herself, and to the stars, hard and bright overhead, although they were rapidly taking leave of her as menacing-looking clouds raced in and gathered from the north.

The place had clearly stood derelict for years. The posts had been stripped of their car speakers and stood in forlorn ranks like bare stalks leftover from some final harvest. The windows and doors of the former projection booth and concession stand were gapes of blackness in the gloom. Their outer walls, and the insides of the perimeter walls, were crusted in spray-painted signs and slogans.

She walked over to the concession stand. It was where her contact said he'd meet her. It was also an obvious ambush site. She stayed on her guard.

She knew she wasn't going to delve deeper into the real reasons behind the skinwalker murders, or the Dog Society's mysterious vendetta for her, without taking some real risks. She'd been forced to confront the fact.

She came within fifteen feet of the door and stopped.

"Hey," a voice said, echoing slightly inside the derelict concessions stand. "I'm in here. Come on in." It was the same voice from her motel-room phone. Whispering, raspy, tentative. If a hunted rabbit could talk it might sound that way.

"Not on your life," Annja said flatly. "I'm not going

in there. You come out. Or forget about the whole thing."

Nothing happened. She started to turn away.

"All right," the voice said around a weedy chuckle. "You're smart. You don't wanna walk in blind where you might get ambushed. That's cool."

She saw motion inside and slipped her hands out of her pockets.

She found herself facing a man. Not a terribly prepossessing one. He looked to be Annja's age, a head shorter, skinny as a prairie weed. He had foxlike features and coarse hair, but his skin and eyes were light and his hair looked brown rather than midnight black. He didn't twitch overtly but never seemed to be at rest. He wore torn, stained jeans, pointy-toed boots, a grimy T-shirt and a scuffed black leather jacket. He looked as if he'd seen one too many James Dean movies.

"You're Creed?" he asked.

"That's right."

He nodded spasmodically. "You can call me Two Hatchets," he said.

It was a pretty grandiose name for someone who looked as if he'd need both arms to raise one, Annja thought.

"What do you have for me?" she asked.

"Right to the point, huh? Yeah. I like that."

Annja turned to walk away.

"Wait! Sorry. Sorry. Listen, the Dogs are planning something. Something heavy. Something bad. Something bad enough to send shockwaves circling the globe. You get me?"

"That's old news, Two Hatchets. Anyway, how would you know?"

"They use me for a runner, like. The Dog Society. Do odd jobs. Gopher. That sorta thing."

"And they let you in on their planning sessions?"

He laughed. "Yeah. Imagine that. Two Hatchets, the errand boy. No. They never tell me shit. But I'm like the janitor, man. Part of the furniture."

He pointed to the side of his head. "They forget I got ears. You dig?"

"I see."

She was skeptical. But it made sense. Back when people had servants their masters always seemed to forget that they had ears, too. Service people still tended to be taken for granted. And she could definitely understand overlooking Two Hatchets.

"So what did you overhear?" she asked.

He shook his head. "Nothing specific. Just enough to know what they're cooking up is big and bad. Superbad."

"Again," she said. "Old news."

"Yeah, yeah." He nodded, as if trying to mix something in his skull. "I'm getting to that. They got a big meet set up. It's key. It's like the final step, man. The final piece of the puzzle. Going down tonight. Tonight, tonight."

He looked up at the sky. "Gotta hurry if we wanna get there."

"You'll take me?" she asked.

"Yeah. Shit, yeah. Show you the way in. I'm not going in myself—no way. But I'll point it out, and if you're bat-shit-crazy enough to spy on these Dog warriors, knock yourself out."

"I'll do that thing," she said.

He started walking toward the gate. Since there were no cars in the derelict lot he correctly assumed she'd parked outside the graffiti-clad walls.

"Wait," she said.

He turned and tapped a pointy, impatient toe on the gravel.

"What's in it for you?" she asked.

"Heh. Payback's a bitch, man. The Dogs make me do their shit work. Treat me like I'm nothing!

"I take you there," he said. "You get what you want. And then you screw those Dog Society warriors. Smash them to pieces."

Annja shrugged. "That's the plan," she said.

13

Two Hatchets guided Annja north of Lawton and east of Sill on Interstate 44. He had her turn off at an exit that led to a strip mall east of the road. Like the drive-in it was abandoned. Big plywood sheets covered all the windows. Instead of public taste passing it by, though, it had fallen victim to a bubble that had burst.

"Turn off your lights and go around the right side," the informant directed her.

Annja did as he said. Built in a sort of bowl its drainage either had been poorly designed or was degrading from lack of maintenance. Parts of the parking lot were pools of scummy-looking water.

"Desolate," she said to her passenger. She wished it wasn't too cold to roll the windows down. Two Hatchets smelled as if he lived in his clothes.

"So they're meeting here?" she asked him, disbelieving.

"What? Are you stupid or what? You think I'd just have you drive in, just like that, if they were? They'd spot us and kill us both, they would."

"Okay," she said, drawing it out. "I thought you might have me do just that, if you were trying something funny."

He laughed. "Everything I do is funny. So funny I forgot to laugh."

Leaving her to digest that odd rendition of the half-forgotten playground saying, her guide pointed. "Park here. South side. Don't go no farther! Park here, here!"

She guided the car against the side of the southern-most wall of the strip mall and stopped. "Now what?"

He grinned. "Now we walk."

As he got out of the car Annja frowned. Two Hatchets didn't look like someone who walked a whole bunch. He was dancing around in a little circle, puffing condensation like a steam engine.

"Follow me, follow me," he said.

He peered around the corner of the building, then sidled around. She followed deliberately. She didn't trust him entirely and wasn't going to. But given that Johnny had sent him to her, she had to take seriously the prospect he might have useful information to convey.

Two Hatchets crouched on the side of the small mall away from the highway, where the early-evening traffic continued to hiss by. He seemed to be peering intently to the northeast, past the loading docks for the stores that no longer existed.

"What are we looking for?" she asked.

He pointed. "There."

She squinted. In a rising moon's light she saw a black

sprawl of what looked like a structure perhaps a thousand yards away.

"What's that?"

"Holly Hills Training Center."

"Training for what?"

"Who knows, who cares? Company building it went tits-up right before it got finished. Contractors cratered, too. Everybody just walked away, left it empty."

"The Dog Society's meeting there?" she asked.

He bobbed his head. "Place is built behind a ridge there, hides it from the highway. Company wanted privacy. Wanted to block some of the interstate noise."

"What about lookouts?"

He laughed and shook his head. "No. Not this way. They're watching the road that leads from the west. Probably watch the back door, east side, just because. Otherwise, zip. Nobody ever comes here, nobody ever goes there. So why bother? Not like they think anything can touch 'em, anyway."

She nodded and blew out a long breath. "Looks as if we're in for a hike."

"*You* are," Two Hatchets said. "Not me. Not me. No how, no way. I brought you here. I pointed you in the right direction. You take it from here. This is where I get off."

"All right, I guess," she said, trying not to sound as eager to be rid of him as she felt. "I can handle it from here. Thanks."

"You be sure to tell Johnny I did this for you," he said. "You be sure. Tell him."

"I'll do that," Annja promised.

TWENTY MINUTES LATER Annja was hunkered down in brush growing beneath a wood of small trees that stood along a creek running from the east down toward the highway. The south wing of the Holly Hills Training Center stood a hundred yards away. A drainage ditch with low grass-covered banks ran around its parking lot. It apparently emptied into the little creek through a small culvert thirty yards to Annja's left.

Annja had picked her way cautiously across the darkened countryside.

Now she was looking at a loading dock. The center consisted of three main wings strung out south to north and connected by covered passageways. The windows of this wing were covered in plywood sheeting like the ones in the dead mall.

She contemplated how to get inside. She already took for granted the Dog Soldiers wouldn't have enough people on hand to secure the whole facility.

Nor did she reckon the building contractors, stiffed and more than likely themselves insolvent, would have wasted much time and energy ensuring no one could get in the empty husk. It almost surprised her they'd bothered to put plywood over the windows.

A flare of white light off to her left made her hunker down instinctively. She saw the glow as a pair of head-lights swung around the southern hip of the ridge that screened the center from the highway. She followed the vehicle's progress.

The south wing quickly hid the lights from view. Annja remained crouched. She waited and watched.

At the center's far end, several hundred yards off, she

saw the headlights sweep across the grassland to the north. Then they cut off.

Somebody was coming in, she thought. Right through the front door, apparently. Good to know.

Annja slipped across the open space down into the drainage ditch. Smelling stagnant water, she leaped a marshy bottom, and ran quickly up the far side and toward the buildings. In the several minutes she'd spent watching she hadn't seen any patrols. It seemed probable that any sentries were concentrated farther north, and doubtless paying more attention to the newcomers than unexpected, uninvited guests.

Annja ran through plots and plans to gain admittance. Could the upward-sliding door of the loading dock itself be unlocked? Maybe she could cut through a plywood window covering with her sword, although she knew from experience that would make a lot of noise.

On impulse she walked up the short flight of steps to the access door beside the main loading bay and tried the knob. It wasn't locked.

"You never know," she said softly, and went inside.

14

Annja froze.

She'd made her way blindly through the dark building until she'd heard voices.

The voices were raised and angry. She could make out no words.

Annja waited, pressed in the shadows as the voices moved from the front of the building toward the middle. They passed in front of her from left to right. There they seemed to stop moving. Other voices joined, and the disputants were gradually mollified.

Annja made her way carefully toward the sound of the voices. In short order she saw the glare of some kind of artificial light shining from her right.

She turned down a corridor. A few steps along, whitish-yellow light spilled onto the concrete floor from an open door. She crept up to it, crouched, then risked a three-second look around.

It was a small room, possibly a meeting or instruction room. A far doorway opened to a larger, central space. In that space lay a jumble of equipment the contractors must have left—ladders, boxes, tangles of utility cords. She was surprised anything at all of value remained.

White tarp or plastic sheeting—from the sheen, she quickly realized it was the latter—had been laid on the floor. A number of men sat on crates and folding chairs. She heard the rumble of voices.

She slipped into the small room adjoining the larger one. The light from the main room alerted her to obstacles inside. Office chairs had been stacked in a clumsy fashion, desks piled one upside-down atop another. She had no clue what they were doing there. Possibly samples delivered by a would-be vendor. Or maybe the company building the training center had gotten ahead of itself and ordered in furnishings before the place was even complete. She was gathering that rational planning had not been their strong suit.

The heaped furnishings made excellent cover. Bent low behind them Annja worked her way close to the door to the big room.

"I offer you, comrades, literally the opportunity of a lifetime," a voice was saying. Its familiarity tickled Annja's subconscious. But it didn't belong to one of the men who'd accosted her in eastern New Mexico. She knew she'd recognize their voices instantly.

"Bottom line, what're we talkin' about here, *comrade*?" The second speaker had the accent of a North American-born Latino. His emphasis on the boilerplate socialist-revolutionary honorific had a distinctly skeptical ring.

"What we all dream of," the first voice said. "Revolution. The end of the white capitalist hegemony. The chance for justice and peace."

"How does that work, exactly?" Annja peered around a desk. The speaker was a black man; the accent was pure New Orleans.

"All we want's a chance to make a stand and take us some payback," another voice said.

Annja realized there were at least four factions gathered there. She couldn't even see the Dog Soldiers, somewhere to her left, so she couldn't say for sure there weren't even more groups represented. She also made out, vaguely, shapes standing along the walls. She figured they were the security contingents for the various spokesmen.

On the right side of the room three African-American men sat, wearing what looked like a kind of civilian uniform—dark glasses, jackets and trousers of some heavy, dark fabric with a bit of sheen to it, over black shirts. They wore their hair cropped close and looked very businesslike. One of them was the man from New Orleans.

To their left sat three Latinos, all wiry and bearded. They wore flannel shirts and jeans. To their left sat three more African-Americans, two with shaven heads; the one in the middle had a medusan tangle of dreadlocks. Even sitting down he was enormously tall. Standing, Annja reckoned, he'd clear six and a half feet easy.

Finally, closest to Annja, sat three young white men—skinny, nervous, hunching forward uncomfortably on their chairs. One had his head shaved, one had long red hair and a beard on his vulpine face. Their central figure had dark blond dreadlocks and tribal tattoos encircling bare upper arms.

Most of these men carried guns, some stuffed improvidently into waistbands, others in holsters. Annja suspected the three identically clad black men were packing under their rather loose jackets.

"We provide the catalyst," the Dog Society spokesman said. "More than that—the first strike. It will have aftershocks. I give you my word as a Plains warrior. And then it's up to you to keep the blows coming until the empire crumbles."

The immensely tall dreadlocked man waved a big hand. "Why you think you can down the empire now?"

"When has the time been better?" the Dog asked. "The oppressors fight dozens of wars, declared and otherwise, across the entire globe. Their enforcers are scattered to the four winds. Their warriors are exhausted. Even their most basic equipment is wearing out and not being replaced, while they pour billions of dollars into fantastic toys like stealth fighters and bombers that are no use to them in the wars they fight. The economy is a smoking wasteland. The pigs at home see their pension funds empty, their paychecks shrinking in value. The people groan for bread, yet there is no bread. Only trillions and trillions for the fat cats who oppress us all!

"The system is not just vulnerable to being toppled, my friends. It cries out for it! It requires only the impetus. The *push*. We, the Dog Society of the Numunu and their allies, will provide that push. Soon, the empire shall feel its foundation crack beneath it!"

"What do you want from us?" asked one of the semiuniformed men.

"Leverage," the Dog spokesman said. "Force multipliers. Once we begin our campaign—and that day dawns soon—the more violent, and more widespread, the additional shocks applied to the system, the greater our chances of crashing it. You all represent sizable networks of fighters for revolutionary justice. If you are concerned with the risks entailed in direct action, you needn't involve yourselves personally at all. I'm sure all of you are well acquainted with any number of hotheads you can persuade to take part in a rising tide of revolution."

The man from New Orleans nodded. "That's fine as far as it goes. But what's in it for us? For *our* movement?"

"The chance to strike off the chains of oppression, of course." The Dog Soldier sounded surprised. "To seize justice in your own way."

"But wait," the dreadlocked white guy said. "If we bring the government down, who'll provide a social safety net?"

"I thought you boys were anarchists," the dreadlocked black guy said, eyeing his white counterpart without favor. "Ain't you all about bringing the government down?"

"Real anarchism calls for the right *kind* of government," the red-bearded man said. "One that's big enough to provide for the needs of the people without keeping them down, or hanging them up in all kinds of rules. And big enough to keep the capitalists from exploiting the people."

"When we have broken the white-supremacist hegemony," the Dog Soldier said, with a rasp of asperity creeping into his distant-thunder voice, "you and your communities will be able to define your own life-ways and walk them, as we Indians do."

The Latino spokesman sneered. "So what you Indians are really saying is, you're just looking to stop paying your taxes? How is the government gonna provide jobs for my people?"

Before anyone could respond commotion erupted from the front of the central building. Two burly men, Dog Soldiers with painted faces, strode into the circle of light.

Between them they dragged the slight form of Two Hatchets. He looked as if he'd been handled none too gently.

"We found *this* creeping around outside," one of the guards said in a deep voice.

"Wait!" Two Hatchets said, wincing as his escorts thrust him forward into the light. "I only did what you Dogs told me to! I brought the spy Annja Creed right to you. She's probably here now, listening to you talk!"

15

For a moment everything stopped dead.

"Did I do right?" Two Hatchets asked, blinking, in a mosquito whine. "Did I? I'm off the hook, right? Right?"

Then all hell broke loose as someone shouted, "It's a trap!"

Guns began to strobe in the meeting hall with a cataclysmic multivoiced roar. One of the first shots hit Two Hatchets in the left temple. The little informant fell on his face on the floor.

The sound of multiple guns firing at once reverberated between the bare concrete floors and ceiling. Annja saw a bullet explode a lantern on a table. Liquid fuel sprayed over a man standing nearby, probably a Dog Soldier by his placement. Hideous light flared as he tottered, blazing, out of Annja's view, waving his arms and shrieking.

Men were struggling. Bright gun flashes made the

hellish scene more so. The smell of burning hair and skin made Annja's eyes water, stung her nose and made her stomach churn.

It all happened in a matter of seconds. She heard the Latino leader hollering about betrayal in Spanish. He was suddenly cut off.

Time to go, Annja thought.

As she turned, rough hands clamped on her arms. Two huge men loomed right behind her. The light of various fires glistened on the paint that obscured their faces, and gleamed on the enamel of teeth bared in feral smiles.

"Oh, *no!*" she gasped, as melodramatically as possible. She slumped dead weight toward the floor.

The Dog soldiers were strong men with strong hands. But they weren't prepared for Annja's sudden boneless, sobbing, whimpering slump. She pulled free and dropped to her knees on the coldly merciless concrete.

"Please," she whined. "Please don't kill me! I'm a journalist! *Please.*"

The men hesitated for just a moment, then one said, "We plan to make an example of you."

Annja concentrated hard as she summoned the sword. As the closer man lunged for her she slashed his legs.

He reared back, flinched and toppled sideways against his partner. The other man yelped like a dog with its tail stepped on and pushed him away as his legs gushed blood across the jumbled furniture, the floor, even the wall.

The other Dog turned back toward Annja, legs braced, raising a hatchet over his head. "I'll fix you," he shouted.

"I think not," Annja said, and thrust the sword into his chest.

She released the hilt. The sword vanished.

The Dog Soldier uttered a gurgling scream and collapsed.

She looked back to the big room. The men were all fighting one another.

All around her men shouted in fury, fear and pain. Whether any or all of the Dog Soldiers' invited guests had believed they'd been lured into a trap, once guns came out it was every radical for himself.

Annja ran. Wheeling right she darted down the corridor. Ahead of her the passageway ended in a space expanding to her left, with a large plywood-covered window beyond. She cut left at an angle across the open space, the size of a largish room, to a corridor she thought led toward an exit from the rear of the central building.

As she passed the black mouth of another cross-corridor to her left, a white light speared from the direction of the exit and nailed her. Her eyes dazzled; she hurled herself left, letting herself leave her feet. A dive into the dark unknown was preferable to what she knew she was otherwise about to receive.

From the corner of her eye she saw the blue-white spot illuminating the red-bearded white radical. He was supporting his taller dreadlocked comrade, who appeared to be wearing a red Raggedy Ann wig over a bloody mask. Then Annja was out of the line of fire, as shatteringly loud gunshots erupted from down the hallway.

She landed hard, cracked her chin, slid along the

floor with bright lights flashing through her brain that had nothing to do with the full-auto muzzle flashes dancing at her back. That brilliant beam, she'd instantly known, came from a ballistic flashlight clamped to the barrel of an assault rifle—a CAR-4, judging by the horrific racket it made. The shooter had presumably illuminated his target as much to make sure he wasn't about to light up some of his own guys as for help aiming. The fractional-second pause as he processed what he saw had given Annja her life.

At least for the present. Despite the pain hammering through jaw and head she forced herself to snap back to her feet and drive on. Behind her, somebody seemed to be shooting back at the man with the CAR, presumably a Dog Soldier, guarding the exit.

She ran into the front-to-rear corridor on the wing's far side. Instantly a couple of male bodies jostled her. Somebody cursed. There was a flash so close she felt the hot slap of the blast. Tiny fragments of unburned propellant stung her neck.

The muzzle flame illuminated the upper torso and strained dark face of a man in a dark quasi uniform. She was sure it wasn't one of the three radicals who'd been negotiating with the Dogs. Probably a bodyguard.

He had opened fire on her. She made the sword appear in her hand, hacked compactly left and right. She felt the steel bite. Heard screams.

As bodies thudded against either wall of the passageway Annja ran on. In a few steps a plywood-covered floor-to-ceiling window loomed on her left.

Annja pulled up short. Turning, she slashed a quick

X through the wet, resistant wood. As she'd feared, it made a loud squealing noise. But at this point a little more noise seemed unlikely to make a bit of difference. She could barely hear it for the ringing in her ears.

Shoulder first she threw herself at the thin wooden sheet. It gave way, though it grasped at her with jagged damp claws. She stumbled out into bracingly cold, blessedly clean-smelling air.

Sword still in hand, she took quick stock of her situation. She stood on a patch of grass in a recess between the central wing and the northernmost one. Hugging the main building's wall she crouched. It was scarcely less black outside than inside; she had a good chance of escaping detection even if somebody outside the recess looked directly at her.

From the tumult of screams and shooting the mobile melee seemed to be rolling north toward where the visitors, and maybe the Dog Soldiers themselves, had presumably parked their vehicles. Shouts drew her attention back to the opening east of her. Two men appeared, running from the south. As one raced onward with the flopping high-swinging gait of sheer panic, the other, a tall, spare man with a bandanna tied around his forehead, stopped, turned and opened fire with a handgun.

A moment later a pair of unmistakable Dog Soldiers dashed out in pursuit.

Annja stayed hunkered down where she was. The commotion continued to the north of her. She heard shots that clearly came from outside on the far side of the buildings, the west. She guessed the delegates to the abortive war conference had more guards stationed out by their cars. They were now presumably shooting it out with their hosts.

After five deep deliberate breaths she decided to make a break.

Quickly she duckwalked to the corner, did three-second looks left and right. No one. As she started forward, she saw a revolver, a Smith & Wesson N-frame, on the ground.

Without hesitation or pause she bent to scoop it up as she ran for the rolling terrain east of the training center. The big Magnum might not be an ideal choice for follow-up shots, but Annja had no fear of its noise or recoil. If she found herself having to shoot, she'd get to cover or drop to the ground, aim and make the last rounds count.

If there are any rounds, she thought. She wasn't about to stop and swing open the cylinder to check, either. Nor was she going to crack the piece open on the run and risk the low-comedy catastrophe of spilling out however many live cartridges remained.

Instead, she pelted flat out across the pavement, vaulted the drainage ditch and was gone with the wind.

Ranging wide to the east before turning north to where her rental car waited, she hoped, undiscovered and unmolested at the rear of the dead mall, Annja had plenty of time to consider what had just happened—and to parse through her options.

She had witnessed an abortive attempt at coordinating terror strikes by terrorist groups from across the U.S. That these particular bands, or their survivors back at their home bases, weren't likely to want to collaborate with the Dog Soldiers did not mean that other groups hadn't already met and made terms. And that familiar voice had made clear that the Dog Society plotted something big—and soon.

Try as she could Annja could not dredge up a face or name to go with that voice. She gave up the effort quickly; she had too much else to think about.

It was cold. Indeed, the wind literally seemed to be sucking the very life from her out through her jacket. She was coming down from an adrenaline jag, which made her knees wobbly and set nausea seething in her stomach. But that was nothing she wasn't used to. She kept her legs moving by force of will, as she allocated at least some of her attention to negotiating the rolling prairie by light of a partial moon.

Two Hatchets had clearly been sent by the Dogs to lure her in. Most likely for capture, interrogation and eventual disposal. That meant the Dog Society had well and truly targeted Annja Creed for death.

They certainly showed signs of arrogance to a near-suicidal degree. But she found it hard to imagine they'd actually told their snitch to lure her into the middle of their big top-secret confab. She guessed her actual reception committee had either been waiting for her in another part of the training center, or perhaps were still waiting futilely somewhere else entirely.

As for why Two Hatchets had done what he had, she guessed he'd either misheard his instructions and screwed up, or had decided to get clever, improvise, presumably impress his masters with his zeal and resourcefulness.

And screwed up. Fatally. From her brief acquaintance with the man that seemed about right.

Annja thought about calling Tom Ten Bears and tipping him off that the Dog Society was cooking up a big steaming cauldron of evil. There was no guarantee he'd believe her. Even if the highway patrol turned out and found signs of a battle royal, it wouldn't necessarily substantiate any wild-eyed claims of a conspiracy to mount a nationwide insurrection. They'd probably think more in terms of some kind of major drug deal gone way off the rails. If the Dogs picked up their casualties before clearing out—and she knew they would—there wouldn't necessarily be any evidence tying them to the massacre at all.

Am I just rationalizing the fact that I really do not want to get hauled in for questioning on this, much less implicated in the bloodshed? she wondered. But no, she told herself, her reasoning was sound, as far as it went.

Besides, what she had witnessed was the sort of massive bloodletting that didn't happen in well-mannered First World countries. Especially the U.S. And when it did, she knew, the authorities clamped an iron lid on tight. So that nothing really happened, after all—as far as the public ever knew.

There was an even more compelling reason not to call the cops, she knew. But her mind shied away from dealing with it. Get warm first, she decided.

Feeling half past dead from cold and exhaustion, she finally dragged her way back to her car. She made herself scope the scene from the night. She saw nothing threatening. When she came up to the car she found no sign the doors had been jimmied, nor were people waiting in the foot wells of the backseat to ambush her.

Annja got in and drove. She knew there was a danger that the GPS record from her phone would clearly show her route to the training center, not to mention her escape. So would the pings from the phone to the relay towers, if anybody bothered to check either. She knew every cell phone sold contained built-in spy and tracking devices for law enforcement. So she paused, regretfully, to delete the memory of her expensive third-generation phone, throw its shell in the Dumpster of one closed-for-the-night business in a not-well-trafficked part of Lawton, and the SIM card, stamped into pieces, in another. She didn't dare use it again, nor allow it to record any more of her progress.

Her real reason for not calling the police, and the biggest reason for not wanting to be tracked, was the sizzling and nasty suspicion that law enforcement in the region was itself infiltrated by the Dog Society. Part of it was hunch. Part of it was knowing more about how law enforcement actually worked than most members of the ever-trusting public.

She was as sure that Lieutenant Tom Ten Bears was clean as she was that the sun would rise in the east in too few more hours. But it didn't mean everybody else in Troop G was. And thanks to the war on terror, there was way too much interconnectivity between forces, departments and agencies for anything resembling real security. It could be someone connected with the Lawton cops, or the Comanche County Sheriff's Department, or even the Feds who used the information she provided to set the death squads on her trail.

It wouldn't even take an actual traitor or a mole to

betray her to torture and death, she realized. Tom and Johnny Ten Bears had both told her there were no secrets in Indian country. Especially when information was so widely disseminated, there was no telling who might brag, or blurt, or wonder aloud—or even make some kind of seemingly harmless comment on what he or she had done at work that day to the family. All it took was for someone to overhear and innocently tell the wrong other someone. And Annja would be dead.

Forty-five minutes after leaving the mall parking lot she walked through the door of the Bad Medicine.

"I need a place to hide out," she told the curious Iron Horse People gathered there. "The Dogs are on my trail."

16

"Lookit," Billy White Bird said around a mouthful of cereal. "Johnny's a TV star."

"With those looks he's a natural," Angel said. "Too bad we're all likely to show up on screen right next to him. Especially you, with that jack-o'-lantern face of yours."

Under the circumstances Annja found it hard to feel more than an academic appreciation for the Iron Horses' gallows humor. They sat in the living room of a club safe house, a sprawling ranch-style set off by itself down a country lane, well screened by trees and surrounding terrain. Evening light filtered in over the tops of heavy curtains.

Shown to a room of her own by her hosts on arrival Annja had slept most of the day. She had awakened to find it had hit the proverbial fan.

The TV switched from an image of a mug shot of the absent Johnny Ten Bears to a newswoman in a rain-slicker standing by a rain-swept gulley as technicians in coroner's jackets hauled out a body bag from behind her.

"The latest victims in today's shocking wave of violence in the Lawton area, which has claimed at least six lives, with several more missing and feared dead, are two of our own—reporter Monica Stevenson and her cameraman, Rondé St. John. They were discovered in this gulley west of Lawton and south of Fort Sill just forty-five minutes ago. Both had their hands bound behind their backs by wire and both had been shot once in the back of the head. Their bodies also showed what a Comanche County Coroner's Department spokesperson described as, 'signs of torture.'"

"Bad sign," said Angel, who sat next to Annja on the couch with her legs drawn up beneath her. Annja hadn't realized before how petite the Comanche biker woman was. She probably wasn't even five feet tall; her leather jacket seemed to dwarf the rest of her.

"Notes discovered on Ms. Stevenson's computer reveal she headed out early this morning to meet with a confidential informant who has been aiding her in an ongoing investigation into a shadowy western Oklahoma Native American group calling itself the Iron Horse People Motorcycle Club. Authorities are blaming the club for the current violent crime wave. Special Agent in Charge Lamont Young of the Lawton office of the Federal Bureau of Investigation has just announced that the Department of Homeland Security has named the motorcycle club a terrorist group. We switch now to a live press conference—"

"Can we change the channel?" Billy White Bird asked. He sat in a reclining chair eating his cereal from an outsize mug. "I hate that dude."

Ricky, who sprawled on the floor with his back propped against the couch next to Angel, clicked the remote. On CNN some newsface was interviewing George Abell by video feed. The Horses hissed like angry cats.

"Whoops," Ricky said. "Let's move on before somebody heaves a boot through the screen." He turned to a cartoon channel.

"Young was involved in the Waco massacre, you know," Ricky said to Annja.

Annja raised a brow. "He seems young for that."

"It's that smooth baby face of his," Billy White Bird said. "Easy to maintain when you don't have a conscience."

"I think he's aching for an opportunity to try again with the same tactics and get a better outcome," Ricky said.

"Why did you say the report about the bodies of those TV people was a bad sign?" Annja asked Angel. "Other than for them?"

"Bad news for us," Angel said. "It means the Bureau's going for a shock-and-awe publicity blitz. They usually don't release details like that, especially while they're hauling the bodies to the meat wagon. It was a setup to naming us terrorists and Johnny as the FBI's Most Wanted."

"You sound very authoritative," Annja said.

Angel shrugged. She looked acutely unhappy.

"She used to work for the U.S. Attorneys' Office," Ricky said.

"She was an up-and-coming young prosecutor," Billy added with relish. "She's older than she looks, too."

"What happened?" Annja asked.

"I grew a conscience," Angel said quietly. "Or it woke up. Whatever."

Ricky patted her thigh comfortingly. "Fortunately it didn't start to age her, like a vampire in the sunlight or whatever."

Billy burped and set the empty bowl on a TV tray beside him. The three Iron Horses had been in the house when Annja emerged sleepily an hour before. They'd pointed her to a well-stocked kitchen, where she'd braced herself with a big slice of panfried ham, eggs and beans.

She was forcing herself to take it easy. She'd driven herself hard for a long time—since weeks before flying back to land hip-deep in the horror that happened to Paul and his associates. She'd traveled long distances and delved deep into sorrow. She'd fought for her life and taken life and fled for her life. All of these things took tolls. On the body and on the soul.

And who knows how long I'll get to rest? she thought. So she curbed her restless nature, her impatient desire for action.

There'll be action enough soon, she reminded herself. More than enough for a normal person's entire lifetime.

"So, Billy," she said, recognizing a need to be distracted, "feel free to tell me this is too personal—but what on earth is that tattoo on your stomach, anyway?"

Angel barked a foxlike laugh, then covered her mouth shyly. "Sorry," she said. "But would he go around without a shirt on all the time if he *didn't* want people asking about that tat?"

"Hey," Billy said, sounding aggrieved but grinning as he pulled up his stained white T-shirt. "I'm wearing something today."

"Just be glad he didn't compensate by leaving his pants off," Ricky said.

Annja leaned forward to peer at the artwork etched on the broad canvas of Billy's belly. She saw it was a beautiful, remarkably intricate work in blue ink, after the fashion of a nineteenth-century newspaper lithograph. It displayed what she took for a Comanche warrior riding his pony away from a small party of U.S. Army cavalry who, from their bearing, she guessed were a general and his staff. The warrior was showing them his bare backside and slapping it for emphasis.

"That's, um, remarkable," she said. "How long have you had it?"

"Since I was a kid. All these years I still kept my svelte shape, you see." He slapped his belly, which jiggled.

Annja cocked a brow. "And you served in the military?"

"Oh, yeah. Where I learned my trade."

"What did they say when they saw that tattoo at boot camp?"

"'*Semper fi,* Marine.'" He braced in his chair and snapped off a perfect salute.

She stared at him a moment, then laughed out loud.

"I served in Iraq, round one," Billy said, leaning forward to settle his beefy elbows on the table.

"He's older than he looks," a voice said from the side. Annja turned to see Johnny Ten Bears, wet hair hanging over the shoulders of his colors, grinning at her from the door to the kitchen. "Not to mention worse."

"Much worse," Billy agreed.

"Have you been here all this time?" Annja demanded.

"Heck, no," Johnny said. "Just came in the back."

"I didn't hear you."

"Good. Injun warriors specialize in sneaking up on unsuspecting white-eyes. I'd have to hand back my Boy Scout merit badge in redskin perfidy if I couldn't pull it off."

"I knew Johnny's daddy, even," Billy said, clearly feeling expansive. "We served in the same Marine Expeditionary Unit. Then again, us Numunu boys always tended to stick together. Kiowai too. All us Injuns did."

He made a face that made him resemble a jack-o'-lantern more than usual. "'Course, old Tom and I come to some pretty opposite conclusions about what a good idea that whole war was."

"He has a habit of coming down on the wrong side of every fence," Johnny said, not smiling anymore. "When he gets off it, that is."

That killed the conversation for a moment. Sorry, Billy mouthed to Annja.

"Where've you been?" she asked Johnny.

Johnny came and sat unselfconsciously on the floor near Annja. "Walking up and down in the world, and going back and forth in it," he said.

"Old joke," she said.

"For you, maybe, Ms. Renaissance Scholar."

"He was probably hiding your rental car somewhere and getting rid of that Magnum you brought back," Ricky said.

"That's right," Johnny said.

"You came in last night?"

"You were snoring like a chainsaw," Billy said. "It was downright cute."

"Uh-huh," she said.

"So was that horse pistol hot?" Billy asked Annja.

"Radioactive," she said. "Probably."

She hadn't wanted to dump it anywhere herself after her escape from the training center slaughter; the chance of discovery was too great. Whereas the Iron Horses had, as she assumed, ways. As indeed it seemed they had.

"You want to know what I did with it?" Johnny asked.

"No. But how about my car?"

"Stashed in a garage in town, in case somebody tracks it. When you need it we can get it back."

"So what are your plans from here, Ms. Creed?" Johnny asked.

"Good question," she said. "I'm still determined to track the skinwalker killer and stop him. I haven't forgotten that even if everybody else has. Also—"

She hesitated. Will I sound too presumptuous? Then she thought, Screw it. My whole life's presumptuous.

"I want to clear your names," she said. "You were right about the Dog Society—all of it."

She had told them what she had seen the night before. "And I was wrong. I don't want to see you suffer for their crimes—past, present or future.

"Don't forget I enjoy pride of place on the Dog

Society's hit list," she said. "I'm the witness who can nail their coffin shut. And they were after me even before I got caught like a complete fool spying on their little terror con fab."

"So why didn't you go to the authorities, Annja?" Johnny asked.

"As in Special Agent in Charge Young?" she said. "Or as in your father?"

"Either one." His gaze and voice were flat.

"You think this is the first time I've lived by the maxim 'if you don't dare call the cops, call the outlaws'?" she asked. "Anyway, isn't that a funny question for an outlaw biker to ask? Especially one who just hit number one on the FBI's Most Wanted list?"

"Not so much, Annja," Angel said earnestly. "I think what we're all wondering is why *you* made that choice," Angel said. "It's not the same as advocating it ourselves, right?"

Annja reminded herself that what looked like a sweet high-school girl playing at running with the pack was a woman who was probably older than she was, and an attorney to boot. "All right," she said, "fair enough. I don't trust law enforcement."

Johnny frowned. "Consider the blatantly obvious question asked."

"I trust your father," she told him. "That doesn't mean I trust everybody around him. There're too many ears in that Department of Public Safety office. Not just his fellow officers. Dispatchers. Clerks. People from other divisions walking by the door. The UPS dude. They don't even have to be moles themselves. All they have to do is tell the wrong friend or family member something exciting they heard. Or even say it in front of the wrong random person."

Billy turned his somewhat scary grin on his chief. "She's a smart one, Johnny. Admit it."

"When did I deny it?" He sounded more grumpy than growly.

"Plus," Annja said, her conscious mind suddenly dredging one of the subconscious warnings that had stopped her last night to the surface, "the Feds are almost certainly monitoring his cell phone."

"You do realize that would be illegal, Annja?" Angel said.

"That doesn't mean they're not doing it—right?"

"Right." Angel shrugged. "Another reason I quit."

"So what do you plan?" Johnny asked, standing and stretching.

Annja shook her head. "I don't know yet. Hang with you guys if you'll let me. Use this as a base. And—"

She drew in a deep breath and sighed it out. "Wait for some kind of opportunity."

Johnny looked to his comrades.

"I like her, Johnny," Angel said.

"Fine with me," Ricky said.

"I think she's a keeper," Billy said.

"What about the rest of the club?" Annja couldn't help asking.

"They're not here," Johnny said. "Okay. Make yourself at home."

"Do you have a better plan? Anybody? I'm asking that seriously," Annja asked.

Johnny shook his head. Then he flashed his dazzling grin. "But opportunity'll break somewhere," he said. "It always does."

Annja might have made some flip, ironic comeback. But she wasn't that person.

She believed opportunity always broke, too. Somewhere.

I just hope it breaks in time, she told herself, before there's a lot more heartache.

She had to admit she didn't like the odds.

17

"So what we got here," Lieutenant Tom Ten Bears said, "is what we call in law enforcement, technically, a big ol' mess."

Actually, Annja was willing to bet they called it something much worse, but she wasn't about to contradict him.

They stood together next to the grid marked out by the OU archaeological dig team. The sticks leaned. The twine boundaries sagged forlornly. The wind plucked them like flaccid violin strings, eliciting no music Annja could hear.

"And we're right in the middle of it," she said.

"That surely is the case. Where've you been hiding from me, Ms. Creed?"

"If I told you it wouldn't be hiding," she said. "Am I in trouble? Have I gotten you in trouble?"

"'Not yet' to both." He chuckled deep in his throat.

"That was a cute trick to set up this meet. Why go all around Kicking Bird's barn to do it, though?"

She had called his cell from a pay phone. She told him to go to where they first met and ask about her. At the ICU of the Norman medical center they had given him a handwritten note. It read simply, "Dig site."

"I don't want to be arrested," she said. "Much less die."

"You don't trust the authorities?" His voice had taken on an edge like the spring wind.

She turned to face him. "No," she said. "You told me yourself—nothing happens in Indian country that doesn't get seen."

He stared at her for a moment. Then, slowly, he nodded. "I see what you mean."

"It doesn't necessarily mean a traitor," she added.

He turned away and sighed a puff of condensation. "But it's possible. Likely, even, now that I think about it."

"Then there's the Feds," she said. "I didn't want to risk them listening to your calls."

He turned back. "You really think they'd—whoa. No need to finish that, is there?"

He walked a few steps away from her. "I'm a patriot, Ms. Creed," he said. "Any true Indian is. Think about it. The American white-eyes beat us. That must make them the best there is, huh? So theirs is an honorable path to follow."

He shook his head. "And it's a good country. The bad things that were done a long time ago—they were plenty bad. They're also long past. In the end your people treated mine better than a lot of conquered peoples have gotten. And we're accepted—mostly."

"Yes," she said. She wasn't sure where he was going.

"I've fought for this country," he said. "Not just in Iraq. And I still believe in it. But—"

He shook his head again. "I can't believe in everything it does. Done in its name. I can't believe in what it some-times seems it's becoming. I see the part I've played in that—and I feel ashamed. Is that wrong? Am I weak?"

"No," she said. "And no."

"Why did you want to talk to me, Ms. Creed?"

"I didn't want you hunting for me."

He laughed. "That's pretty up front."

"I also don't want to lie to you, Lieutenant. Mainly, I don't know if I could get away with it. Is anybody looking for me?"

"No. Not…formally."

That set Annja's danger antennae to quivering. "What does that mean?"

"Well, that George Abell from the Nation's special investigative unit has been putting the word out he really wants to talk to you. Seems he thinks you're part of the problem."

A chill ran down Annja's back like meltwater from a snow-covered branch. "And you're not going to hand me over to him?"

"Him?" Ten Bears laughed. "Georgie's always been strong in the body, and he's anything but stupid. But he still's never showed many signs of being worth much. He likes to lecture people on the glories of our ances-tors riding across the Plains, but he's always done most of his riding on his daddy's coattails. Him and his little rich-boy pals, they went off to school and got law degrees. Then they come back, and the next thing anybody knows, they got 'em this shiny new SIU. Most folks hereabouts just reckon that's another toy his daddy, Rich Ronnie Abell, bought for him."

"So that's a no. Even though you're a stand-up lawman."

"Having a fancy badge don't make you a lawman in my book, Ms. Creed," Ten Bears said. "George wants to talk to you, let him do some real police work for once and run you down himself. Anyway, I still want you helping me track down this serial killer. Not like anybody else is looking for him."

He stuck his hands in his jacket pockets. "Brr. Cold out here. Dunno how the ancestors put up with it without pockets."

"What do you mean, Lieutenant? About nobody looking for the skinwalker?"

"We been passed by," he said. "We're old news. All these poor, dead people—nobody's interested in that now. Serial killers were all the hot thing a few years ago. Now it's terrorists."

"They pulled you off the investigation?"

"No. Only just about everybody else."

She drew a deep breath. "I saw something," she said. "The other night."

"What?"

She told him what she'd witnessed in the training center. She left out any indication she'd done anything other than duck and run—and, of course, all mention of the sword. She let him think she'd escaped by a combination of resourcefulness and dumb luck.

"Why didn't you call me, then?" he asked when she'd finished.

"You already know that," she said. "The Dogs had already set me up for abduction. Then I went and blew up their terror confab. How do you think I'd have wound up if I blurted that on the phone?"

"Like that poor reporter girl yesterday," he said. "I knew her folks, you know? She interviewed me a few times."

"I'm sorry."

"Hey, if bad things only happened to people who deserved them, people like me'd be out of a job. You, too, I think."

She sucked in a breath.

"Now, why'd I go and say a fool thing like that?" he said. "You're just an archaeologist, right? Anyway, it looks like we've got us a full-blown war between rival gangs of would-be terrorists on our hands."

"What do you mean?"

He shrugged. "From the news it surely looks like the Iron Horses have struck back at the Dogs."

"You believe them?"

"They got evidence," he said. "Monica—Ms. Stevenson—was investigating the Iron Horses. So who else was it went and did her and that poor camera fella like that?"

The Iron Horses tell me otherwise, she thought desperately. They figure the Dogs must have been setting Stevenson up for this for weeks. To frame the Horses.

She believed them. For one thing she'd seen both the Iron Horse People and the Dog Society up close. She knew which bunch kept trying to kill her.

But she couldn't tell *him.*

"Where you been keeping yourself, Ms. Creed?"

"I have contacts in the area. From my college days." It was true, as a matter of fact. Also irrelevant. "I've got help," she said.

He looked worried. "You sure you know what you're doing?"

"No. But it's what I have to do."

"Don't play this too cute," he said. "The stakes are too high. The game is too ugly."

"I'll try not to. I don't want to end up like Ms. Stevenson. I promise."

"Let me give you one bit of advice—stay clear of the Iron Horses. And especially John."

"What about you?"

He looked away from her, squinting up into the rain that began to spit from cloud bellies the color of bullets.

"I'm gonna find him before anybody else does. That's a promise."

"And then?"

"And then—well, a man's got to be able to shoot his own dog."

"You TALKED TO THAT policeman," the woman named Snake said the moment she walked in the safe house door that afternoon.

And here I was thinking our inevitable eventual encounter couldn't get more uncomfortable, Annja thought. She was sitting on the couch, looking at her computer.

"Yes," she said, shutting the laptop and placing it beside her.

Snake coiled her sinuous length onto a footstool and regarded Annja without friendliness.

"So you're crashing here with us?" Snake asked.

"Wait," Annja said. "You're not going to accuse me of selling you out?"

"You're not stupid," Snake said, "even if you don't always have much sense. We're your only chance of survival, as long as you stay in the area. You think the Dog Soldiers couldn't reach out and touch you if you were locked up in a cell?"

"No. I know perfectly well they could."

"You could always fly away home to New York."

Annja wasn't at all sure that would work. If she left, law enforcement was likely to take an unhealthy interest in her. She felt, possibly irrationally, that her best chance for avoiding that kind of uncomfortable scrutiny was to see this thing through.

For that matter the Dogs weren't likely to give up on her scent, either. As long as they were at large and scheming they threatened her.

"I'm not leaving," she said. "I still have my friend's death to avenge."

"You mean that? I thought you liberal white college girls didn't believe in vengeance."

"I do."

Snake shrugged. "Point to you."

"Also," Annja said, "I don't want to see the Iron Horse People made the scapegoats here. I feel responsible in some way."

"You aren't," Snake said. "This was going on a long

time before you got here. Probably go on a long time after you're gone."

"Some of it, maybe. But I'm not going anywhere until I see things settled with the skinwalker. And the Dogs."

Why am I so convinced that they're tied up together in this? Annja wondered.

There was way too much coincidence involved. The skinwalker and the Dogs seemed to be coming from the same direction. With this wave of murder breaking things wide open, the terrorists and the shadowy serial killer *had* to be working together by now. If they hadn't been all along.

Snake gave Annja a sidewise glance. "Johnny likes you."

He does? Annja's heart did a little bounce.

"And that's a problem for you?" she asked.

"It distracts him. At a time like this that's not good." But the long, lean Cheyenne woman wasn't meeting Annja's gaze, Annja noted.

"I think he'll manage."

Snake stood. "He'd better," she said. "He's a great man. He has the potential to be a catalyst. Help people create serious changes—changes for the better. I won't let anything happen to him."

Annja met her gaze. "Good," she said. "I hope you're right."

CAPTIVITY QUICKLY BORED Annja silly. Her natural drive to be off and doing things soon turned into a caged-panther frustrated pacing. She didn't even dare log online to get e-mail.

At least Doug can't bug me here, she said, thinking of her Chasing History's Monsters, producer, Doug Morrell. It was a blessing that law enforcement hadn't released to the media any of the details identifying the I-40 Killer as a skinwalker. Otherwise, he would have been after her to follow up the monster angle with an eye to doing a show about werewolves.

Fortunately her few friends and her co-workers were accustomed to her dropping out of sight for protracted periods. They had convinced themselves she contracted out to do things, like help authorities in far-flung countries track down relic poachers. And occasionally that was even true.

Fortunately Annja kept a large selection of books and researched papers on her handy little computer.

But she could only spend so much time reading.

She wasn't literally a prisoner. Not of the Iron Horse People, anyway. She wasn't sure why they treated her so hospitably, although the more contact she had with them the more she found herself liking them. And vice versa, apparently.

But if she left the isolated safe house she risked being trolled in by law enforcement. Or abducted by the Dog Soldiers. And there always remained the chilling possibility that they could amount to one and the same thing.

Annja didn't even dare go for a run in the hills—that would increase the risk of being spotted too much. She could go outside in the yard and do some practice with her sword. The house had no clear sight lines for any great distance, especially to any road or neighboring dwelling.

The majority of the time she had the place to herself.

Clearly the club had other safe houses and secret hideouts. She figured most or all the Iron Horse People had some other occupation than mere motorcycle outlaw—especially since she knew that selling drugs, the popular income stream for modern biker gangs, was something they didn't do.

They seemed in many ways oddly prim for a band of outlaws who carried weapons and were willing to use them. Their day jobs were going to be threatened if it was known they belonged to what the FBI now loudly trumpeted as a domestic terrorist group.

Annja felt safe swinging the sword in the backyard. And in bumming around the house in general. So much so that habits from her rare and cherished intervals at home in her own Brooklyn loft began to kick back in.

And so it was the second afternoon alone that Annja emerged from the bathroom after the shower for the short walk down the hall to her sparsely furnished but comfortable room wearing nothing but a fuzzy towel wound around her long wet hair in an impromptu turban…

And promptly found herself face-to-face with Johnny Ten Bears.

18

"Is this what you've been doing all this time?" Johnny Ten Bears asked her. "Running around the house buck naked? Sorry I've been away so much."

Annja felt all too aware of his presence. His very *male* presence. He was a big, healthy, young masculine animal who smelled of outdoors and motor oil and a hint of sweat, dressed in his colors and olive drab T-shirt and faded jeans. He stood within her usual personal space for the simple reason that she'd all but walked into him when she came out of the bathroom. And he stood there smiling appreciatively at her and did not step back.

She felt a surge of fear. How well do I know this guy? she thought. I'm totally in his power. As far as he knows.

The sword's constant absent presence was, as often, a comfort. But not a major one. He was strong and panther-quick, she knew. And well trained. She should never forget he'd been an Army Ranger in Afghanistan. At these close quarters he might well immobilize her before she could summon the sword, or even disarm her if she did.

As was her reflex when ambushed, she counterattacked. "A gentleman would look away," she said tartly.

He laughed. "I'm not a gentleman. Not exactly part of my cultural heritage."

Damn it, he *is* attractive, she thought. The European concept of *gentleman* may have been alien to his tradition, but his bearing was as beyond-confident assured as any medieval lord's. She began to understand just why the Comanches had once been called Lords of the Plains.

She stomped past him down the hall and slammed the door to her room behind her.

Her philosophy was, if you crash your plane, you need to get back in the air as soon as possible. So within five minutes she was dressed in jeans, a T-shirt and a bulky man's flannel shirt her hosts had lent her. She even put on socks and shoes, instead of going barefoot or in stocking feet as she usually did. Then she stalked out to the living room.

Johnny sat talking earnestly to some of his bikers. When one's glance registered her, he looked back over his shoulder and grinned.

"Got all dressed, did you? Don't feel obliged to do it on my account."

"That's precisely why I did it, Johnny."

The others laughed. "You're not afraid to stand up to anybody, are you?" Johnny asked. "In any circumstances."

"I haven't met everybody," she said, "nor under every circumstance. So I can't say for sure. But so far—no."

They all laughed at that. Angel, who was on the couch, invited Annja to sit beside her. Annja did. It seemed safest all around.

More members came in as they discussed the difficulties they were having trying to earn a living, much less trying to track down their rival Dog Soldiers without getting picked off, either by the Dog Society or law enforcement.

"FBI's living up to its reputation," Ricky reported. "Basically they trample around alienating everybody."

"Standard operating procedure for the Bureau," his girlfriend, Angel, said.

"Bigger trouble is the Staties," Ricky said, with a sidelong glance at Johnny, who was eating a pear.

"Because of my father," he said.

Annja frowned. She felt a burning urge to argue the case with Johnny. It seemed vital to her for any number of reasons—not least the fact she found herself liking and respecting both men—to somehow find a way to get the two past their mutually interposed walls of pride and misunderstanding.

But it didn't seem the sort of thing to discuss in front of the rest. It felt too personal. Besides, she was pretty sure that in front of his clan Johnny would feel especially challenged, and resist listening to anything she had to say.

"So we're keeping out of the way of trouble," Johnny said. "But that's not getting anywhere. We can't afford to play a waiting game for very much longer. Sooner or later they'll start to run us down."

"The good news is the Dogs haven't stuck their ugly heads up much since they went on their killing spree a couple days ago," Billy reported. The TV news had reported three more bodies found. "The bad news is, we can't turn up any trace of them, either."

"Maybe they're afraid they overstretched and have shut it all down," Ricky said, reaching for a handful of chips. Fruit and various snacks had begun appearing periodically as the discussion went on.

But Johnny, who for once had bound his hair back in a ponytail that hung well down his arrowhead-shaped back, shook his head. "We wish. They're *preparing*. The casino opening's tomorrow. They're using their success in transferring the heat to us to get ready for their final move."

"But what will that be?" Angel asked. She absently tousled Ricky's hair, which he wore relatively short.

"That's the bitch of it," Johnny said. "The clock's running on us. But all I can see to do now is sit tight and wait for their next move. And that truly sucks."

He looked at Annja. "Unless somebody has a better idea?"

"I wish I did."

"One thing on our side," Billy said, sitting back in his chair and putting his hands behind his head.

"Do tell," Johnny said.

"We may be running out of time, but what we don't have is a definite deadline. The Dogs do."

"The casino opening," Annja said.

"Got it in one."

"Well, we just have to hope that's enough," he said. "Now, who wants something serious to eat? I'm hungry."

"So isn't that a strange activity for outlaw bikers to take up?" Annja asked, picking up a slice from one of the pizzas someone had brought and plopping it on her plate. Outside the windows, night had arrived. At least a dozen of the Iron Horse people had gathered in the safe house living room. Disregarded, the television flickered in the background. "Fostering a barter network among the Comanche and Kiowa communities—even whites, if I'm hearing you correctly?"

"So you figure we're not doing enough armed robberies, then?" Johnny asked.

She shook her head. "It's not that at all. You're just being difficult."

Johnny held a piece of pizza in the air, tipped his head back like a hungry baby bird and bit off the dangling tip. "You expected something different?"

"Well, we ride bikes," Billy said. "And we do things we think are right, whether or not they're strictly legal. So I guess that makes us outlaws. So, outlaw bikers, huh?"

"Tell her about the project you and Snake cooked up, Billy," Johnny said.

Annja craned around to look at Snake, who sat on a footstool off to one side with her tattooed arms crossed. The woman gave her a thin smile.

"It's about getting people set up for small-scale power generation," Billy said enthusiastically. Windmills, solar—there are some really exciting technologies coming up the pike, make localized and even household-level power generation more and more feasible. Snake there handles the technical aspects. She was a real black-program electronics whiz for some DARPA-connected company before quitting to go in the wind."

"You're kidding."

"Not a bit of it."

"Okay, here's something else I don't understand," Annja said. "Aren't you supposed to be big on restoring your native traditions? And yet here you are trying to promote some pretty high technology."

"Them high-and-wide old days on the Plains," Billy said, "they're gone forever, Annja. And we wouldn't bring them back if we could."

"I'm officially confused now."

"We're exploring," Johnny said. "Experimenting. Trying to find the proper balance. Even that's not the right word. What we're working on is finding and making use of the best of the old and the new."

"So we're looking to maximize our advantages," Billy said.

Annja cocked a brow at him.

"Don't mind Billy," Johnny said, helping himself to another slice of pizza. "He got himself a degree in economics a couple years back. Pretty much the only dude in the OU program to do it while working full-time as a fleet mechanic for a local trucking firm."

Annja looked around at the dark, cheerful faces. "Is this some kind of PhDs-only motorcycle club?" she asked.

"Well," Johnny said, "we *are* a motorcycle club. We all love to ride—love the sense of freedom it gives you.

And freedom's what it's all about for us. But you're right—that isn't all we are."

He picked up a napkin and dabbed grease from his lips. "I didn't start the Iron Horse People, see. That was Billy, years ago. He started—you'd call it networking now—getting together with some like-minded people. People interested in getting off the grid. People interested in trying to build a society that'd work without involving the government at all."

"In some ways the luckiest thing ever happened to us Comanches and Kiowa was getting screwed out of our reservations by the government," Billy said.

"Reservations were always just a nice name for concentration camps," Snake said.

"That's true," Billy said. "And reservation Indians have always been wards of the state. Any crazy-ass bit of social engineering theory that came up, they got force-fed like laboratory guinea pigs. They basically have no control over their own destinies. Their own lives. One week the official policy is to wipe out Indian culture and force everybody to be a fake white man. Next week suddenly they're trying to preserve traditional ways. Only those 'traditions' are what some bureaucratic hobbyist in Washington thinks they are."

He shook his big round head. "No wonder people take to the bottle so much."

"What about the income from casinos? That seems to be making a lot of money for a lot of tribes," Annja said.

"Which mostly winds up lining the pockets of the tribal governments," Johnny said, "and their cronies."

"Is that why you're opposed to the new casino

opening tomorrow? I mean, I'm not sure how much power the Comanche Nation government has, since they don't have a reservation to administer."

"Increasing income to the Nation from casino receipts can only centralize wealth and power," Billy said. "Encourage people to support a sort of top-down model—those up top bestow largesse on those below. Saps the independence of the people, too. Makes 'em dependent. The polar opposite of what we're about."

"So you think it represents voodoo economics?" Annja asked.

"I thought it was more the way socialism works," Johnny said. "The notion that concentrating wealth and power and calling it 'the state' will somehow help the masses."

Annja shook her head. "This is all pretty wild. Half the time you talk like total radicals. Half the time you sound like some kind of militia types out of the nineties."

The Iron Horses looked at one another and laughed. "Looks like you're starting to catch on," Billy said, helping himself to pizza.

AS IT GOT LATE the Iron Horse People began to drift away to wherever they'd lie low for the night. Because of their strong comradeship, which Annja found so appealing, they were willing to risk bunching up for limited periods of time. But they understood the value of dispersal—a single bad break wouldn't wind up with all of them dead or behind bars.

When the crowd had thinned Annja went into the

kitchen, where she found Johnny Ten Bears elbow-deep in foamy water.

"What kind of biker lord does the dishes?" she asked, propping her rump against the edge of the kitchen table.

"The kind whose turn it is to do the dishes," Johnny said. "Anyway, you already know we're not exactly an orthodox motorcycle club. And besides, the word *lord* sure doesn't apply to me. The concept's not part of South Plains Indian culture. You should realize by now these particular misfits are the very last people on earth who'd submit to any kind of lord."

"What are you, then?"

He shrugged. "Speaker. Guide. It's all by consensus. Persuasion. Everything is voluntary. That's a tradition we definitely want to keep. Nobody has power over anybody else. Nobody wants it—nobody'd consent to letting anyone have power over them."

"I can see why your ancestors had such a hard time adjusting to the European-derived overculture."

"Well, some of us adapted way too well."

"So, Billy didn't resent your taking over as—whatever you are?"

"Oh, hell, no. I do take responsibility for keeping us together and seeing everybody's cared for. Road boss is probably the best term for what I actually do. Billy's good at doing things, and he's more than a bit of a dreamer. A hell of a dreamer. But he isn't fond of respon-sibility."

"So how'd you get tied up with the Iron Horse People, anyway?" Annja asked.

"Well," he said, setting another dish in the rack to

dry, "I've known Billy White Bird my whole life. You probably noticed my father and I don't see eye to eye. It's always been like that, ever since I was little. He wanted me to play GIs and Nazis—I wanted to play cowboys and Indians. And have the Indians win. Billy was an old war buddy of his who turned into something of a surrogate father to me."

"Oh," Annja said. She wanted to encourage him to open up, but didn't feel she could say something like, "I see." Because she wasn't sure she did.

"When I got back from my second tour in the 'Stan I was pretty messed up. Not physically—I was lucky that way. Not even psychologically, like so many of the people I served with. That's one place a lot of us Indian types have an advantage. Comanches are still a warrior culture. We know what we're getting into."

"So how were you messed up, then?"

He shrugged. "Morally, I guess. Let's just say it turned out we weren't fighting for what I and most of my buddies thought we were. And I began to see how that reflected a country that had turned into something other than what I thought it was. Except, as I started to study a little deeper, I came to see maybe there hadn't been such a big change, after all—that the country wasn't about things like freedom and opportunity and tolerance that we'd always been taught it was, and never had been. That it was all a bill of goods we were sold so we'd line up and turn into obedient little consumers and conscripts."

"That seems like kind of an extreme reaction."

He looked back at her. "I'm not asking you to agree with me. You asked a question. I'm trying to answer."

"You're not interested in persuading me?"

"Not really," he said, turning back to the dishes. "We mostly look to help people who look to help themselves. Opinions don't matter much one way or the other—actions do. Anyway, if people need to be talked into being free, what's the point?"

"Hmm," she said.

After a few moments she said, "You and your father should try to work things out. Seriously."

He put the last dish in the rack, pulled the plug from the sink and, turning to face her, leaned back against the counter.

"Kind of ambitious given that he's set on hunting me down."

"But that's all based on misunderstanding. The way— the way your whole relationship with him seems to be."

He laughed. "Now you're an authority on Ten Bears family politics?"

"I've met and spoken to you both," she said. "I respect you both. And it doesn't take any kind of expert to see what's going on. It's so obvious. Unless you're too close to the situation to see it. And too blinkered by pride."

"It's not just pride. We're, like, polar opposites, him and me. You know how I said earlier that some of us adapt too well to the white man's ways? My father's exhibit A. A classic case. Always making jokes and playing up to the white folks. Doing everything but tugging the forelock or strumming a banjo."

"But your father uses his sense of humor, don't you see? Whether it's to fool suspects into underestimating him or showing up pompous whites without them even knowing it. It's not any kind of self-abnegation. If anything it's a kind of assertion of self."

"Or passive-aggression," he said mockingly, "or whichever shrink-speak catchphrase you care to use."

"You're both strong men," she said. "You're both looking for ways to face the future without losing your identity as individuals or as a culture. Your solutions aren't all that different, really, if you just look at them. Even your political beliefs aren't as far apart as you think."

He gave her a skeptical look.

"Your father's adopted the overculture's ways," she persisted, "but his outlook is wholly his own. Even his humor's an Indian tradition itself. I don't pretend to be an expert on Native American cultures any more than on your particular family. I do know enough Indians to know what kind of sense of humor so many share."

"I've been a rebel all my life," Johnny said. "I tried to fit in. That was part of what joining the Army was about. And what I learned from the Army was—I didn't want to fit."

"But you're not a terrorist. I may not be onboard with everything you believe, or even do. But there's no need for you and your father to be enemies or even at odds. It's just such a waste."

He shook his head. "No. We're doomed to disappoint each other. That's just the way it is. Good night, Annja. I'm going to bed."

For a full minute she stayed alone in a kitchen dimly lit by the single fluorescent fixture over the sink.

"Why do I have this feeling," she asked herself quietly, "that could have gone better?"

SUNLIGHT LIT UP the curtains of her bedroom and made a bright band across the top as a brisk, insistent knocking on the door roused her.

"Ms. Creed," a feminine voice she didn't recognize called. "You should probably come pretty quick. We got a situation."

19

Snake, Billy and Ricky were in the kitchen when Annja entered. Billy was pouring coffee into mugs.

A small TV on the counter by the fridge was on. A glum-looking man in a tan trench coat stood in the right foreground. To the left, a block or two behind him, many vehicles with flashing lights surrounded a white building with a peaked roof standing well up above the budding trees.

"No change in the hostage situation in an Assembly of God Church in eastern Lawton," he was saying into a mic.

Without conscious intent Annja accepted a steaming mug from Billy. She frowned. "This sounds bad," she said, "but how does it concern us?"

"Comanche Star Casino opens today," Snake said. "Do you believe this is a coincidence?"

"But what does a standoff at a church in town have to do with the casino opening twenty miles out in the county?"

The newsman was describing how no demands had yet been made by the hostage takers. Nor had they identified themselves when they had called an area radio station an hour earlier to announce that they had taken hostages.

"Now, we're getting reports in the newsroom that there have been no indications of crimes or police pursuits taking place in the area that might have led fugitives to take innocent people hostage," he said.

"As of now nothing is known except that the pastor, a maintenance man and two parishioners are being held captive by unknown gunmen. Or at least that's all the authorities are telling us."

"Good diversion," Ricky said.

Annja could hear others coming in. Obviously the safe house was an emergency mustering point for the Iron Horses. She felt a spike of alarm.

"Is it a good idea to bring everybody here?" she asked. "I mean, the police and Feds are going to be made berserk by this. If this place is compromised, wouldn't it give the Dogs and the FBI the Waco-style extravaganza they both want?"

They looked at her. "Not bad for a white chick," Snake said.

Johnny came in, smelling of cold air and outdoors. "She's right," he said. He was in an elevated mood; color glowed on his cheeks and his eyes shone like obsidian chips in sunlight. "I wasn't thinking too clearly when I put out word to gather the tribe. Well, we'll use the chance to make sure everybody who's here is on the same frequency, wave off the rest and split up again."

He sat down in an incongruously prim-looking wooden kitchen chair. It was painted white, with colorful flowers.

"You'd think I'd be mindful of the dangers of clumping up, especially since our whole thing is decentralization," he said. "Not to mention I've spent three years fighting people we were never able to win any kind of lasting victory over precisely because they didn't centralize. They didn't depend on chains of command—didn't have a single head we could chop off."

"Human tendency's to seek comfort in one another's company in trying times," Billy said. For once his manner seemed serious. It made him look older than his usual mad-goblin humor did. "Even us crazy-individualist Plains warrior types. No harm done, Johnny. Feds've got their hands full right this minute, even if somebody drops a dime on us. So pat the brothers' and sisters' cheeks and send them on their way with a glad heart."

Johnny grinned and nodded. He got up and went out. Annja observed how the others watched him with a look of reverence. Even the hardcase Snake. Johnny had just done what no conventional leader or commander would—admitted a mistake. To an outsider. And it hadn't diminished his standing in the eyes of the club a bit. Meanwhile Billy, who'd dropped his clown mask to play the wise elder, was nodding to himself with a smile of pleasure, as if he'd invented Johnny.

Interesting, she thought, and sipped her coffee.

A moment later she heard many powerful V-twin engines roaring alive outside. Johnny came back in. "Okay. We're not all sitting like ducks on a pond now, anyway. They'll spread the word to everybody else to stay sharp and wait for the word to move."

"How will you get the word out?" Annja asked.

"Boys and girls'll go deliver the word in person, as much as they safely can," Billy said. "Beyond that, we got us walkie-talkies."

"But the Feds can listen in on that."

"Might be a little tricky with the encryption Snake set up on our sets," Billy said. "Anyway, even if they crack the crypto—well, let's just say them Navajos weren't the only code talkers in World War II, even if they do get all the ink."

Annja stared at him. Then laughed. And quickly sobered.

"But it's not like they can't find Comanche speakers around here, either," she pointed out. She hoped the obvious example—Lieutenant Tom Ten Bears, OHP—didn't have to be enunciated.

"Do you think we're total idiots?" Snake asked. "We've been playing this game awhile, even if the stakes have started rising dramatically."

"Our Ms. Creed doesn't like to take things for granted," Johnny said, pulling a chair around backward and sitting down facing her with his arms across the bowed wooden back. "Do you, Annja? She wanted to make sure we had it covered."

"We got code phrases and such in Numunu," Billy said. "Same thing the code talkers from all the Nations did in World War II, in case the Japs caught Indians and made them translate. 'Course, they never caught 'em carloads of Comanches the way they did them poor Navajo fellers in the Philippines."

"That was MacArthur's fault," Johnny said.

"True enough."

"So what can we do about this?" Annja asked. It was seeming less and less likely to her that this hostage taking was coincidence, the more she thought about it. "We—you can't very well go out and try to throw a cordon around this new casino. The cops would scoop you up like a bunch of tadpoles in a net."

"I think she's getting the hang of our folksy Western metaphors, Johnny," Billy said.

"We can wait for what happens next." Johnny seemed supercharged, more truly alive than she had yet seen him. It made him more even magnetic. Like he needs that, she thought.

"Then what?" she asked.

He grinned like Billy. "It depends," he said.

Johnny, Snake, Billy, Ricky and Annja remained together in the kitchen. Johnny cooked a breakfast of eggs, ham, hash browns, wheat toast. It wasn't exactly a demanding menu but he did it to perfection, while keeping up a high-energy stream of banter with his companions. Annja guessed that anything he did, he'd make sure to do it well.

The television kept up its own stream of excited non information. Apparently nothing more was being heard from hostage takers or hostages. Though nothing was said explicitly Annja and the rest got the strong impression the authorities were trying to prepare themselves to rush the place.

"They like to negotiate when they can," said Angel, who came in at midmorning. "Good PR. Even makes sense if they can resolve it that way. Less risk of what they call collateral damage."

"Though they seem to care less about that every day," Billy said.

"True. But here at home, anyway, they're still shy about pulling really scaly stuff in view of the whole world, which any media situation like this is these days. But it also makes them crazy when they can't get anybody to talk back to them. Can't negotiate one-way."

"Most likely," Johnny said, "there's all kinds of feuding all the way up the law-enforcement ladder about whether to pull elements off the Casino for this. Even postpone the opening."

He was truly enjoying himself, Annja could see. He thinks we're about to see action, she thought. And he loves it.

She couldn't honestly say she didn't feel the same way. She still wasn't sure whether it was a good thing or a bad thing. But she was personally going nuts sitting still and not being able to do anything.

"Nation won't let them put off the grand opening," Billy said. "Got too much riding on it—money, reputation. They'll take it all the way to the top if they have to. And no politician's so highly placed he or she'll turn down nice gifts of Indian-casino cash."

Johnny held up a big hand. "Wait," he said sharply.

"We're getting reports now of an explosion near an

elementary school in Lawton," an older reporter was saying on the screen. He had piercing blue eyes, silver-white hair shellacked into unlikely waves and a voice like molten amber. Apparently the station's big gun had been rolled out to break the new development.

"Holy shit," Ricky said. "Let me go check the police scanner." He disappeared through the rounded archway of the door to the rest of the house.

As the group sat and listened tensely in the kitchen more information filtered in from various sources. The story played out that a car had exploded and burst into flames on a side street a half block away from the school. The students had been inside at classes; there were no reports of injury.

"Why would the Dogs take so much trouble to avoid hurting people if they're starting a terrorist campaign?" Annja asked.

"It's smart," Angel said. "They want to frighten people and shake up the authorities without making everybody hate them. Killing kids will pretty much unify the country against them."

"Speaking of the old militia types," Billy said, "not that I knew any. They used to say after the Oklahoma City bombing that if McVeigh hadn't blown up those kids at the daycare in the Murrah Building he'd have been considered a national hero. Now, I'm not saying I agree with that, but they did have a point."

"And even setting off a bomb *near* a school will freak everyone out completely," Snake said. "No matter what's going on elsewhere the pigs have to respond to this one. Big-time."

"So," Johnny said. "*Two* diversions. That'll shake everybody's shit loose."

"Except the Dogs'," Snake said coolly.

"Look, I'm as skeptical of the authorities as anybody else," Annja said. "But won't they see these have to be diversions, too?"

"Oh, hell, yes, Annja," Billy said. "Even Lamont sees that."

"Even if they recognize it's a feint, what else can they do?" Johnny asked. "As Snake says, threatening a school's the thermonuclear option. The authorities have to jump all over it."

"So now what?"

"Dog Soldiers're about to make their move," Billy said, draining his fifth mug of black coffee. "We sit tight and hope to spot it in time to put a stick through their front spokes."

"How're you going to do that if—"

"You were going to ask, 'if the Feds can't?'" Johnny laughed. "What did I tell you? Nothing happens in Indian country—"

"That people don't know about. Yeah. But you guys had no clue about that terrorist confab at the training center," Annja said.

"The Dogs were being ultra-hush-hush about that. And we weren't looking for it. This is the Dog Society making its big play—whatever it was they wanted those other radical fools to jump in on. It'll be public, splashy, and we're on full alert for whatever it turns out to be."

"Like the government, we got eyes and ears everywhere. Only ours are human," Billy said. "Advantage—us."

"He's right," Snake said. She seemed amused.

And as if cued Ricky appeared in the doorway. He held a small yellow push-to-talk radio to his ear.

"I think we got a hit."

20

A half mile ahead, it rumbled along parallel to their jouncing, hurtling course, throwing up a big wave of yellow dust from the indifferently graded road.

"A hijacked gasoline tanker?" Annja said. Actually, she yelled it at Johnny Ten Bears' back, trying to make herself heard above the singing of the wind and the snarling of the motorcycle's big engine. "Don't the Feds have some kind of security measures to prevent that?"

"They got a program," Johnny called back. "More paperwork than implementation so far. But you have to know by now the Dogs have their snouts in the Federal trough somewhere, too. If there were safeguards, they circumvented them."

At unquestionably unsafe speed they rode a dirt road southeast of Lawton. A dozen or so of the Iron Horse People charged behind them on their big stripped-down bikes. They'd gotten the tip from an old buddy of Billy White Bird's. He was neither a member of the Iron Horse People nor an Indian, Annja gathered. Rather he was a participant in the underground-economic network, the establishing and maintaining of which seemed to be among the club's main purposes.

"But how do we know it's really been—oh, my God!" Annja's question turned to startled outcry as she saw a swarm of bikes and a pickup truck following in the tanker's dust. They immediately began to peel off to intercept the fast-closing Iron Horses. Some cut down a connecting dirt road to cross their path.

En route Johnny had shouted an explanation to Annja that this area had been grid-graded in preparation for an entire phantom subdivision—investment homes, products of the real-estate bubble now burst. The houses would never be built; the roads remained, turning gradually into arroyos from rain and wind.

Annja could make out the black-painted faces of the approaching riders. Most wore buckskin leggings and went bare chested despite the overcast cold. They were pretty seriously committed to this reenactment stuff.

Some raised hands toward the Horses. Thin gray smoke gouts were whipped away by passage wind as they opened fire. The bullets came nowhere near as far as Annja could tell. No spouts of dirt or miniature sonic booms of high-velocity projectiles passed by. Not surprising, given their terrible firing platforms.

"What do they think they're reenacting," Annja called, *"The Road Warrior?"*

With a snarl of a big V-twin engine Billy White Bird pulled alongside them.

"Do you see that posse of posers?" he shouted. "They're wearing feathers."

Annja saw it was true. At the back of most of the enemy riders' heads flapped an eagle feather. The missing ones, she suspected, had been plucked away by the breeze.

And leading the procession down the connecting road ahead, right in front of a pickup truck full of men with M-16s, rode a man on a motorbike who sported a full flowing Plains feather bonnet.

"What an asshole!" Johnny cried over his shoulder. His own long hair was tied in a ponytail and tucked down the back of the olive-drab T-shirt he wore beneath his colors, to prevent it flapping in Annja's face. "You're supposed to get awarded those feathers one by one for counting coup!"

"I think it's a case of entitlement gone amok," Billy shouted, "since if you look real close that's little Georgie Abell wearing the tourist curio. The fat bastard's been behind this all the fucking time!"

"Holy shit," Johnny said. "You're right."

"We'll clear the way," Billy called. His grin widened and he wound out the throttle.

"Better haul out that piece we got you," Johnny called over his shoulder to Annja. "You probably won't hit anything with it, but you'll give the bastards reason to stand back."

"Already on it," she called, pulling her Glock 23 from a holster at the small of her back.

She wished she dared pull back the slide enough to confirm a round was chambered—as she'd been rigorously taught to do whenever a firearm came into her hands, to confirm its status as loaded or empty, and regardless of whether she'd just watched someone else do it. She'd reaffirmed the handgun was loaded several times already; the impulse was pure habit. But it was a good habit.

Dog Soldiers on dirt bikes had cut cross-country. They began passing through the Horse column, firing handguns and even CAR-4 full-auto carbines one-handed. Annja blazed away at a couple, missing as Johnny had predicted. Well, she'd expected it, too. Hitting a fast-moving target from a platform that was also moving, and moreover bouncing all the hell over the rutted road, was basically impossible save by mad accident. And indeed when the Dogs began swirling around in the field beyond for another pass, a quick look around showed no Horses had fallen.

"Told you!" Johnny called.

"But they're on dirt bikes!" she cried. No motorcycle expert, she did know the smaller machines were more agile, far better cross-country than the burly Horse choppers, which were optimized for long-distance highway cruising.

"Yeah, but our target's bound tighter to the road than we are," Johnny called back. "And these Dogs don't live to ride, the way we do. Buncha dilettantes."

And indeed Annja saw several of the Horses vault defiantly from the saddles of their bikes to stand one-footed on a side peg, before hooting and resuming their seats. The Comanches had always been reputed among the very best horsemen among the horse-worshiping Plains nations; apparently her comrades took the whole Iron Horse thing literally.

"Impressive. But what about the pickup with all the guys with guns?"

"Watch Billy," Johnny shouted.

The crossroad still lay a quarter mile ahead.

Bent low over his handlebars Billy rode straight at the big pickup truck. The Dog Soldiers in the back were firing furiously over the top of the cab with full-size M-16s and obviously missing. Billy leaped up to stand on his seat, giving them a double-barreled finger as his machine slowed with his hand off the throttle. The bike wobbled. He jumped back down to the saddle as lightly as a gymnast, grabbed the bars and veered off into the grass as the truck roared past.

The road had a drainage ditch running alongside it. Drawing his pistol, Billy circled back around and into the dry, weed-choked ditch, following the big truck.

The Dog Soldiers in the back had jostled one another all out of any order when he went past the first time. Some grabbed for handholds in case the massive Harley slammed head-on into the truck. Others swung around shooting, hoping with wild optimism to hit him.

They were still untangling themselves when he rolled up the inner bank onto the road next to the truck, almost inside arm's reach. He pushed out the chunky revolver until its four-inch barrel was almost pressed to the front tire, then blasted off two shots. He yanked his front wheel right, hard, putting a boot down and taking off at a right angle to the road.

"Yeah!" Johnny crowed. "Classic buffalo-hunter move!"

The tire blew. Before the driver could do much about it the truck veered into the ditch. The truck slammed onto its side, bounding over the winter-tan grass. Dog Soldiers and their long black rifles spilled out.

They were picking themselves up and helping one another to their feet as Johnny whipped past them up the crossroad in pursuit of the runaway tanker. Though she had no way to be certain Annja thought none seemed badly injured. They were certainly hard core, these Dogs, dilettantes or no. And she already knew they were deadly dangerous.

A swirling battle had developed. Or rather the Dogs on their more agile machines swirled around the Horses, who charged on single-mindedly after their quarry. Both sides shot at each other but if anybody went down Annja didn't see.

Annja leaned forward into Johnny's back. Conscientiously she kept the Glock pointed skyward with her trigger finger braced on the frame instead of inside the guard. "What's the plan?" she shouted.

"I'm open!" Johnny said. He sounded as if he were totally enjoying himself. As if he'd enjoy it, live or die.

"Get in close to the tanker's rear," Annja said. "I'll climb up the back and go for the cab. Take out the driver."

Johnny turned his head briefly to blink back at her through his aviator shades. Mirrored in his eyes she saw the very question she was asking herself. Did I actually just *say* that?

"You're crazy!" he shouted.

"Of course I'm crazy. Look, I can do it. It's the only way. Unless you trust me to drive the bike while you climb up."

By the tensing of his shoulders she could tell what he thought of *that*. About the same as she did, actually.

But it was true. They weren't going to be able to shoot out enough of the big rig's eighteen tires to slow it down. And there were three bad boys riding up top the tank itself, armed with full-length M-16s, lying down and aiming, at least sort of. They'd likely pick off any Horses who got close enough to take a moving shot at the driver in his high cab. And as Johnny turned onto the road behind the tanker Annja saw yet another long black barrel sticking out the passenger's side window of the cab.

"You mean it?" Johnny called.

"Just do it, before I come to my senses!"

"I'll call the club to give you fire support."

"Wait! On a tanker full of gasoline?"

"Tank'll probably self-seal, if our bullets can even punch through," Johnny shouted. "Those puppies're tougher than you think. Anyway, bullets don't start fires for shit. Even in gas. Believe it—I know."

"Go for it," she said. She heard him speaking for the benefit of the microphone on the radio headset he and the other Horses wore. She couldn't make out the words. Since they were doubtless in Comanche she knew it didn't matter.

With a full-throat snarl a bike pulled up beside them. Snake was riding it. She caught Annja's eye, gave her a thin smile and a salute with her .45. Then she swerved off the road and gunned ahead to shoot at the gunmen atop the stolen tanker.

The rear gunner man lay on his bare belly shooting single shots. That metal must be cold, Annja thought. A shift in the flow of movement caught her eye. She looked aside in time to see a riderless Horse motorcycle bounce across the prairie for twenty yards before veering to one side and toppling in a cloud of dirt and bits of dried grass. She grimaced. She wondered who it was, hoped he hadn't been badly hurt.

Or she. Even Angel, who looked fourteen and, like her name, rode with the club to battle this morning. It wasn't the traditional Plains way. It was the New Traditional Iron Horse way.

Yellow muzzle flames flared like suns, right toward Annja. Bullets cracked by her head so near she turtled down inside the borrowed leather jacket she wore.

Johnny whooped, put his head down between his handlebars and gunned the engine. Despite its double load the powerful vintage bike leaped ahead at crazy speed. It caromed high off the bumps and rattled as if coming to pieces. Annja wasn't sure how he could possibly keep the machine on course. But he did.

She tucked her stubby Glock back in its holster and clung to him hard.

Gunfire crackled from close behind. Iron Horse People were closing in, firing at the tank-truck gunner as they came. Annja hoped they had the sense to aim high. It would really suck to take a round through the back of her head from her own guys.

The gasoline tank's rear loomed before her like an oval silver cliff. The gunner up top winced as a bullet whanged off metal near him. He jumped up, trying to keep Johnny and Annja in his sights as they got close to the bumper.

The Horses loosed a rapid-fire volley at the Dog Soldier. Glancing around, Annja saw the head of Black Bull Jake, a Kiowa, snap back as he took a bullet through the forehead. Riding at his side Snake had to veer wildly off the road to keep from being knocked down by his out-of-control bike.

Then Johnny was up alongside the left end of the tanker's big corrugated-metal rear bumper. Not letting herself think about it, Annja grabbed his shoulders. Using him to brace herself she clambered up onto her seat. Then she jumped for the bumper.

She got a foot down on it. And found herself falling forward helplessly.

21

Annja's momentum carried her across the sheer face of the big silver-gleaming tank's end. She got a hand on one of the steel rungs welded to the back of it and clung like a monkey. Her right leg flopped down off the bumper. The toe of her shoe kissed the road winding by below. She felt a terrible tug for a moment, then yanked her foot back up onto the bumper by sheer force of will.

She may not have had the upper-body strength of even a substantially smaller man, but Annja was still strong. She got her other hand on a rung and hauled herself upright.

Riding hard alongside the bumper's left side, Johnny gave Annja a grin and a thumbs-up. And out of the grassland came George Abell, his ridiculous feather bonnet flapping behind him, straight into Johnny's blind spot. Annja screamed and pointed.

Abell swung a hatchet in a gleaming silver arc. It

struck Johnny on the back of his head. He fell off his bike, narrowly missing the tank-truck's bumper, to roll over and over in the road.

Annja heard the Horses scream in rage. Abell accelerated rapidly away cross-country as bullets cracked around his feathers.

Annja saw Johnny stir, start to pick himself up. She hoped desperately he wasn't badly hurt. But a crackle of full-auto gunfire from above told her she had no more time to spare him.

She swarmed up to the top of the tank twelve feet above the dirt road. Empty casings fell on her in a glittering cascade. A glittering *hot* cascade. One seared her cheek painfully, just glancing off.

The Dog gunman was standing straight up with legs braced right above her. But he was looking back, not down. The pack of Horses following close in the tanker's dust cloud whooping vengefully and shooting at him seemed a far more credible threat than that some crazy white-eyes chick would actually jump onto the truck and come after him.

It flashed through Annja's mind that he probably had a point.

But she wasn't just *any* crazy white-eyes chick. She was Annja Creed. She reached up, grabbed his right ankle and yanked.

With a screech he flew off the tank and over her head. He struck the road sideways and rolled.

The Horses broke to either side of him to prevent being knocked over. Though he'd lost his rifle he was actually hard core enough to get right back up again with his back to the tanker.

And Snake, who'd fallen behind after being forced off the dirt road and was pushing hard to catch up, yanked the short front fork of her sled up into a wheelie. Spinning fast the front tire promptly came down again, catching the dismounted Dog Soldier full in the face like a combination of a tomahawk and a circular saw.

Annja looked away. And realized she was dangling one-handed from the back of a speeding hijacked tanker loaded with gasoline.

"Focus," she said aloud. She got both hands and feet on the cold steel rungs. Then she peered over the upper rim.

Two Dog Soldiers crouched on the roof, one shooting left, one shooting right. Ducking down and taking another quick look around Annja realized that the Dog Solder bikers were pressing the Iron Horse People hard. The most her friends could do to help her with the tanker guards was keep scattering the occasional shot their way.

Fear for Johnny jabbed her hard. Annja felt a fondness for all the Iron Horses, even the intractable Snake, and a desperate desire they should all pull through unscathed. That was already impossible, she knew. Jake was certainly dead. She had exchanged perhaps a dozen words with him; she recalled he had a five-year-old daughter.

And Johnny—he was definitely not unscathed. Annja could only hope against hope that neither the hatchet blow—which had been hastily delivered, after all—nor the ensuing fall from his bike had done him irreparable damage.

But she couldn't worry about that now, any more than she could ponder just why she felt such concern for Johnny Ten Bears. Instead, she flung herself up and over.

Suppressing the memory that she was on the back of a gasoline tank jouncing down a dirt road, Annja bull-rushed the nearer gunman. Focused on his weapon and his targets he didn't even notice her in his peripheral vision until she was almost on him. Then it was too late.

He swung the long barrel of his rifle toward her. She put her shoulder down and slammed into him, hoping her unexpected momentum would knock him off balance and allow her to pitch him overboard.

But the Dog Soldier was a powerful man, built low to the ground—or in this case, the steel runway along the tanker's spine. He held his ground. He might have quickly overpowered Annja, but she grabbed the ribbed plastic forearm of his M-16 and wrenched it. He refused to let go.

Instead, he started swinging his upper body from side to side, hoping to fling Annja away from him and off the truck. As he did she saw the other gunman, at the front of the tank, do a double take as he noticed their dance of death. Then he swung his rifle toward them.

The man grappling with Annja spun her counter-clockwise. She quit resisting. That caught him by surprise. He swung her clear around, legs swinging dizzily over empty space, so that when her feet came down her back was toward the other rifleman.

Catching the M-16 with both hands, she used it like a trapeze and swung herself between the Dog's wide-braced legs. As she did, his partner's rifle opened up with a shattering noise. Her opponent grunted as the needlelike .22-caliber bullets lanced into his unprotected flesh.

Annja popped up on the far side of the Dog Soldier. Spinning, she caught him as his considerable weight slumped toward the runway. Leaning her shoulder into his bare back, which despite the chill was slick with sweat, and grabbing the waistband of his buckskin pants, she ran him toward his companion. Perhaps trying to keep himself from falling over the side, the wounded man stumbled through several paces. Screaming, his buddy pumped burst after three-round burst into his chest and belly.

Annja felt the man slump. Screeching her own hawk challenge back at the other man she charged him.

The Dog Soldier jumped back. His flinch yanked his rifle barrel up and off-line. Risking all, Annja vaulted the bullet-riddled man as he dropped onto his face on the ribbed steel of the runway.

The sword came into her hand.

The other man's eyes went huge in his black-painted face as he saw the three-foot blade materialize in her hand out of thin air. Shock-slowed, he threw up the rifle before his face to protect himself. She started swinging the sword before her feet touched steel.

Shock ran from Annja's hand up her sword arm. Annja swung the blade again. She struck him in the forehead.

He stared at her for a disbelieving moment. Then he slumped onto his face.

Annja let go of the sword, allowing it to vanish back into the otherwise, rather than risk being dragged off the tanker with him as his body rolled down the gleaming steel flank and fell from view. She crouched, securing her balance as the immensely heavy tank-trailer jumped into the air over a particularly bad rut. Then she dashed forward the final few steps to leap over the gap between the gasoline tank's front and the green roof of the tractor's little overcab apartment.

All this time the rig had been driving arrow straight, north on the dirt road. Suddenly it swerved beneath Annja. The violent surprise direction change threw her off balance. She tumbled off the cab to her left.

Recalling the sword she reversed grip and plunged the blade down through the thin-gauge metal roof of the cab. Her legs swung wildly over space. Metal tore with a scream.

Tires grinding the packed and rutted dirt of the road, the tractor veered left. Annja was snapped onto her back on the overcab apartment. Momentum slid her across it on her rump until her heels thumped on the roof of the cab itself, in front of the raised apartment. She barely kept her grip on her sword's hilt.

If she let go it would vanish again. It was the only thing keeping her from being thrown to the road in the tanker's path.

The cab roof shuddered beneath Annja's feet. Silver holes appeared in the green-painted metal, punching upward. The passenger was shooting blindly, hoping to hit her.

Frantically she yanked her feet back up onto the apartment roof. The driver cranked it right again. This time she felt the rig's wheels rise all along the left side. The coupling between tractor and tank squealed in protest.

Annja's breath caught in her throat. He's willing to risk losing control to shake me off, she thought. Again the tractor swung left.

She released the sword and flung herself forward. As she did she recalled the mystic weapon yet again. She plunged its tip downward through the left side of the roof.

She heard a scream as it transfixed the driver from above.

Bullets stitched through the roof right beside her rib cage. Then the shooting stopped. The truck headed off the road to the left.

Abruptly it cranked right again. Held on the cab by her death grip on the sword's hilt Annja realized the man riding shotgun had grabbed the wheel from the out-of-action driver and was hauling back clockwise to avert disaster. Except he was seriously overcorrecting.

She looked down. The road wasn't moving all that fast below her. But she knew the burly tractor, and its massive load of liquid fire, had momentum.

Once more she released the sword. Then she jumped for the ditch.

Even as she flew through the chill morning air she heard a tremendous ripping noise behind her as the big rig jackknifed. The mass of the tanker and its thousands of gallons of gasoline was driving the tractor down the road sideways, stripping tires from rims.

Annja hit. Feeling flash gratitude for gymnastics training as well as some instruction in parachuting technique—specifically *landing*—she let her legs flex and went into a roll.

Her vectors were a little more complex than what she compensated for. What was intended as a forward roll turned into a weird sort of corkscrew, flopping her over and over across prickly bunchgrass and the hard earth beneath it. After what seemed a really long time Annja came to rest facedown in the dirt.

Annja raised her head to look toward the eighteen-wheeler in time to see it crash into the right-hand ditch. She saw the tanker split open like a sausage flexed violently in giant hands. Then a white spark.

She buried her face in her arms. With a colossal hollow *whoomp!* the load of gasoline ignited. A shockwave rolled over her, stinging her bare wrists and the back of her neck like dragon's breath.

But the laws of physics were on her side. She risked a glance over her arm. Its fine pale hairs were kinked by heat. The truck was crumpling, screaming, glittering steel and a vast yellow fireball that tumbled away from her across the prairie. With a sigh she collapsed back onto the ground, luxuriating in its cool embrace.

She was completely spent.

For a time she just lay there. She relished the sense of numbness that enveloped her. Too soon, she knew, it would give way to something a whole lot more like a full-body bruise. She'd been here before.

She heard a snarling of multiple motorcycle engines, forced herself to roll over and sit up, reaching for the Glock. It was still in her small-of-the-back holster, she knew. Its imprint, and that of its holster, had been embossed deeply into her flesh by her madcap roll across the landscape. That was the risk of wearing a holster there, although she was smart enough to wear it to the right of her spine to avoid serious damage.

To Annja's surprise and double relief she saw Johnny Ten Bears. Beside him rode Billy White Bird; between them they steered an untenanted Iron Horse bike with one hand each on the handlebars. They came to a stop near her.

"Johnny!" she exclaimed. Despite the throbbing agony now starting to seep through her body she leaped up and ran to embrace him. He put his cheek to hers and hugged her.

"Not too tight," he said. "I don't reckon we're either of us in shape to stand up to much punishment right now."

She pushed him away to arm's length—still being cautious to keep her finger off the Glock's trigger, and not cover either man with the muzzle. "It's so great to see you! You look awful!"

And he did. His handsome face was brutally bruised, one eye almost swollen shut. His jeans were torn, and the leather jacket he'd worn against the cold had little tufts of grass sticking out at random angles, as if indifferently sodded. His hair had escaped the ponytail; its left side had been turned into a lank, faintly rust-hued mat by the blood that had soaked it and begun to dry. A pressure bandage had been hastily taped to his head.

"I may not be much of a gentleman," he said, laughing, "but my sense of self-preservation's strong enough to keep me from commenting on your appearance."

He pointed at his head. "That fat bastard Abell's so

hung up on his fantasy reenactor thing he tried to scalp me. Almost brought it off, too. Too bad for him he forgot to kill me first."

He shook his head in annoyance. "Damn! Son of a bitch got the better of me *again*."

"Not a bad bit of work there, Ms. Creed," Billy said, holding the extra bike balanced. He nodded his chin toward the furious red blaze of the big rig and the thick column of black smoke that rose out of sight through the cloud cover. "Looked like you were swinging a pretty big blade up there up top that truck, the few times I had a chance to look over."

"A machete," she said with practiced ease. She hated to lie to a friend, especially one who was now a comrade in arms. But she had no choice. "Took it off the one dude before his buddy shot him."

Billy's cheeks rode up to turn his eyes into little narrow fingernail slices of skepticism. "That was one mighty big machete."

"Isn't that kind of a personal remark, Billy?" she asked sweetly. She laughed as his dark complexion flushed deep red.

She turned to Johnny. "I take it we won?"

His smile vanished. "We accomplished the mission," he said in a flat tone. "By definition, that's victory."

"Once the truck blew, the rest of the Dogs ran off tail-high," Billy said.

Annja frowned in sympathy—and her own pang of loss. "Did we lose many?"

"Coulda been worse," Billy said, "but any's plenty bad."

"None of us is expendable," Johnny said, and his voice was broken now. "No one."

Annja shook her head. "I'm sorry. We—we did something big here. Saved a lot of people. That has to count for something."

Slowly Johnny nodded.

"Weren't any draftees out here today, son," Billy said. "Leastwise, not on our side."

The noise of the flames was like the wavering, shifting boom of the wind intensified a hundredfold. A shift in the actual wind brought the stink of burning gasoline to wrinkle Annja's nose.

"It's Jake's bike," Johnny said, indicating the spare bike. "He's wasted. We got a couple trucks following behind. They'll pick up him and the…others."

"Then can we go home now?" Annja asked.

He looked at her a moment, as if having trouble processing her words. Then a slow half smile winched up one side of his mouth.

"Yeah," he said. "Let's go home. The good guys won. *This* time."

22

The good guys won.

The surviving Iron Horse People celebrated at the Bad Medicine that night.

"Listen up, everybody!" Johnny Ten Bears shouted. "Let me salute the real heroine of the hour. Without her, the world would be a darker place for everybody, and especially us. So let's give it up for Annja Creed!"

The Iron Horse People cheered and clustered around her. They were all smiles, hugging her, shaking her hand, thanking her. Even Snake caught her eye and gave her a nod.

And if I ever have to earn an acknowledgment bigger than that, Annja thought, I probably won't survive.

When the crowd broke into smaller groups, Annja found herself sitting with Billy and Johnny.

"I want to give you my own thanks, Annja," Johnny

said, leaning his head in close. "You saved my bacon, in particular."

She nodded, then smiled, a little sadly.

"I'm glad I could help," she said. "You were innocent. And we stopped the guilty."

Billy bellowed a laugh and slapped the table. "We did more than stop them," he said. "We kicked their asses, we took their names, and the brothers and sisters are drinking their beer!"

Suddenly people were shushing one another and bidding Ed, the bartender, who was actually cracking a smile, to crank up the volume on the TV set over the bar.

Annja looked up at the screen and laughed out loud. "That's the last person I'd expect the Iron Horse People to turn up the volume for," she said. "Special Agent in Charge Young!"

"You're saying, Special Agent Young," the reporter stated, "that in effect George Abell of the Comanche Nation's special investigative unit, and the secret organization he apparently heads, this so-called Dog Society, have swapped places on the Most Wanted list, and as a designated terrorist organization with John Jacob Ten Bears and the Iron Horse Motorcycle Club?"

"In the wake of today's events," Young said, pudding bland as always in face and voice, "we can confirm that the Dog Society is the object of the recent months-long investigation by a multiagency task force, and that they were responsible for the recent wave of killings and disappearances."

"What the hell?" someone shouted. "The Dogs were *part* of the multidisciplinary task force!"

"And they were also behind the attempt to run a hijacked gasoline tanker into the front of the Comanche Star Casino during the opening ceremonies?" the reporter asked.

"Precisely. As you know, through testimony by surviving terrorists, as well as physical evidence collected this afternoon and evening, we can definitively pin responsibility on these extremely troubled and violent individuals."

Information had come out by dribs and drabs in the media and on the Internet that afternoon. Though badly burned and battered the man riding shotgun in the tractor of the hijacked tanker had survived. And he'd been spilling his guts. The Dog Society's intention was to spark a race war—"first, Indians against white-eyes, then all oppressed minorities against the whites." They planned to make their opening statement by plowing the stolen gas tanker through the crowds attending the Comanche Star Casino opening and ramming the entrance.

In his most sensational revelation, the survivor had named the Dog Society's chief as none other than George Abell—head of their new special investigative unit. Apparently a bunch of George's well-connected buddies had been working days in SIU and playing Dog Soldier by night.

The media theorized that a last-minute falling out among the actual terrorist strike team had resulted in the spectacular flaming crash of the hijacked truck, as well as strewing the countryside outside Lawton with Dog Soldier bodies.

"You see, Jerry," Young was saying to the white-haired reporter, "sometimes misdirection is required to smoke out particularly diabolical terrorist conspiracies. Hence, the recent public characterization of the Iron Horse People Motorcycle Club."

"So John Ten Bears is no longer a person of interest to the Bureau?"

Young looked directly into the camera. "John Ten Bears has never been a person of interest to the Bureau," he said.

"You lying sack of shit!" somebody shouted.

"Standard Bureau word mincing," Angel said. She stood by the bar with Ricky's arm around her. "If you're Most Wanted, that's not a 'person of interest.' Different categories. So as far as he and the Bureau are concerned he's telling the truth."

The TV coverage had switched to a press conference held earlier that evening by a spokesperson for the Oklahoma State Attorney General's office, thanking the Federal Bureau of Investigation, and complimenting the Department of Public Safety, the Comanche County Sheriff's Department, the Lawton police and, improbably, the law-enforcement division of the Comanche Nation for their work in bringing an end to the most serious terrorist threat to the state and people of Oklahoma since the 1995 bombing of the Murrah Center.

Their battle that afternoon hadn't been without cost. Along with Jake, two other Iron Horse People had died, including a young woman. Five more had been injured badly enough to require medical attention, including Johnny. One man had broken his neck; he was in a coma and was almost certainly crippled for life.

The merriment in the Bad Medicine had a brittle quality. Despite the nature of the club's victory, and the inevitable rush of elation when you face deadly danger and survive.

Annja could see Johnny felt it more than anybody. His brave and cheerful demeanor was a mask to hearten his comrades. "Are you okay?" she asked. "This must have taken a real toll on you."

"I'm touched by your concern," Johnny said. "But I'm fine."

"Really?"

"Really."

He shook his head. "I wish there were some other way to do this. But if we don't stand up to people like the Dogs, what do we stand for at all?"

"Compassion without softness," Billy said, nodding approval. "Hard to beat that combination." Annja wasn't sure whether he was talking about her or Johnny. Maybe both.

Johnny smiled a strained smile and pushed back from the table. "Well, I should probably circulate. This is something we need to celebrate. Especially given what it cost us."

Shortly thereafter Billy went off to play pool with Snake, who trounced him soundly. Annja was content to sit quietly by the sidelines. She enjoyed the all-too-rare sense of belonging, tinctured with sadness as it was. She knew it wouldn't last for long—she'd be gone in a few days, and unlikely ever to return.

But maybe not *that* soon, a small persistent voice in her head reminded her. The skinwalker's still at large.

Not one word had been said about the I-40 murders amidst the extensive and continuous coverage of the foiling of the Dog Soldier plot. Yet Annja remained convinced some connection must exist, at least between the attack on the Oklahoma university dig and the no-longer-underground war in Comanche County.

Just as she found herself starting to give in to fatigue the party began to break up. Angel and Ricky drove her back to the safe house and dropped her off. Johnny hadn't yet returned. Annja decided that might be for the best. She barely had energy to totter to her room and collapse on the bed.

A KNOCK ON THE DOOR frame woke her. Despite fatigue that still weighed her down as if the bedsheets were made of lead Annja snapped fully alert.

She opened her eyes. Snake stood in long lean silhouette against a jittering spill of colored light from the living room. "Annja," the Iron Horse woman said. "You need to come. Now."

Annja wore a long T-shirt over her panties. She hurriedly added a blue-checked flannel man's shirt from the closet and hastened to the living room, disregarding the cold air on her bare legs.

Johnny and Billy were there, along with several other Horses. They all stared, grimly rapt, at the widescreen television.

On it, George Abell was speaking to what was obviously a handheld camera.

"We call upon our brothers and sisters of color to rise to join us in our righteous rebellion against the capitalistic, paternalistic, racist United States. We have fought from within as long as we could. Now the time has come to strike."

Abell wore buckskins, war paint, a bone-bead breastplate, all dominated by a slightly tattered-looking eagle-feather war bonnet. He seemed to be standing in front of the white-painted interior wall of a house to make his manifesto.

"They posted the video on YouTube twenty minutes ago," Billy said in a low voice when Annja perched on the arm of the sofa beside him. "They apparently also e-mailed copies to various TV stations and the cops and FBI."

"Today fascist, reactionary elements interfered with our direct action against the opening of a new casino to exploit the Comanche people and the greed of consumerism-maddened whites. Lest you think, though, that the revolution has been thwarted—or that the Dog Society can no longer strike effectively against the oppressors—we offer this evidence."

The scene changed to the dimly lit interior of what seemed to be a normal residence. The viewpoint, once again evidently a small handheld camera, proceeded down a hallway.

A figure lay in a side doorway. The camera swooped down to look at it.

Annja sucked in a horrified breath. Dr. Susan Watson lay on her back, moaning softly. Her handsome aquiline face was masked in blood; her nightgown was torn and darkly sodden.

"Let me go!" an angry young female voice shouted

in fury. Watson stirred as if trying to rise, but even the sound of her daughter in peril wasn't enough to overcome her injuries.

The camera turned up and around. A burly man in dark clothes with his face painted black emerged from a bedroom with a furiously struggling Sallie Ten Bears trapped under his arm.

Annja turned to look at Johnny, who stood by the far end of the couch with his arms folded over his muscular chest. His expression was as set as a stone statue's.

When she looked back at the screen Abell was on again. He seemed to be having a hard time suppressing a smirk.

"We have taken captive the daughter of one traitor to the Indian people and sister of another," he said. "Now we call out to Special Agent in Charge Lamont Young, the Federal Bureau of Investigation and their famous Hostage Rescue Team. Bring it on. You love war. We will give you war.

"You have heard of us as the Dog Society. Now you may call us the Crazy Dogs Wishing to Die. I have spoken!"

A cell phone rang. Annja jumped at the jarring sound.

Johnny turned to pick the phone up from the table. He flipped it open.

"Yes?"

Sensing that she urgently needed to hear what was said, Annja moved close to him. Rather than resent the implied intrusion, once he heard the voice on the other end of the line the tall, long-haired man turned the phone away from his ear enough to allow her to listen, as well.

"Did you like my little show, asshole?" George Abell's voice was saying. "We've got your sister."

"I saw it," Johnny said in a voice flat and hard as the top of an anvil. "I also saw you call out the FBI. Young is itching for a Waco-style extravaganza. You're looking at a real bloodbath, you know that?"

The other man uttered a shrill hoot of laughter. "That's what we want! We want the blood to run in rivers and outrage all the Indian nations of North America. We Dogs are happy to die as martyrs to the cause. And I'm personally going to make sure Sallie dies, too."

"I'll find you first, Abell," Johnny said. "I'll find you and I'll kill you."

Abell laughed again. "You're so predictable. Why do you think I'm calling you? I'm generously going to give you first crack at dying in a futile attempt to save your sister. *If* you're smart enough to find us.

"You can't beat me, Johnny. You never could. You were always a punk. And you're going to die a punk."

The connection broke. Johnny stared at the phone for a moment. Then he shut it with a snap.

The video statement had ended. A glum-looking female newsreader was saying that Dr. Susan Watson remained in stable condition at Albuquerque's University Hospital and was expected to survive. Thank God for that, Annja thought.

"I'm gone," Johnny said to Billy. "I have to talk to my mother. Get everyone ready to move on a moment's notice."

"You want me to come with you?" Billy asked, standing with alacrity belying his bearlike bulk.

Johnny shook his head. "I ride alone."

"No," Annja said. "Get me a bike, too. I'm going with you."

23

"What are *you* doing here?" Johnny asked. His voice had the same tone as when he'd talked to George Abell on the phone.

Lieutenant Tom Ten Bears, wearing a crumpled-looking Oklahoma Highway Patrol uniform, froze halfway out of the chair from which he'd begun to rise when he heard steps approaching his ex-wife's hospital room. Dr. Susan Watson, swathed in bandages with a tube in her nose, lay propped up beside him. Her normally spare features were puffy and discolored. Her black hair with its light streaking of silver lay spread out on the pillow.

The sight of her was like a knife in Annja's ribs. She looks just like Paul did, she thought.

"What the hell do you think I'm doing here?" Tom said.

"I think he's wondering how you got here so

quickly," Annja said, pushing in past Johnny to interpose herself between the men.

Tom caught her eye. He scowled. She held his gaze. He sat down heavily.

"Ms. Creed," he said, "I could probably ask you the same question, couldn't I? What are *you* doing here?"

"It's obvious, Thomas," the injured woman said without opening her eyes. "She's serving as a control rod to prevent a critical testosterone overload."

Then she did open her eyes. "Thanks for coming, son. I take it you brought Ms. Creed?"

"I told her not to hang around with him," Tom grumbled. "No one ever listens to the old man."

"Tom, everything isn't about you. If *you* listened more you might not have so much to complain about. And we might still be a family. Although it was dear of you to come." Her hand found his and squeezed it.

"As for how I got here," Tom said, "the department sent a plane. Looks like the skinwalker case is active again."

"So you're back on it?" Annja asked.

To her surprise he shook his head. "They let me ride along as a courtesy. I'm on administrative leave with full pay. Hardship leave, they call it. A nice way of suspending me because they're afraid I'll deal out some old-school Comanche justice if I get to these kidnapping bastards first."

He sighed. He sounded as weary as he was angry. And he sounded as if the rage simmered like magma deep inside him. Waiting to erupt.

"After a quarter century of busting my hump twenty-five hours a day to be the best trooper there was, I'm out of it. They don't trust me."

"I'm sorry, Thomas," Dr. Watson said. "You deserve better from them."

Annja looked back to the injured woman. Dr. Watson's eyes were bright and keen and fixed on her.

"I may look like death refried," Watson said, "but it's mostly cosmetic damage—various contusions, gouges and bruises. I have some cracked ribs and some torn muscles in the abdominal area. It hurts, but it's not life threatening."

She closed her eyes and seemed to sink into the bed again. "The dog saved me. Eowyn. The nurses tell me she'll be fine, too. She has a broken leg and a big knot on her head."

"I'm so sorry about Sallie," Annja said.

The eyes half opened. "You didn't kidnap her. Those monsters did."

"But it's my fault," Annja said. "I brought you and her into this. If I hadn't contacted you—"

"Is she not sleeping well, son?" Tom asked. "Usually she thinks clearer than that. I think the boy and I have a little more to do with this than you do, Ms. Creed."

"But I led the skinwalker to you," Annja said. "It was the skinwalker that did this to you, Dr. Watson. Wasn't it?"

"Yes. And it was clearly working with that fat little bully George Abell. All grown up into a pudgy big bully, I suppose. He was there. The creature didn't seem to care for them much, either. I think it doesn't like people."

"Will you tell us what happened?" Annja said.

"It was late at night. We were both in bed. I was

asleep—I think Sallie was reading Carrie Vaughn's latest book. She loves the Kitty Norville stories." She smiled slightly. "The heroine's a werewolf. Ironic, I suppose."

A look of pain crossed her face. Annja doubted it had much to do with her physical wounds. "I heard a tapping at my window. Then—John's voice. I thought. He said, very softly, he needed to talk to me. Asked me to let him in."

Annja flicked a look to Johnny. He had tied his hair back in a black bandanna and stood with his arms crossed over his chest. His face was set again, masklike almost; but a muscle twitched in his cheek.

"I've been following the news, obviously. I know he's been in trouble. And then suddenly he was supposed to be cleared. But I was still worried. Had something else bad happened to him?"

"So you opened the front door to him," Annja said.

The two men were looking impatient. However, Dr. Watson was addressing Annja as if neither of her menfolk were there. Annja got a sudden insight into why Johnny had turned out as he had—and found time to wonder how a marriage between two people as hard-headed as the professor and the highway patrolman had lasted as long as it had.

Watson moved her head in a faint nod on the pillow. "To *it*. Something strange—I heard a hissing sound as I approached the door. I thought I might be imagining it. When I opened the door I saw nothing in the porch light. So I opened the screen and stepped onto the porch—and *it* appeared. I never saw more of it than a shadow. But it had—seemed to have—the head and jaws of a wolf, but it could stand upright like a man.

"It rushed me, snapping with its jaws. I fended it off with an arm, got that well bitten. It fought me all the way back into the hall. Then it got me down in the doorway to my bedroom and began to rake my stomach with its claws. That's when Eowyn jumped it. Actually knocked the thing off me. It lashed out at the poor pup. I guess it had an arm like a man's, but when she was slammed into a wall I saw big gashes in poor Eowyn's side."

"What happened then, Mom?" Johnny asked.

"Those men burst in. With their faces painted black. I recognized Georgie, anyway. The Navajo wolf seemed not to like their presence—seemed almost frightened of them. It darted off before it could finish either Eowyn or me."

Tears welled up in her eyes. "I tried to stop them," she said, gripping her ex-husband's big hand so tightly the bones stood out on the backs of her hands. "But I had lost so much blood fighting with that—that thing. I was so tired. Even when Sallie screamed, I couldn't get up. I tried so hard, Tom. I *tried*."

"It's okay," Tom said. "You did what you could. You fought the thing. That took plenty of courage."

"And you survived," Annja said. "That's the important thing."

"No," Watson said flatly. "The important thing is that I could not protect my daughter. I failed her."

"We'll get her back," Annja said. She raised fierce eyes first to Johnny, then to his father, daring them to contradict her. All she saw on either man's face was pain threatening to break through their granite-hard reserve.

"I'm sorry," the nurse said from the doorway. "You'll have to leave now. Dr. Watson needs to rest."

Tom Ten Bears rose, then bent down gracelessly to kiss his ex-wife's cheek. Then he shuffled aside, not looking at Johnny, as his son stepped up to kiss her, as well.

"Ms. Creed?" Watson said.

Annja bent over her. The doctor reached up and with surprising strength pulled her down to kiss Annja's cheek.

"What happened isn't your fault," she said. "But I know there's more to you than there seems to be. You're the responsible adult here. You make sure the boys work together.

"Get Sallie back. And kill the men who took her."

She released Annja. Annja stood. "I will," she said.

"I thought you were the big liberal, Suze," Tom couldn't help himself saying from the doorway. "What's with the call for blood and vengeance?"

She smiled. "Well, you know what they say about liberals getting mugged? I'm a mother first. Then, I find, I am a Kiowa, the daughter of warriors. As well as ex-wife and mother to them. My political beliefs come after those things. And don't get smug. What happened doesn't shake my core beliefs in social justice. And if anything, it drives me closer to Johnny's crazy libertarian beliefs than your right-wing ones."

Tom shook his head mournfully. "See what I had to put up with all these years, Ms. Creed? I can't get any respect."

"Don't even try that on me, Lieutenant," Annja said.

When they walked out through the hospital's sliding doors the sun was just rising into some baguette-shaped clouds above Sandia Crest. Early rush-hour traffic was already beginning to clog Lomas Boulevard in front of them. The high-desert air was crisp, but far less bitter than the Great Plains winds Annja and Johnny had pounded through on their full-throttle nocturnal ride from western Oklahoma.

Jake's widow, who didn't ride herself, had consented to allow Annja to borrow her late husband's bike. Annja had pushed it hard to keep the taillight of Johnny's motorcycle in view, worrying alternately about running foul of traffic cops and losing control of the overpowered chopper at a hundred miles per hour in the dark and the wind.

But they crossed the windy Plains and the pine-forested ramparts of the Sandia without incident, and rolled down a largely empty I-40 into the heart of the city by the Rio Grande.

Tom Ten Bears stopped outside the hospital entrance and glared at his son. "If you'd just been there for your sister, instead of riding around playing rebel without a clue—"

Johnny's eyes flashed. "Big talk. You're the one who drove Mom off because you always had to be right about everything—"

Annja—had had enough.

She stepped right between them. Despite the fact she was taller than the older man, and had plenty of presence herself, she felt like a poodle getting between a rottweiler and a wolf.

In such circumstances, Annja Creed knew only one thing to do—attack.

"Put your manhoods back in your pants and *talk* to

each other. And just for a change, try *listening!* If you can't tone down the roar of testosterone enough to hear each other now, then Sallie will die, there'll be a major massacre and both of you will be complete failures as fathers, brothers and men. Comanche warriors, my ass! You're just a pair of egotistical babies having temper tantrums at each other."

And she folded her arms and turned away.

As she hoped they would the two men at once became shocked and conciliatory.

"Holy shit," finally came from Johnny's mouth.

"It's the family curse, son," Tom muttered, shaking his head. "To be attracted to women stronger than us."

That made Annja frown. It also made her turn around and reengage. "Okay. Now shake hands."

Her tone of voice and her body language did not suggest that was a request. Nor did it leave much room for anything but meek compliance. She now felt like a lioness laying down the law to a pair of unruly cubs.

The two men hesitated, then shook hands. Her brow furrowed warningly, but neither tried any hand-crushing games.

"Now promise you'll work together," she said.

They looked at her, then at each other. She waited, drawing in an ominous breath.

"Screw this," Tom Ten Bears said. "I may not be much of a dad, but I'm the elder, and it's my place to do what needs to be done. So I'll back down. I'm sorry, son. I'll do anything necessary to get your sister back. I reckon you will, too. So, yeah. I'll work with you, Johnny. Whatever needs done, we'll do it."

Johnny nodded. "Yeah," he said.

"Say it," Annja hissed.

He laughed. "Yes, I'll work with you—Dad. And Annja. You're part of this, too."

"Of course," she said. She rubbed her hands up over her face and back over her hair, which was starting to escape from the borrowed green bandanna she'd tied around it.

"Now that everybody's settled down, what's next? Are you willing to play things by the book and let the authorities handle this, like good little citizens?"

Johnny snorted.

"Well, now," Tom said, "that Special Agent Lamont couldn't pour piss out of a boot with the instructions printed on the heel. So I'm sayin' that's a *no*."

Annja raised a brow at him. "So there's *something* you both can actually agree on, right?"

Tom shrugged. "Since I'm suspended, anyway, I don't reckon I have to play this by Oklahoma Department of Public Safety rules."

Johnny gaped at him. "You? Mr. Law-abiding White Man's Indian talking about breaking the law?"

"Well, you know, son," Tom said, "it turns out—since my breakfast this morning is crow, with ashes for an appetizer—that you're right. The *right* thing really isn't always the *legal* thing."

A big grin split his face. "My bosses are afraid I'll go looking for old-school frontier justice. Then they went and cut me loose. So what say we go deal out some, son?"

Suddenly the two men were embracing. So fervently

Annja was actually afraid they'd dislocate something. Then they broke apart, looking half sheepish and half defiant. As if maybe hearing a chorus of their past selves hooting at them.

"Now," Annja said, "speaking of breakfast—unless ashes and feathers are enough for Tom—can we go get something to eat? I'm starving."

24

"So what's our next move?" Annja said.

"If the FBI finds out where Abell is holed up first he'll get the bloodbath he desires," Johnny said, sipping coffee. "And that'll be it for Sallie."

He looked at his father as if expecting him to jump to the defense of his fellow law enforcers. Tom simply nodded.

Johnny blew out a slow, frustrated breath through flared nostrils. "Problem is, I don't know how to start. We've got no means of tracking these self-proclaimed Crazy Dogs Wishing to Die."

"What does that even mean, anyway?" Annja asked.

"Another North Plains thing those boys picked up by way of the Cheyenne," Tom said. "For a bunch who claims to stand for traditional Comanche values they sure borrow a lot that doesn't come from the People.

The Crazy Dogs Wishing to Die were an Absaroka thing—what white people used to call the Crows."

"They say it means *sparrow hawk*," Johnny said.

"You're not even supposed to call them sparrow hawks, anymore," Annja said. "The birds, I mean. They're American kestrels now. Turns out they're not even related to hawks. DNA analysis says they're descended from parrots."

"You have got to be kidding me," Johnny said.

"Jesus Christ," his father said. "Maybe the End of Days types have a point, after all. *Parrots.* I bet the Absaroka are pissed about *that.* Pardon my French."

Annja smiled over her coffee cup. "I've heard worse."

Tom shook his close-cropped head. "Anyway, the Crazy Dogs were a flavor of Contraries, the warrior society whose members did everything butt-foremost."

"Early Native American frat rats," Johnny said. "With a murderous streak, granted."

"That's dead-on appropriate for Fat Georgie Abell," Tom said. "But the real Crazy Dogs were pretty serious dudes. They used to tether themselves to the ground and fight—and die—where they stood."

"You think Abell and his friends will live up to that?" Annja asked.

"You worked with him," Johnny said to Tom, with a touch of reproach.

"Easy now," Annja said.

"I did because I had to," Tom said. "The Department of Public Safety wanted us to play nice with them because they were a pet project of the council. Which meant George's dad and all his rich cronies. Many of whose kids were SIU, and are now holed up somewhere with my daughter and a bunch of feathers stuck to their heads. They were all college-educated ding-dongs playing cops—now they're college-educated ding-dongs playing Che Guevara."

He took another sip of coffee. "And like that spoiled rich-boy Ernesto Guevara, they got them a nasty streak. Basically they're what you kids today would call 'drama queens.' So, yeah, I'm afraid they will carry through with it. Leastwise, until it's way too late to change their minds. Special Agent in Charge Young and those trigger-happy FBI SWAT shooters of his won't be eager to give them a chance to, if they ever catch up with 'em."

"So how can we find Sallie?" Annja asked. "*Before* the Feds do?"

"I got a way," Tom said with assurance.

Johnny looked at his father in honest puzzlement. "But you're on leave. The Staties will never share any kind of tracking info the FBI or NSA picks up on the Dogs with you."

Tom shook his hand. "You were a good soldier, son," he said, "good enough you coulda even been a Marine. And I don't doubt you're good at whatever it really is you do now. You always had to be the best at anything you did. I reckon you thought that'd make me approve of you. Problem was, that wasn't what I wanted. All along, I wanted you to be something you couldn't ever be."

"What was that?" Johnny asked.

"Obedient."

Tom held up a big, scarred hand as if to forestall argument. Annja could see the groove the wedding ring had worn into his stubby finger, even though she guessed he hadn't worn it for years.

"Look. I'm comin' clean, here, son. 'Fessing up. I was the adult, and your mom was right. I didn't act like one. I acted like a little spoiled child myself, holding my breath till I turned blue because my boy didn't turn out exactly like I wanted him to be.

"I know I'm rambling here, and we don't have much time. But believe me, son. You're good at anything you do, but you've never been a cop."

"Okay," Johnny said, "granted. Your point?"

"Abell was. A crappy half-assed one, maybe. But he was also tied into the whole Homeland Security thing. That was another reason the Nation went for his shiny new SIU, along with the fact he was Rich Ron Abell's son. He was real good at sucking up to the Feds. Brought in tons of money and aid. And all that high-tech stuff the Feds love to use instead of their heads or their shoe soles. In place of actual police work, I mean."

"So you're saying he knows all about electronic surveillance," Annja said.

"More'n any of us does. That's a flat fact. Boy got no sense, never had him a lick. But he's not stupid—no way. Anything the FBI or even NSA can use to track him by, he ain't doing. They already know that video of his was posted by somebody tapping into some random badly secured wireless network right here in downtown Albuquerque. War driving, they call that."

Annja slumped. "So we can't track him."

"Didn't say that," Tom said. "Said the Feds can't track him."

"All right," Johnny said, exasperated. "How can we track them if they can't?"

"I thought you were the self-reliant, antigovernment type."

"Lieutenant…" Annja warned.

"Okay, okay. Just having some fun. Only 'cause I know things are about to get deadly serious. Emphasis on *deadly*." He wiped his mouth with his napkin and tossed it on his well-cleaned plate.

"Feds can't track these bad boys," he said, "but old Injuns can."

THE MEN CAME and went from the large living room. Between massive dark roof beams, and the red Santillo-tiled floors strewn with rugs in bold stripes and jags, it had been turned into a war room for Tom Ten Bears' Indian old-boy-network and their hunt for his kidnapped daughter. It smelled of wool and age and the piñon fire crackling enthusiastically away in the big fireplace.

Annja sat to one side on a sofa that, like all the big ranch house's furniture, seemed built to withstand a bomb blast. She watched, sipping coffee. It wasn't that she was deliberately excluded—the elder Ten Bears always paid careful heed to anything she said. And Johnny, restless as a leopard in a zoo, wasn't any more hooked-in than she was. They simply were not what their ever-congenial host characterized as old Indians.

Their host was one. Santo Domingo Pueblo Indian

Edgar Martínez was an amiable adobe brick of a man, with iron-colored hair wound into a short, thick queue.

He wasn't a cop. To Annja's surprise, far from all members of the network Tom Ten Bears had summoned to his aid were current or former law enforcement. Martínez had spent decades traveling the world as a machinist and mechanical engineer working oil fields. Then he retired to a sizable spread he'd bought in the piñon hills north of Santa Rosa in eastern New Mexico along I-40. There he presided over several generations of descendants and a number of enterprises, from running rangy cattle out in the chaparral to repair and remanufacture of parts for heavy equipment.

Martínez, Ten Bears father and son, and a half dozen assorted network members were poring over U.S. geological survey maps spread out on a low coffee table. Having worked dig sites across America, Annja knew those well. They covered an area ranging from the Rocky Mountains in the west through northeastern New Mexico, the Texas panhandle and western Oklahoma to Lawton, and from Interstate 40 north to southern Colorado.

It was the second day since the triumph Annja and the Iron Horses had bought so dearly had been turned to ash by the mauling of Dr. Watson and Sallie's kidnapping. A huge flat-screen TV fixed on one whitewashed wall showed one of the news channels, all of which were giving the hostage hunt in the American West constant play. The sound was muted. Every now and then someone glanced toward the TV to see if anything new might be breaking.

"Oh, no, thank you," Annja said when Martínez's

wife came bustling in with a tray of pastries steaming from the oven. Maria Martínez smiled, nodded and moved on. She was of all things a Norwegian. An anthropologist who specialized in Norse and Celtic cultural interpenetration during the Viking epoch, Maria was a stocky, pink-faced woman who affected the flowing velvet skirts and boots of a Pueblo woman, and kept her ash-blond hair wound into a Pueblo hairstyle that reminded Annja irresistibly of Princess Leia.

At odd moments Annja found herself talking shop with her hostess. She enjoyed it. Dr. Skarsgaard, as she was professionally known, was a remarkably erudite woman even given her profession. It was certainly not every day Annja talked with somebody who was fluent in both Old Norse and Keresan, along with her native tongue, English, and slangy New Mexican Spanish.

Despite having come remarkably far afield of both her homeland and her scientific discipline Maria seemed to thrive in these New Mexico hills. She proved an avid and adept cross-cultural cook. It was just that it was too early in the day for *lutefisk empañadas*. As far as Annja was concerned it was always too early for them.

Annja did accept a refill of her coffee from one of the Martínez granddaughters, a fourteen-year-old who dressed like a cowgirl. Edgar and Maria's sons and daughters, their number indeterminate to Annja, seemed to share their father's predilection for blondes.

"Why are you so convinced they're in the area, Tommy?" asked a tall, spare man with gray braids. Frank was a Minnetonka Lakota from Minnesota, who'd worked for the BIA in the Southwest for years before retiring to fish Conchas Lake, which lay fairly nearby to the northeast.

Tom's Indian old boys weren't all South Plains or Southwestern types. They weren't even all Indians. A few New Mexican Latinos and a few Anglos had passed through in the past day or two.

What all the old boys did have in common was that they were one and all military veterans, mostly with combat experience. Over the decades Tom had met them in American Legion and VFW outposts, at state fairs and gatherings of Nations. It turned out to be a very effective form of networking.

"Well, see, Frank," said Miguel Escobar, a retired Jicarilla Apache tribal cop with prominent cheekbones and sunken intense eyes. "They hit Albuquerque two days ago."

"Which means they could be anywhere in the whole wide world by now," Frank replied.

"No," Tom said, shaking his head. "These boys won't want to wander too far outside their comfort zone."

"Typical perps," Escobar said.

"Also, they're making a political statement," Tom said. "They're playing to Indians, and the South Plains peoples, in particular. Although they're also trying to stir up every random revolutionary wannabe in the entire United States."

He cast a quick glance at Annja. She had told him, belatedly, about the battle in the abandoned training center outside Lawton. He in turn had passed the tip along to his fellow Staties. They had found the site cleaned of bodies and most evidence—but despite extensive cleaning, lots of spilled blood hadn't been eradicated. Tom had not been pleased with Annja for holding out on him. Although he did claim he understood her reasoning, especially now that the Dogs were revealed not just to have infiltrated law enforcement, but to all intents and purposes *been* law enforcement.

"So this is where their target audience is," Tom said, tapping the maps strewn across the massive coffee table, "not Idaho or Mexico or Kabul."

"But with satellite news and the Internet they can still deliver their message from those places," Frank said.

"They want the FBI to spill Indian blood on Indian land," said Aldo MacArthur, a wiry little Navajo who had fought as a RAG-boat gunner in the Vietnam War.

Frank straightened up, jutting out his jaw and nodding. That argument had force to any Indian who still felt the ties of the old culture.

Standing outside the circle of sagely nodding men, Johnny caught Annja's eye. He jerked his head toward the door. Brightening, she nodded and stood preparing the excuse of going outside to stretch her legs.

The old boys were so into it they never noticed the young folks leaving. Or more likely, Annja suspected, they paid no attention. Tom Ten Bears never missed a thing; she was certain some of his cronies were equally sharp.

I just hope they're sharp enough, she thought.

25

"So what's this thing between you and George Abell?" Annja said as she and Johnny walked along the lee of a ridge, where the piñon and juniper scrub had given way to scrub oak. "If it's not too painful to talk about, I mean."

In response to Annja's question concerning his history with the Crazy Dog leader, Johnny shrugged and laughed. It wasn't a very cheerful laugh.

"Might as well talk it out," he said. "I can't think of much else right now."

"Understood."

It was a bright day, with high clouds like white horse-tails brushing across a high wide sky of almost-painful blue. The wind blew chill. Annja kept her jacket zipped and her hands in the pockets.

She liked walking and talking with Johnny Ten Bears. His company felt comfortable. Even if his charm and sheer masculine presence was a constant reminder of the sort of thing she tended to miss out on in the life-way she had half chosen, half had thrust upon her.

"George was totally my bête noire growing up," Johnny said. "He was a year ahead of me, and we were always in the same school. And he had a real passion for picking on me. He and his rich little toadies."

"Why?"

"He was wealthy and a jock, even though he never got rid of that fat gut. I was a skinny kid who spent way too much time with my nose buried in a book—that was something George had in common with my dad, disapproving of that."

"But I thought your father was a big believer in education," Annja said. "He married an anthropologist, after all, just the way our host did."

"Yeah. Well. We're complicated." He grinned at her. "I guess you picked up on that. Lot of us Kiowa and Comanche are big believers in education. But there are contradictions, too. We still grow up with the old-school warrior-hero-jock ethos of our Plains forefathers. And then there's that whole military-cop thing. You know my dad's not stupid—might surprise you to know I never thought he was. But the larger the mind, the more room there seems to be for contradictions, you know?"

"Oh, yeah."

"So, anyway. George didn't like me. I didn't like him. Then there were our dads. Ronald Abell didn't like my dad. My dad returned the feeling with interest. Abell loved money and was never too scrupulous about where he got it. Dad was the ultrazealous cop type you've come to know so well. He was always looking to bring

Abell down, from the time he was a common trooper right out of the academy. Thought he was a crook."

"Was he?"

"Are you kidding? The man's a politician."

He shrugged. "But Dad never could nail him. There were times he got close—some shady financial dealings were too big to keep covered up, some ugly incidents with hookers. Both Abells like hurting women. And Ron always had enough influence, not just within the Nation but with the city and county and state governments, to cover it all up. He did a lot of contracting for Sill, too, construction and such. He had pull. Even when my dad busted George for breaking his cheerleader girlfriend's jaw, his senior year at school, he never spent a night in jail. Georgie was lifting weights and lettering in football and wrestling by then. And still a fat bully. Just a real strong one."

"I'm surprised George was able to get into law enforcement, then," Annja said.

"Are you really? Didn't take you for that naive, Annja. Cops get away with that shit all the time. And politicians' sons."

"I guess you're right. But why wasn't Ron Abell able to get your father fired?"

"Not for lack of trying. But Dad was a good cop. He always felt he had to be twice as good as the white-eyes to get the same recognition they did. And we were well into the racial-preferences epoch when he joined the patrol. The Department of Public Safety has always been eager to recruit and keep on Native Americans. So Dad had political shielding, as well. Enough that all Ronnie's plunder and pull couldn't mess with him."

He shook his head. "Dad always did have a gift for dealing with people. Making friends. And yes, I was way too quick to put that off on sucking up to the white man."

"You both have a conspicuous talent for turning your charisma off when the other is concerned."

"Ouch. Well played."

"So about you and George—"

He laughed. "Yeah. Sorry—funny how everything seems to keep coming back to Dad and me."

"But not surprising."

"So George improved his school days by giving me noogies and making me eat dirt. Hell, I guess I have to credit the bastard for my getting into shape and getting into athletics. It was a matter of sheer survival."

"And you did well," Annja said.

"Yeah. Had a knack for it, I guess. Anyway, I did better in sports than on the academic side. I still loved my books. Loved learning stuff. But school bored the crap out of me."

"No surprise there, either."

"Problem was, George was always better. At least, he was stronger. I could run his fat butt into the dirt in track and field, eleven times out of ten. But he never got into that much. He turned out to have a knack for power lifting, and he liked sports where his brute strength gave him the edge. And, of course, where he got to hurt people. He's always loved that."

He went silent then. As they walked Annja felt a chill emanating from Johnny that had nothing to do with the wind that stirred the chaparral.

"You're thinking about Sallie," she guessed.

"Yeah. Great to think a sadistic freak on a terror rush has her completely in his power." He ground his teeth so loud she could hear him above the restless rustle of the wind.

Annja pressed her lips together and exhaled forcefully. "This may be a really terrible way to comfort you, Johnny," she said. "I know it's awkward. But if Abell was hurting your sister—torturing her—he'd be showing that on YouTube, too. Until it got taken down. Right?"

He sucked in a deep breath. For a moment Annja feared she'd overstepped.

He exhaled explosively. "Yeah. You're absolutely right. He understands the purpose of terror is to terrorize. If he was…hurting her, yeah, he'd be showing the world in gruesome detail. It'd be all over other sites even after YouTube yanked it."

He frowned then, and looked at her. "Which begs the question—why *isn't* he?"

"Well, you know him better than I do."

But I've had extensive experience with terrorists, she thought, as well as serial killers and drug warlords and pirates and secret policemen and other such evil men. But she couldn't exactly say that. Even to him.

And that was why she didn't dare open up to Johnny Ten Bears the way she longed to. She had way too many secrets that had to stay that way.

"I think, for what it's worth," she continued, "that he's saving her for later. Savoring it. The anticipation of—*you* know. And, I hate to say it, he's probably enjoying her emotional and psychological distress."

She watched him closely. But he nodded slowly. She knew her words caused him pain, but she respected the man too much to tell anything but the truth. Not *all* the truth, granted.

"So what role is your little pal the skinwalker playing in all this?" he asked.

She shook her head. "I wish I knew. He's—well, a lone wolf, to use a cliché. But that's what a Navajo wolf is—deliberately isolated from his people and his family."

"Which the Athabascans are even more big on than most Indians."

"Yes. Cutting yourself off from your clan is as huge and terrible a step as immersing yourself in ghost magic, I gather. Although I also suspect he may not be an actual Navajo."

"Why?"

She shook her head. "Gut feeling. Also—all respect, but I've known a fair number of Navajos. The deep-res types, the ultratraditionalists—and you have to be really into the traditions to go to the lengths to violate them that a witch does—tend to be some of the most bigoted people I've met."

"No kidding," Johnny said. "They don't like outsiders, period. White-eyes or Indian."

"So our killer seems to care an awful lot about the ancestors of modern Pueblo and South Plains Indians, neither of whom the Navajos ever got along with real well."

Since first talking to Johnny's mother—who was recovering nicely and had been moved out of ICU, thank goodness—Annja had done some reading of her own.

"Yeah," Johnny said. "You're right. Navajos'd probably think whoever made that site on the Continental Divide were Anasazi—which I think's an anglicized version of their term for *the enemy people*."

Annja looked at him. He shrugged. "All right, so I always got along better with Mom, okay? I picked up on some of her interests."

They both laughed. Annja found it surprisingly easy to do.

A drumbeat of horse hooves sounded behind them. As they whirled, their hands sought the handguns they each carried. Annja had her borrowed Glock in a Kydex holster on her right hip, beneath her puffy down jacket. Johnny wore his Glock in a holster of similar material, dropped well below his belt with its lower end strapped to his lean blue-jean-clad thigh.

Annja and Johnny each had the training and the presence of mind not to draw the pieces prematurely. Riding bareback toward them was a grandson of their host's.

"Annja, Johnny," he cried as soon as he saw them. "We need you back at the lodge. They got a hit!"

26

The ever-present wind whistled through the long tan grass around them and tried to pluck the map of Harding County from the fingers of Eugenio Rocendo of Jemez Pueblo and whip it off the hood of the white Range Rover where Annja and her companions were studying it. Rocendo was seventy years old and vigorous, a former USAF security patrolman and LANL security officer. All around them Native American vets were unloading horses from trailers. And unlimbering a startling assortment of scoped bolt-action rifles, lever actions and even WWII-era Garands.

"Okay, there's been activity at this old abandoned house here on the Rabbit Run Wash," said Chuck Mason, a local Kiowa rancher, pointing at a spot near the tiny town of Roy a few miles south of the Kiowa National Grassland. "Tends to kind of stand out.

Harding's the state's least populous county. And New Mexico ain't a populous state."

The clans were gathering at a crossing of dirt roads. It was dry and forbidding grassland where the Great Plains met the Southwestern desert. As Tom Ten Bears had promised, his network, including its members' extended families, had turned up results before the government did.

"There've been some strange Indians seen in the area," Mason said. "Some threats made to locals."

"Not too smart where all forty people in the county have a rifle rack in the back window of their pickup truck," Billy White Bird said to Annja. He wore a ball cap and an Oklahoma Sooners blazer over his big paunch. He had his hands in his pockets.

She nodded, trying to take in the details of the terrain. The old Otero place seemed to lie in dead ground, with land swells surrounding. Like the training center outside Lawton it seemed to have been chosen for being hard to see at any distance, rather than defensibility. If the objective was to play hard to get, and then make a final stand that could never succeed, anyway—but the more bloodshed, the bigger the win—it made a twisted kind of sense.

She looked around. "What's all this costing, anyway?"

"Don't worry about it," said Edgar Martínez, who'd come with them to be in at the kill. "Some of us are doing all right. We're happy to help out a longtime comrade like Tom where his family's concerned."

"And we've shed a lot of blood, sweat and tears for

this country," Rocendo added. "These terrorist bastards are striking at that while giving us all a bad name."

"And never underestimate the power of an old man's vanity," Mason said.

"The 'last ride syndrome,'" Johnny said with a lopsided grin.

"Yeah, and in another forty years it'll be biting your ass, too, Sonny. So you can just wipe that smirk off your smug mug."

Johnny laughed. "Believe me, Mr. Mason, I understand. And I'm grateful for what you-all are doing."

There were maybe a dozen of the oldsters, and nine Iron Horses in addition to Johnny, including his lieutenant and chief wrench, Billy, Snake, Ricky and Angel.

"The Bureau's afraid we'll do better at finding the Crazy Dogs than they will," Angel had explained succinctly when she and Ricky arrived that morning. The others had trickled in since the word went out to the Iron Horse People the previous afternoon—get here if you can, quick as you can. "We're off the bad-guy list but we're still marginal social types. So they can get away with squatting on us. A lot of us are under surveillance and didn't dare come here."

Johnny's mask of stoic good cheer slipped just a bit, giving him the momentary aspect of a skull, with sunken eyes and hollow cheeks.

The life of one single human being lay at stake. Sallie Ten Bears. Innocence personified and endangered, Annja thought.

"Something we need to think about," Angel said. The wind whipped her long dark hair in front of her face. "The Dog Soldiers who were part of the SIU were connected with Federal antiterrorism efforts, right?"

"Yes," Tom said.

"That means they'd have access to a lot of high-tech equipment. Such as radio direction-finding gear. So, is any of that missing?"

Tom Ten Bears looked uneasy. "The Feds don't seem to want to talk about that. From what I hear from my buds back in Comanche County, the scuttlebutt around the Lawton PD and the Troop G barracks is that lots of stuff is missing."

"So we can't use walkie-talkies or cell phones too close to our objective," the pretty young woman said. "We have to assume they'll spot us. And that won't be good."

"So we can't use electronics at all?" Johnny asked, looking alarmed. Every person on the scene carried at least a cell phone. Some of the old guys' trucks fairly bristled with antennas, like FBI surveillance cars.

"We should be okay outside of maybe a mile," Angel said. "They can't get too twitchy about signals farther out than that. Even as sparsely populated as the area is, everybody's got cell phones, radios, whatever. You'd be surprised how many transmitters you find even out in the boondocks these days."

She bit her lip. "We might want to ask people who don't absolutely need them to switch off their electronics, though. They spot too big a cluster, they'll get antsy. And once we break up to start our approach, even outside the mile limit, probably only one person per group should have a live unit. They're paranoid."

"Just because you're paranoid doesn't mean

people aren't plotting against you," Frank said. "Evidence—us."

Everybody laughed at that. Maybe a bit too readily. They'd gotten word from their own spies in the nearby regional U.S. Attorneys' Offices that the FBI thought it had a fix on the hostage takers' location and were expecting to strike soon.

Despite her distrust in Lamont Young's competence, and general skepticism of the FBI, Annja hoped they got the right location. It would be beyond ironic if she and her friends took down the Dogs—only to have the goal of setting off a bloodbath fulfilled when the FBI landed hard on somebody else.

"What about satellite surveillance?" Annja asked.

"Any access to overhead observation would require passwords to get the tasking," Tom said. "Those've been canceled by now. Even the Feds aren't that dumb."

Annja caught Snake lifting a skeptical eyebrow. Maybe it shouldn't surprise me that a former DARPA wonk is conspiracy minded, she thought.

The old boys were discussing alternate communications methods. "We'll just have to rely on a system of bird and animal calls," Frank was saying. "Just like our ancestors did."

"Wait," said Mark Running Bull, a tall and spare Cheyenne. "I can't do bird and animal calls."

"What? Didn't you learn how as a young man?" Frank asked.

"Did I go to some kind of school to learn how to be an Indian? My dad worked for AT&T. I grew up in Wichita."

"No, not Indian school," Frank insisted. "You know. Boy Scouts."

"The rebels in Afghanistan always got the best results against us when they used the lowest tech," Johnny said. "Not exactly hard in that godforsaken part of the world. For those who don't know them, I can teach everybody a set of simple hand signals pretty fast."

"What about different groups?" Tom asked, sounding as if his patience was straining. "How'll we know when everybody's in position? Send smoke signals?"

"Not a bad idea," Frank said.

"I got a better one," Juan Tenorio said. He held up a hand. Something winked dazzlingly. "Apache telegraph. Or as the white-eyes call it, heliograph."

"You'd better get moving," Mason said, holding his cell phone to his ear.

"Why's that?" Johnny asked.

"FBI is rolling," he said. "They're estimating two hours from now to the target."

Annja looked to Johnny, who shrugged.

"Wait," the elderly Kiowa said. "There's more. There's *another* convoy, well on its way out of Albuquerque. Looks like somebody from the U.S. attorneys' Office is trying to preempt the FBI, with a little help from the New Mexico State Police and Harding County Sheriff's Department."

He shrugged. "The sheriff's my son-in-law. One of his deputies is my nephew. So let's just say we got the word from inside."

"Why would the U.S. Attorney be trying to steal a march on the FBI?" Annja asked.

"Two possible explanations I can think of," former federal prosecutor Angel said. "Either they're hoping to grab the credit themselves. Or they want to put a spoke in SAC Young's and Abell's mutual scheme to stage a massacre."

"Humanitarian motives?" Billy asked. To Annja's discomfort several of the senior posse—former lawmen or attorneys themselves almost to a man—laughed out loud at the notion.

Angel shrugged. "Not everybody in the justice system lacks a conscience."

"Maybe," Ricky said, hugging her. "But you're here with us now, so who knows?"

"But let's say some of that," she suggested, "plus a desire to avoid the PR hit to the government if there's major bloodshed."

"Well," Billy said, opening the lever action of a Marlin .44 Magnum carbine, "we're planning on shedding some major blood ourselves, aren't we?"

"In part precisely so it *won't* be the government doing it."

"I hate taking the government off the hook." He slammed the lever home with a loud clack.

"Me, too," Johnny said. "But my sister's life's at stake."

Billy looked chagrined. "You're right, John. Sorry."

Men started leading over saddled horses. "Y'all best cut stick and go right now," Mason said. "The bunch from Albuquerque will be here way ahead of the FBI."

"What about you?" Annja asked. Eight of the elders would ride out with Annja, Johnny and the Iron Horses. The rest would stay behind with the vehicles blocking the closest access road to their target.

"We're gonna keep the law at bay," Mason said.

She looked around in alarm at the heavily armed old men. "You're not planning to *fight* the authorities, are you?"

The men looked at one another and laughed. "Oh, hell, no," Frank said. "We're just human shields."

"Violent terrorists are one thing, Ms. Creed," Martínez said. "The federal government is not about to bulldoze a posse of well-respected Native American senior-citizen war heroes. Nor are the New Mexican authorities. And the Harding County Sheriff's Department sure isn't."

"Better not," Mason said. "Otherwise Sheriff Phil is cut off forever."

"You kids go with good hearts," Martínez said. "Us old farts should be able to keep the cops negotiating long enough for you to do what needs done."

"Okay," Johnny said, swinging aboard a palomino gelding. "We ride!"

ANNJA CREPT THROUGH tall grass. Along with Billy, Snake and a gangly Cheyenne kid named Cody Hawk, she was circling to the south of the abandoned adobe ranch house where George Abell and his Crazy Dogs were holed up with a captive Sallie Ten Bears. They hoped.

Annja carried a Ruger Mini-14, a handy, reliable

carbine that fired the same .223-caliber cartridge as the M-16. She knew a shotgun usually served better for close-in work. But there was a major prospect they'd have to shoot it out with the hostage takers before busting into the house. She preferred something she could shoot accurately at range. Anyway, for infighting she carried the borrowed Glock.

And she always had the sword, of course.

Snake carried a Mossberg 500 combat-style shotgun in 20-gauge. When Annja cocked an eyebrow at her choosing that over the more conventional 12-gauge, the tall, tattooed woman had shrugged, smiled and said, "Three-quarters the killing power for two-thirds the recoil. I like the trade-off."

Billy and Cody Hawk both carried lever-action carbines chambered in .44 Magnum. Billy claimed those served as well as a semiauto rifle like the Mini-14, even in close-quarters battle; and while the needle-like .223s had a lot of penetration, the big blunt Magnum had torque. Like Annja, the three Iron Horse People carried holstered handguns as well as long arms.

They had ridden horseback as close as they could get to their objective without being seen. Annja decided she wasn't surprised that her biker buddies knew how to ride flesh-and-blood horses as well as iron ones. It fit perfectly with their philosophy of combining the best of the old with the best of the new.

When they had ridden as far as they were going to they dismounted. Four of the elder warriors stayed to tend their young horse herd well behind the line of fire. The other four had gone to position themselves under cover. They would provide long-range fire support for the younger people assaulting the ranch buildings.

"You wouldn't think some of them would make it across the room," Johnny said, shaking his head as the four snipers disappeared. "But they move like mist out here in the weeds."

"Don't underestimate your elders, cub," Tom said gruffly. For a moment Annja worried the truce between him and his wayward son was about to break at the worst possible moment. But then Tom's seamed face split in his engaging grin, showing he'd been kidding. And to her relief Johnny laughed.

They gave the old boys ten minutes. For Annja it was like squatting in boiling water, trying to contain her eagerness and awareness that the clock was running. Then they split themselves into three teams and moved out.

The lone road to the Otero place ran up and over a low ridge from the west. Annja's group intended to take up station on the far side, covering the back of the house from the cover of dry Rabbit Run Wash; they had the farthest to go. Johnny's quartet would approach from north of the drive, his father's from the south. The three parties were positioning themselves in an approximate equilateral triangle, to allow them to catch their opponents from flank and rear while minimizing the danger they'd cross fire one another.

Annja had fretted about how willing Iron Horse bikers would be to put themselves under the command of a cop, much less their beloved chieftain's until-recently estranged father. But Tom's team, Angel and

Ricky, plus a Kiowa named Satanta, seemed to respect the older man.

It's all going so smoothly, Annja thought as she duck walked along with carbine in hand. That's what worries me.

When they had reached a point Annja reckoned was due south of the house, she held up a hand to halt.

"Let's take a look," she said softly. "Get our bearings."

The others nodded. Even more than concern over Tom's reception, Annja had felt trepidation about how Snake would respond to being effectively under her command. But Snake just kept acting with her usual cool matter-of-factness. The running fight with the stolen tanker seemed to have won her respect.

They went to their bellies. The earth was cool beneath Annja. She wore a light jacket over jeans and hiking boots. Working her way to the top of a low rise she peered through the yellow wraparound lenses of a pair of shooting glasses.

Despite being built of stabilized mud brick the main house looked like a conventional contemporary ranch design. Maybe a three-bedroom. It still had glass in the windows; Annja guessed it couldn't have lain derelict that long. Of course, out in the middle of nowhere untended window glass might have a greater life expectancy than, say, back home in Brooklyn.

A maroon SUV was parked in front of the ranch house. To the west lay a garage and a small prefab building that might have been a shed or a workshop. Past a corner of the house Annja glimpsed a small barn made of poles and sheet tin.

"All right," she said. "We're on the right track. We better move." Once they reached their attack positions they'd use a mirror to flash quick signals to the other two groups.

Snake caught her forearm in an unsettlingly hard grip. "Wait," the tattooed woman said tersely. "What's going on over there?"

She pointed off to the northwest. Annja saw a commotion in the tall grass.

A heartbeat later Johnny Ten Bears rolled into sight, grappling for his life against a bulky, bare-chested George Abell. A knife flashed in the Crazy Dog chieftain's hand.

"Freeze where you are!" a voice barked behind Annja.

27

Annja was already in motion upward with no ready way to stop. She also knew that people who were talking didn't usually shoot. It took time, and generally an act of will, to shift state from *talk* to *shoot*. So she took a calculated risk and turned.

Of course, she anticipated a loud noise, and shattering impact, and blinding white light for every millisecond of the movement.

Annja already knew what she'd see. Three stocky guys in Old West Indian-reenactor drag pointed thoroughly modern assault weapons at them.

The Dogs didn't bother blacking their faces anymore; they were out in the open, as it were. Instead, they had painted themselves with various symbols in assorted colors. They wore buckskin pants, bone-bead chest pieces and eagle feathers.

She gave points to the guy who went shirtless. The air was cool. The relentless Great Plains wind turned it into knives.

"Way to walk into the trap," one warrior said. The Crazy Dogs were all keyed up on adrenaline; from the looks in their eyes, they had been for days.

Annja's comrades stood and turned to face the men who had the drop on them. They held their long arms loose in their hands, muzzles angled down.

"Throw down your weapons," the bare-chested leader directed.

Gunfire broke out to the west. Annja felt suddenly nauseous. But the diversion was a welcome assistance to what she was about to do, anyway. Try not to think you're probably listening to friends dying in ambush, she told herself, and dropped the Mini-14.

She kicked it toward the three painted gunmen.

As Annja made her move she'd noted the flicker of three sets of eyes turning reflexively toward the sound of shooting. The drop-kicked carbine sailed up toward the face of the man in the middle. He reacted by reflex. And his immediate instinct was to guard his eyes, not shoot.

He yanked up his own rifle to block the flying weapon. Annja was already in motion. The sword sprang into her hand. She slashed at him.

But he had already flinched back so far from the object flying unexpectedly up in his face that he over-balanced. He backpedaled madly. He bounced the Mini-14 off his own rifle. Then the sword slashed his M-16 across the receiver. Its tip only gashed his cheek.

She was already whirling right. She cut the man on

that side across the chest as he raised his rifle. He spun away from Annja as if propelled by the blood gushing from his chest.

Behind her a gunshot cracked. Then more, rippling like sudden hail on a tin roof. She flinched. I'm dead, she thought.

It took little time to realize that wasn't the case. She wheeled, sword still in hand. Its miraculous blade gleamed in the sun.

She caught an impression of the third Dog gunman falling, dropping his M-4 carbine. With an eagle scream of fury the leader whipped his long black rifle to his shoulder, aimed it squarely at Annja's face and pulled the trigger.

Annja's sword stroke had split open the M-16's chamber. The easiest path for the terrible fire and force unleashed by the primer bursting was *not* pushing a jacketed lead pill out of the cartridge neck and forcing it to screw its way down a long grooved barrel. It was to jet out like a superheated knife into the leader's painted face.

He never had time to scream.

Annja turned to find Snake and Billy in Weaver combat stances, staring over the front sights of their respective handguns. Cody Hawk still stood with his own rifle in hand. His dark eyes were wide.

"Whoa," he said.

Annja realized the other two, having dropped their long arms and with handguns still braced and leveled at the air their opponents had occupied moments before, had clicked their eyes to her. Theirs were pretty wide, too.

"Later," she said. "First, survive until later."

A brisk firefight was going on to the west of the main house. Despite having obviously been ambushed by the Crazy Dogs, as well, the other two parties were making a fight of it. Johnny! she thought in sudden terror. And stepped hard on the thought.

"So much for the Feds being smart enough to kill the SIU's passwords," Snake said, relaxing out of firing position. She ejected the 1911's partially depleted magazine onto her palm, tucked it away beneath her bulky Army jacket before popping a fresh one into the well. Meanwhile Billy was ejecting the full-moon clip from his big revolver and reloading, too.

Annja recovered her fallen Mini-14. She jacked back the charging handle far enough to confirm a round was still chambered, because she was properly trained, too. She also gave the bottom of the thirty-round black stamped-steel banana magazine a whack to make sure it hadn't come unseated during the acrobatics the rifle had been called on to perform. If it had, the weapon would lock up when she fired the chambered cartridge.

"Cody," she said softly. The boy continued to stare at her. "Cody."

She sharpened it up as much as she dared. She didn't want her voice to carry, although with all the shooting going on—gunfire was coming from the house now, as well—it was unlikely any Dogs could hear anything but their own caps busting.

The young man blinked. She took that to signify he'd returned to earth. "Watch our tails for us. We don't want any more bad guys sneaking up on us like that. You got that?"

"Oh, yeah." He nodded feverishly, firmed up his grip on his lever action and started sweeping the surrounding grass with wild eyes.

Annja went to a knee and peered up and over the low crest. She felt Snake and Billy slide up on either side of her.

For the moment the battle had devolved into a static firefight. The Horses had gone to ground and traded shots with Dogs firing from behind the outbuildings and the SUV. Annja had no idea how any of her friends had survived being cut down or captured—they had walked into ambush as flatfooted as Annja and her team had.

She heard a strangled scream, saw a Dog who had spun back behind the garage reach up to the red spurting gape where his jaw should've been.

"The old-guy snipers!" she exclaimed. "They're picking off the Dogs!"

Annja could see no sign of Johnny and his burlier foe. She didn't know if that was a good sign or not. She never thought for a moment either side would pack it in just because a leader fell.

Only death would keep Johnny or his father from rescuing Sallie—or wreaking bloody vengeance on her kidnappers if they were rash enough to kill their captive. And for the other Horses this was personal. They were going to settle the score with their bloody rivals.

"Don't forget," Snake whispered, "the choppers are on their way."

"And that's not a good thing," Billy said.

Annja nodded. "One thing to do," she said.

"Of course," Snake said.

"Damn straight," Billy said.

"Cody," Annja called. "We're going in. Follow us."

"Straight in?" he asked. They'd be approaching the ranch house from the side, not the back as planned.

"Seconds count," she said.

She'd figured out a plan. They could bring flanking fire on the Dogs shooting from outside the house. But the quartet of old Indian lawmen who had hidden themselves out in the tall grass had that covered. They could continue to work their way around to come in from the west as planned. But aside from the fact that would take them through the fields of fire of Johnny's bunch, if any were still firing, that would take a long time.

And it wasn't just the FBI kill team coming closer with every sweep of their choppers' main rotors. The longer this went on the greater the likelihood the Dogs would kill Sallie. Or even that a stray bullet from her rescuers would do the job.

There were no good answers. So Annja opted for the quickest.

She jumped up and charged the house.

28

Speed was everything. There was a window in the wall that faced them. Curtains hung in it, their patterned dark cloth long since bleached by the sun to a mottled gray-brown. Annja saw the curtains twitch. Then glass exploded outward as full-auto fire erupted through the window.

A second burst blew curtain tatters flapping out the window. Cody grunted and fell headlong to the dirt. His limbs flopped as he rolled.

A tremendous boom burst from Annja's left. A head Annja had only just spotted fell away inside the window. Snake had paused just long enough to take quick aim before firing her shotgun.

Annja scattered shots through the window to keep the defenders' heads down. Shooting blind might endanger Sallie. But if somebody picked her, Snake and Billy off as they covered the last few yards to the house, she was likely dead, anyway.

Half turning Annja pressed up hard against the wall between the window and the back of the house. Snake slammed up beside her.

A moment later Billy joined them, his short, bowed legs pumping determinedly if not exactly fast. Although he puffed like a steam engine he rumbled right past the women, heading for the back door. Bending low to avoid being spotted out the kitchen window Annja followed. She felt more than heard Snake come after.

Holding his carbine across his chest Bully kicked at the back door. "Damn!" he yelled as his boot rebounded.

Annja slid up to the side of the frame. Keeping the foot-thick wall at her back, she grabbed the knob and turned.

The door opened.

Billy kicked it again. It whipped inward. Annja heard an impact, a soft cry. Then Billy's .44 Magnum roared.

Snake slipped inside. Annja came right after. As she stepped left automatically to clear the doorway's fatal funnel a yellow light and terrible noise filled the gloomy kitchen into which they had intruded.

"Missed!" Snake shouted, racking her slide. She had shifted right on entering. She unleashed another head-burstingly loud blast into the far wall, hoping to blow through and nail the Dog who'd peeked out and then ducked to cover on the far side. But instead of lath-and-plaster or drywall the interior wall turned out to be adobe, too, when the pellets blew a divot of painted plaster off. Like the outer walls it would shrug off hits all day.

Annja slipped forward around a wooden kitchen table set against the wall. A man lay on his back in the middle of the floor with his arms raised over his head and a pair of eagle feathers splayed out on the warped floorboards. He had obviously taken Billy's bullet through the chest.

Her head reeled. She put out an arm to steady herself against the nearest wall. Annja wasn't squeamish. She wondered what would be making her feel so shaky.

Snake fired another shot through the open doorway that led past the hall to the living room. Annja guessed it was to make the man who'd escaped her earlier keep his head down. The brutal noise in such enclosed quarters was making her head ache.

Annja dropped the Mini-14's magazine from the well and stuffed it in her jacket pocket. Then she jacked the action and caught the brass cartridge as it spun glittering from the receiver. She dropped that in a pants pocket. Kneeling, she set the unloaded Mini-14 down on the floor. Short and handy though it was, a handgun was even more effective in close quarters. And she was a lot more used to fighting at face-to-face range.

From the front of the house came a mutter of voices. Louder voices barked questions at each other down the hallway that led right to where the bedrooms and bathroom presumably lay. Sallie was almost certainly down there, as well—if she were indeed being held there.

A hard choice faced her would-be rescuers. They could drive straight for Sallie and get shot in the back by the men in the living room. Or they could deal with them first, putting themselves in danger from whoever was lurking down that hall, and increasing Sallie's exposure time to lethal danger.

The plan could've been better, Annja thought. Then again, this wasn't the plan. It was improvisation forced on them by the fact the Dogs were fully aware of their approach. And the original plan had been pretty ad hoc to start with, given they had no recon and no time, but had to trust the maps, their allies and their own resourcefulness to get in and save a captive child.

"Cover my back from the dudes in the hall," she muttered to her comrades.

A shout and a shot erupted from the corridor as she raced past. Both missed. Then she burst into the living room like a hand grenade, her sword appearing in her free hand.

The two Crazy Dogs kneeling by the windows to either side of the door pulled back from the windows where they had been trading shots with the Iron Horses, stood and begun swinging around to cover their backsides with their long black rifles.

They were too late. The closer man had yellow lightning bolts painted on his cheeks. Annja launched a forehand stroke. The sword slashed across the painted face diagonally. The Crazy Dog toppled backward, clutching at a gush of blood with futile hands.

Still running Annja brought the sword up and around, swung down and right. The second man, one half of his face painted black, the other white, was trying to bull-rush her, with his long black M-16 held transversely across his torso as if at port arms. The sword caught him at the juncture of thick neck and powerful shoulders. The blade bit at an angle deep into his chest.

As he fell Annja became aware that she'd heard the sound of the shotgun, a booming noise that seemed to rattle the abandoned but still-sturdy house to its foundations, and the crash, less loud but more eardrum-punishingly intense, of the .44 Magnum carbine. A second shot from Billy's carbine followed. Annja returned the sword to the otherwhere.

Then Snake stood beside Annja. She held her shotgun, muzzle up. Her usually narrow eyes were wide.

"Clear," Annja told her. The other woman nodded. She had remarkable presence of mind, Annja had to acknowledge.

"Ready?" Snake asked.

"Oh, yeah," Annja said. "Billy?"

"Here," he called. He was kneeling on the kitchen side of the hallway, leaning his bulky body out far enough to cover down it.

He fired again.

"Gotcha!" he grunted. "Bastard stuck his head out from the bedroom, down the hall."

"Right," Annja said. "Sallie'll be at the rear of the house. Take the first door, we cover."

She glanced back at Snake and mouthed, "Then we

hit the next one." Snake's thin lips curved in a slight, feral smile. She nodded.

Annja moved to the opening to the hallway, standing far enough inside the living room to remain invisible from the hall. "On one," she said aloud. She flashed a V sign with her fingers to Billy. He grinned.

"Two," she said.

As she'd signaled him to do Billy launched himself on the second count. He caromed off the corridor's far wall, pushing off to kick the first door on the right with the heel of his boot. Though intact, the house's interior doors were not nearly as stout as the exterior ones. The door splintered under the impact.

Annja hit the rear corridor wall as Billy's shotgun bellowed. A ring of gunshot echo told her he'd just cleared the bathroom. Snake knelt by the front wall of the hallway, aiming down the passage.

Billy erupted out of the bathroom and hit the closed door across the hallway with his shoulder. The door shattered. He fired through the gap, then, dropping the carbine, plucked his one-piece steel hatchet from his belt.

"Hello, boys," he said. And vanished inside.

As screams and thumps came from the front bedroom Annja and Snake dashed down the hall. A man lay slumped in the door of the far bedroom. The back of his head was missing; Annja didn't worry he was playing possum. The right-hand door was closed.

She stopped just shy of the open door and leaned forward over the body, covering the room with the fat white dot painted on her front sight. Nobody. If somebody was lurking out of her field of view on that quick peek she'd just have to risk it. They were out of time.

Sallie had to be behind the last door. If she was there at all.

Annja flung herself to the end of the hall, gouging her left arm on a handle of the linen cupboard set in the end wall above a set of drawers. She flattened herself as best she could. Then she caught Snake's eye where the woman stood posed on the door's far side.

Snake went to one knee. Luck or her subconscious had set them up perfectly—Annja was right-handed and Snake shot lefty. Annja reached down and carefully turned the knob. Then she yanked back her hand.

As she did, shots ripped through the door, knocking long thin splinters from the plywood. A second gun voice joined. At least two gunmen inside were burning up their magazines in one desperate spasm. No three-round burst regulators for these bad boys, Annja realized. No doubt SIU had gotten the federal armorers who'd provided them the automatic weapons in the first place to disable those.

A handful of hypersonic bullets all but grazed Annja's sucked-in belly. She actually felt their passage-shock slapping the front of her Windbreaker. None of the nasty little copper-jacket needles hit her.

Sudden echoing silence broke out over the ringing in her ears. Goodbye, more of my hearing range! Annja thought. She grabbed the knob again, twisted and threw the door open.

There were two of them, crouching by the back wall. Their M-4s lay on the bare pine planks before them with charging handles locked back—empty. Their eyes gleamed crazily from faces painted black from cheeks to hairline.

One Crazy Dog held Sallie Ten Bears pinned between them by the blade of a huge Bowie knife to her throat. The other pressed a 9 mm pistol to the side of her pigtailed head.

29

"Back off!" the man with the knife screamed. "We'll kill the little girl."

Annja cut her eyes to Snake. The other woman caught her look. She nodded once, barely perceptibly.

The two warrior women fired as one.

Both Dog Soldiers fell as one. Each sported a hole dead between staring empty eyes.

Sallie flung herself forward, sobbing, and caught Annja in a ferocious embrace. Annja hugged her briefly, keeping her pistol tipped toward the ceiling so as not to endanger any of her friends.

"Your mom is fine," she said, in response to what she thought were the questions the shaking girl was sobbing into her sternum. "Your dad and brother are outside. We need to get you out of here. Let's go out the back door."

"No!" Sallie ripped herself free. Her face was suffused with blood and twisted in panic. "We can't!"

"Why not?" Snake asked, hunkering down so as not to loom above the terrified child. She kept switching her eyes from rear window to hallway door, taking nothing for granted.

"There's something out there," the girl gasped. Fear seemed to constrict her like a giant python. "A *monster*. Even the bad guys are scared of it. They told me it would rip me apart if I ran away. They—they showed me pictures of all these torn-up dead people!"

"The skinwalker," Billy said. He stood in the hallway behind the women. He had sheathed his hatchet at his belt and picked up his gun.

Annja drew in a deep, shuddering breath. "She's probably safest staying put, then. Sallie, go in the bathroom. Will you do that for me, honey, please? Lie down in the bathtub. That'll keep you safe from bullets."

Unless the FBI sprays the house with bullets from a helicopter overhead, she thought. The clock was running out. Outside, the firefight had resumed. And on top of everything else the Navajo wolf was apparently somewhere on the scene.

"But I want to watch!" Sallie said.

"Please," Annja said. "Do it for your mom and dad and Johnny. If you get hurt they'll never forgive themselves, ever. Understand?"

For a moment the girl looked mulish. The stubborn family temperament bred true, it seemed. Then she nodded. "All right."

She went into the bathroom and closed the door behind her. Through what little was left of it Annja saw her climb into the bathtub, cross her arms and pout.

"Good enough," she said.

Having seen something curious when she checked the bedroom across the hall, Annja ducked down below window level and went inside. Sure enough, computers and flat-screen monitors were set on a wooden desk and a card table.

"Damn," Snake said, running eyes over the displays. "They really did watch us the whole time."

"Wouldn't they have to task a satellite especially for it?" Annja asked.

"There's way more surveillance-capable satellites over our heads than most people realize." Snake gestured. "This might not even be from an American bird. It could be a real-time feed purchased from anybody. Even Russians or Chinese. Your tax dollars at work."

Staying low, they moved to the window and peered out.

"Oh, no," Annja said.

"What's the matter?" Billy asked, hunkering down behind them.

The shooting was picking up outside. "The Dogs have come out from under cover," she said.

"Signifying what?" Snake asked.

Annja gave her a worried look. "Maybe some of our snipers have been taken out by the skinwalker."

"Damn," Snake said. "And no way to warn the others."

Billy laid two fingers on Annja's shoulder and pointed. "Look!"

Johnny Ten Bears emerged from the tall grass on the north side of the road that led to the derelict Otero house. He was walking bent over and holding his Glock ready in his hand.

From beyond the garage George Abell suddenly rushed him. The Crazy Dog wore fringed buckskin pants. His broad flabby torso was bare from the waist up. In classic Comanche fashion his hair was divided in two large braids. A narrow scalplock streamed behind him like a cavalry pennon. He caught the unsuspecting Johnny from behind and slammed him to the ground.

As if the participants were stopping to spectate, the gunfire slackened. Annja could plainly hear Abell bellow, "I got you now, punk! You never could beat me. And you never will!"

Straddling Johnny's back he grabbed handfuls of his long black hair and started pounding his face into the hard-packed ground.

Annja raised her carbine and lined the front sight post on Abell's head.

"No," Billy said. The weapon was gently pushed off-line.

"You don't know Johnny the way we do," Snake said. "He needs this. Live or die."

"So what if he does die?" Annja asked, alarmed.

Snake shrugged. "If Georgie wins, then we kill him."

"Deal."

Johnny Ten Bears got an arm under himself and pushed upward. So focused was his opponent on hammering the ground with Johnny's face, he'd risen up on his legs for better leverage. Johnny's hips were no longer pinned by Abell's great weight. The Iron Horse war chief half rolled onto his left side and scissored his right thigh up into Abell's crotch.

From sixty yards away Annja saw the strike lift the bigger man. His grip loosened on Johnny's long black hair. Johnny threw him off and came up to one knee with a fist on the ground.

"Didn't think that crotch shot'd do much to Georgie," Billy remarked. "Not much by way of a target."

Abell recovered quickly. He was up almost at once, charging his kneeling foe like an angry rhino.

To Annja's surprise Johnny launched himself not backward or away, but forward. He rolled right into Abell's shins. The rogue SIU chief was even more surprised than Annja. He took a header over his opponent and landed heavily on his face.

"Whoa!" Billy exclaimed softly. "That registered on the Richter scale."

Abell got right back up, only a lot more slowly. Too slowly. Johnny popped upright and skip-stepped toward him. As Abell reared up on his knees Johnny caught him in the left side of the face with a beautiful roundhouse kick that snapped his opponent's head around.

Annja winced. She had distinctly heard the blow land. Only the bearlike thickness of Abell's neck saved him from having it broken by that kick.

Abell toppled backward. Johnny danced in with his knee still raised like a kickboxer. Abell lashed out with a leg in an attempt to sweep Johnny's limb from beneath him.

But Johnny wasn't caught out. One-legged, he hopped straight in the air. Abell's short but massive leg passed harmlessly beneath. When he landed, Johnny used the momentum gravity gave him to stomp Abell in the side of his big jiggling paunch.

Abell bawled like a fighting bull stuck by a picador. Far from being stunned by what had to be a painful hit he lunged for Johnny. Johnny had to leap back so fast he almost overbalanced and went over backward.

As Johnny caught himself Abell got back to his feet. He raised half-furled fists by his face. The left side was swelling, the eye reddened and half-closed. Deliberately Abell advanced on his foe.

"Dad's watching," Billy said.

Unwilling as she was to look away from the bare-hand duel for even an instant, Annja moved her gaze left. Tom Ten Bears, dressed in a red flannel shirt that had come untucked and hung down in front of his jeans, stood watching his son battle for his life from twenty yards away. Out of his gray-on-gray Oklahoma Highway Patrol uniform he looked vulnerable. His big hands were empty, but Annja noticed his .41 Magnum still rode in its holster at his right hip. She'd bet the safety strap was unsnapped.

Snake nudged her with surprising gentleness. Annja looked to her. She nodded off to the right. Annja saw a Dog Soldier, shirtless like his leader, who had emerged from cover and was hunkered down, peering around a corner of the shed at the death match. He was mostly hidden from view from the combatants' direction—but plainly in sight of the house. It suddenly struck Annja that, as far as he knew, he was still safe in the hands of his revolutionary martyr-wannabe comrades.

A quick check around showed at least two more surviving Dog riflemen, like the first, concealed if not covered from Johnny and his friends to the west—and in easy view of Annja, Snake and Billy. She grinned briefly. She wasn't worried about notions of fair play. Not with violent criminals who had committed mass murder, attacked an innocent woman and kidnapped her even-more-blameless child.

Besides, Annja knew perfectly well the Crazy Dogs were only taking a quick time-out from trying to kill her and her friends. They had less sense of fair play than she did. They just wanted to watch a good fight.

So did Annja. She enjoyed a battle between experts. For all his bulk and general loathsomeness, Abell was very good.

And so was Johnny Ten Bears. He and his foe traded jabs, ranging shots that had no visible effect. Johnny tried a feint wheel kick at head level in Abell's face, just to let him know he had it in his arsenal. It was risky kicking above the waist in a real fight; but if you were good enough you could get away with it sometimes. As Annja had herself in her time.

Abell lunged at Johnny, diving at his thighs to take him down. Johnny countered with a classic sprawl. He danced back, putting his hands on the backs of Abell's immense shoulders and pushing him down on his face. Instead of diving atop his grounded foe Johnny jumped back, cat-graceful.

He doesn't want to go strength to strength with Abell, Annja thought. Smart man.

Once more Abell was quickly back to his feet. For a
time the two men punched and kicked each other.
Johnny landed more often than Abell, and they were
strong, solid blows, too. But along with his strength
Abell showed a bull-bison's ability to absorb punishment. For all his wiry strength Johnny didn't seem to
have the power to put his broader foe down. His lone
hope seemed to be to wear his man down by attrition.

Johnny tried no more fancy high kicks. He did
manage to crack a few shin kicks into Abell's bowed legs.

And then Abell, once again moving with unexpected quickness, trapped Johnny's left leg with a
grab to the knee.

Johnny wrenched it free at once. But the trap kept
him in range of Abell's terrible power a beat too long,
and breaking the hold put him off balance. He fell off
onto a left foot planted too far behind him.

Abell rocked Johnny Ten Bears' head back with a
lead left that seemed too powerful to call a stiff jab,
though technically it was. Abell had a weight lifter's
arm strength and the technique to step into the punch.
Nailed squarely in the face, Johnny staggered. Annja
cried out as she saw him sag.

Showing true killer instinct Abell closed with his
stunned foe. He pistoned short but monstrously
powerful hooks and crosses into Johnny's short ribs.

Johnny caught Abell with a lead right hook of his
own. But his old enemy leaned in so that the blow
mostly glanced off the back of his skull. Johnny started
to push him off.

Abell brought up the point of his left elbow in a

rising smash that caught Johnny right under the point
of the chin. His jaws clacked together.

The taller, lighter man reeled backward. With a roar
of triumph Abell rushed forward and seized him around
the middle in a bear hug. Johnny called out in pain as
Abell locked hand on wrist behind his back and brought
down crushing pressure on his bruised and cracked rib
cage.

30

Triumphantly George Abell hoisted his imprisoned foe into the air. And Annja, who had long since forgotten to breathe, filled her lungs in one big gasp. Abell had allowed his overconfidence to run away with him. In his eagerness to crush his hated rival, he'd left Johnny Ten Bears' arms free.

It was a novice brawler's mistake—and whatever he was, Abell was no novice. For a moment it looked as if he hadn't miscalculated, after all. Johnny hung limp, bowed back against the killing pressure of those thick arms, his long hair falling unbound across his face. He seemed too stunned and badly hurt to resist the relentless pressure which must soon either break his spine or asphyxiate him like a python constricting a rabbit.

But then without raising his lolling head Johnny clapped his hands sharply over Abell's ears. Abell cried out with startled shrillness as his eardrums imploded.

Johnny jackknifed forward and smashed George Abell's nose with a head butt.

George bellowed and dropped him. Abell staggered back as his free-flowing blood painted a moustache and beard of red down his lips and chin. Johnny's knees buckled as his feet hit the ground.

He had barely lurched back to his feet when Abell put his head down and charged. He rammed the point of his skull into Johnny's stomach.

But Johnny Ten Bears bent forward to meet the flesh-and-bone battering ram. His right arm encircled Abell's throat, slipping just beneath his powerful chin.

As Abell's head hit his gut Johnny pushed hard off the ground with his legs. He used the force of his enemy's charge to drive his legs and torso upward. Confused, Abell reared upright, boosting his opponent higher.

Johnny did a front roll right over the top of Abell's vast back. As his feet came down behind him Johnny surged forward with all his strength. His arms, themselves now locked beneath Abell's jaw with left hand gripping right wrist, dragged Abell's head back and over Johnny's right shoulder. Johnny leaned forward, pulling on the captive head and thrusting with his legs as if trying to tow a Greyhound bus by a rope across his shoulder.

George Abell's neck snapped.

His dead weight dropped Johnny Ten Bears beneath it to the ground. The victor lay unmoving.

The first Crazy Dog Annja had noticed, the one crouching behind the shed, raised his M-4. Annja already had her Mini-14 shouldered. She lined a flash sight picture between his bare shoulder blades, let out half of a breath and squeezed the trigger.

The carbine had little kick. It came back online so fast she was able to double-tap her foe as if it were a handgun. He was already slumping toward the dirt. The second shot hit him in the back of the neck.

Billy's .44 Magnum lever action roared, temporarily deafening Annja's left ear. Another Dog went down as he tried to draw bead on the Iron Horse chieftain, who was feebly struggling to extricate himself from beneath his enemy's dead-buffalo bulk. Tracking her carbine left looking for other targets, Annja saw Tom Ten Bears quick draw his big-framed Smith & Wesson revolver, present it into a fast modified Weaver stance and blast out two rapid double-action shots. Another Crazy Dog Wishing to Die fell forward into sight from beyond the garage, an M-16 falling from his hands.

He'd gotten his wish.

Like a sudden rain squall gunfire broke loose again. Another shirtless, gaudily painted Crazy Dog raced madly around the rear of the maroon SUV with a short M-4 carbine in one pistoning hand. Black holes appeared on his bare chest, and red mist puffed out ahead of him as at least two bullets holed him back to front. He fell and slid five feet on his face and didn't move again.

"I guess not all the bros and sisses were watching the fight," Billy said. Snake had an M-16 recovered from the dead guy in the doorway up and was squeezing off aimed single shots at a target no one could see.

Abruptly the shooting stopped. No targets presented themselves to the trio crouched in the front-bedroom-cum-command-post. It seemed that the other surviving Horses had run out of bad guys to shoot at, too.

"I guess we won," Snake said, not raising her eye from her rifle's battle sights.

"Maybe so," Annja said.

Tom Ten Bears knelt by Johnny's side. During the resurgent firefight he helped his savagely battered son work his way out from under the corpse of George Abell. Johnny had promptly collapsed on his back.

Another motion drew Annja's eye outward to her left. Angel was kneeling in the grass, cradling something in her lap. Her head was tipped forward, her long black hair hanging to obscure her beautiful face. The shaking of her shoulders in the outsize leather jacket told Annja all she needed to know and more than she cared to. The young ex-attorney was cradling the head of her dead fiancé, Ricky, in her lap.

The wind shifted to blow straight from the west, in through the window of the bedroom. Though it was tainted with burned propellants and lubricants, and more organic smells, it still tasted fresh after the more concentrated gunsmoke and spilled blood smells in the room. Its chill seemed to cleanse Annja's nostrils, throat and lungs and acted like a dash of icy water on the face.

Yet at the same time she felt an increased sense of the light-headedness from before.

Annja breathed deep. Shaking her head and blinking back tears, Annja pushed away from the window. She stayed hunched over. No point standing bolt upright and giving some bitter-ender Crazy Dog a free shot at her from hiding.

"I'm going to go check on Sallie," she said.

Then she turned and froze.

Sallie stood in the bedroom doorway. Her eyes were huge.

"Sallie," Annja said, "it's not safe yet. You need to stay in the bathroom."

"But I heard shooting," she said. "Where's Johnny? Where's Daddy?"

"They're fine, sweetie. We're almost through this. But not yet. We—"

"Annja," she heard Snake say in a peculiarly taut voice. As she did the gunfire erupted anew, with a frantic vigor Annja hadn't heard earlier.

Electrified by horror and fear, Annja ran forward two steps to grab and hug the gangly girl against her. Blocking the child's view of the window with her body Annja looked back over her shoulder.

Like a great gray dog it bounded from the yellow grass. It covered ground with such amazing speed that it looked like a blur. In fact, its outlines seemed somehow to *shift* as it streaked toward the ranch house.

Holding his revolver in both hands Tom Ten Bears rose from his son's side and stepped quickly into the gray shape's path. He fired twice. To no effect.

The beast reared up. Now it seemed to be a man with the head of a wolf. It struck Tom with its claws, driving him back. Snouted jaws snapped for his neck.

The highway patrol lieutenant fell, blood spurting from a ripped-out throat. With a desperate cry Johnny flung himself at the monster. Ignoring him it leaped over his supine father and raced on, intent on the house. Johnny collapsed in the dirt as his strength failed him.

"Oh, shit," Billy White Bird said.

He turned for the door as Snake began firing at the creature. Outside, the surviving Horses and what Annja thought were at least two of the old-boy snipers were firing furiously. They must be dumping boxes of bullets into the thing. Yet its step never faltered.

"What? What's going on?" Sallie demanded. Annja yanked her back against the far wall of the hallway as Billy churned past on his short legs. Snake followed right behind him.

Annja still had her Mini-14 in her right hand. Sallie broke free and tried to run past her to the window. Frantically Annja clutched at her arm.

"For God's sake, stay back!" she screamed at the girl. She thrust her into the bathroom and raced down the short hallway. From the living room came the thunder of Billy's lever action carbine, cranking out shots. Somehow she knew it wouldn't be enough.

She had a dread sensation all the firepower in the world wouldn't be enough. The skinwalker was like a force of nature, like a hurricane or a volcano's glowing cloud. Yet unlike those impersonal yet irresistible forces of destruction it seemed to give a black radiance of evil that penetrated the thick adobe walls like gamma rays.

Billy bellowed. Annja reached the end of the hall in time to see the burly man grappling with the gray-furred shape. She heard snarling and the tearing of leather and cloth and flesh. Billy's furious outcries turned to gurgles.

The monster cast the torn body away like a rag doll. For a moment it stood on its hind legs, growling a deep, savage growl, seeming to fill the doorway with its black presence. Its outline still seemed to shimmer, as if Annja—not twenty feet away—was seeing it through a haze of midsummer heat.

The flash and boom of Snake's 20-gauge pump gun filled the empty living room to overflowing. The shadow shape flinched back. Then with a snarl it sprang at her.

Snake racked the action with speed like that of the fang-bared totems tattooed on her wiry muscled arms. Her courage was as impressive as her skill.

Neither helped. The beast lashed out with its right arm. Black talons gashed open Snake's left side and flung her clear across the living room to slam against a huge fieldstone fireplace. Her head slammed back into the slate mantle and she slumped, the shotgun dropping from limp fingers.

Now it was Annja's turn to face the horror. She had the Mini-14 shouldered. The monster of constantly shifting gray shadow filled the space between the steel ears that flanked the front-sight post. She began to squeeze off shots, compact surprise breaks, well schooled to the end.

She *saw* her bullets hit. Saw the fur fluff out where they went home. They had no effect.

The creature sprang at her. She thrust the carbine crosswise into gaping yellow-fanged jaws. They ground together, crunching the brown-stained wood. Its breath stank of corruption from beyond the grave.

For a moment her gaze met eyes that seemed to glow with their own blue witch fire. It snarled and struck her.

The carbine's forestock splintered as she managed to interpose the weapon to take most of the force of the blow. Yet it still threw her over to slam onto her back and slide across the bare wood floor of the hallway.

She came to a stop with her head and shoulders right in front of the open bathroom door. Sallie stared down at her in horror.

She threw a hand toward the child. "Stay! Get back!"

Low growling dragged her reluctant eyes toward the mouth of the hall. On all fours now, its back fur bristling, the shadow monster prowled around the corner. Its tongue lolled over lips that seemed to grin. Triumph glowed in the blue-hot flames of its eyes.

"You're enjoying this," Annja croaked. Though bruised and battered, her body feeling as if it had turned to lead and her limbs to string cheese, she thrust her torso up off the floor with her left hand while she held her right wardingly toward the beast.

It stopped. Its shadow shape contracted as it cocked itself like a spring to strike.

Like a living spear of righteousness Annja Creed flung herself to meet it. The sword came into her hand. She just had time to wrap both hands in a death grip on the hilt and thrust with all her might before she struck.

The sword met the leaping monster in midair and drove deep into its chest where its neck blended in between the muscles of its forelegs. Its snarl of triumph turned to a yowl.

The hurtling mass crashed upon Annja and drove her back. Hot stinking breath surrounded her head, stinging her skin like acid mist. With the skinwalker lying atop her Annja slid down the corridor on her back. She knew with frightful certainty that she dare not let go of the sword—dare not let it vanish back to the otherwhere. Not until its work was done.

The back of her head struck the drawers at hall's end. The beast's forepaws drove into her belly. But they weren't raking her, tearing her belly open and spilling her guts as they had poor Billy's. Instead, it was an ineffectual scrabbling that weakened, heartbeat by heartbeat.

With no more strength in her arms she held its snapping jaws away from her face by the sheer power of her will, pressing the sword's hilt against the gray-furred chest. The monster writhed. It uttered a long agonized cry.

She felt the monster die.

She released the sword. It vanished. With the last of her resources Annja half steered the limp body to her left as it fell, half pushed herself out from under it. It landed diagonally across her hips.

She didn't lose consciousness then. Not quite.

"Annja! Annja, are you all right? Oh, please, don't be dead!"

A child's hands and a child's voice tugged at her, dragging soul back into her body and mind back behind her eyes. She opened them.

Sallie Ten Bears was holding Annja's right wrist in both little hands and pulling for all she was worth. Then Snake appeared, tugging at the dead thing that lay across Annja, trapping her.

When the fearful weight came off her legs Annja

managed to climb to her feet—slowly, and with more help from a young girl than she'd care to admit.

"Snake," she rasped through a throat that felt sanded. "Are you all right?"

"Nothing that won't heal," the tall Cheyenne woman said. The left side of her black T-shirt was sodden. From the labored whistle of her breath she had broken ribs, and possibly a raw end threatening to pierce a lung. But she threaded Annja's left arm over her right shoulder as Sallie inserted herself under Annja's right arm, bracing her armpit with her shoulder, like a living crutch.

"Who the hell is that?" Snake asked, nodding at the shape that lay rolled with its back against the hallway wall.

Annja looked down. A man lay there, naked but for the tattered head and pelt of a wolf. His pallid skin was punctured by innumerable small round holes that bled a tracery of blood, black in the gloom. He had a bit of whitish stubble on his gaunt cheeks, and his wide-open blue eyes seemed to gaze sightlessly upon their own damnation.

"Dr. Yves Michel," Annja said. "The U.N. guy. The skinwalker expert. I should've known."

The woman and the girl walked Annja out, through the living room and out into the healing sunlight and cleansing wind. Annja made herself look at the torn wreckage of Billy White Bird's body as they passed.

There was something pressing outward from within her. Something she must say.

"Thank you," she croaked to her supporters. "The sword—please…don't tell anyone."

Snake shook her head. "I won't," she said. "That's between you and your Power. It's not mine to give."

"I didn't see anything," Sallie said determinedly, and Annja again heard that Ten Bears stubbornness ringing in her voice.

The disparate pair managed to support Annja across the yard and up the road, to where Johnny Ten Bears knelt with his father's head cradled on his thighs.

The sight of her dad lying there was too much for Sallie. With a broken scream she launched herself from beneath Annja's arm and fell across his bloody chest, sobbing wildly. Snake caught Annja as her knees buckled and kept her from falling, despite the pain it must have cost her.

Tom Ten Bears somehow retained the strength to lay an arm across his daughter's heaving back. "You're all right," he said in a faint voice.

"Tom," Annja said.

"My daughter is safe," he said to her. "My son lives. It is a good day."

Johnny raised his face to hers. His lean, bruised cheeks ran with tears.

"My father," he said, reaching down to stroke the back of his sister's head. "I found him. Now I'm losing him."

"Your brother will take care of you, Sallie," Tom said. "He is a good man. I…am proud."

His head lolled to the side and the life left his eyes.

And then the thunder of rotors swept over them like

a Great Plains thunderstorm. Annja looked up at the great shark shadows that seemed to fill the sky with their rotors sweeping overhead. It was too much.

She slipped into darkness.

31

Everybody was arrested.

After Annja came to and was herded to join the others sitting under the guns and black-visored gazes of the FBI SWAT unit, Annja learned the day's terrible toll. Of those who'd gone with Annja, Johnny and Tom on their last ride, only she, Johnny, Snake, Angel and Lonny Blackhands survived. The others had died. Ricky had succumbed to his wounds, Angel told her in a lost and quiet voice, while shooting at the charging skinwalker. Angel herself had been shot through the upper arm.

The skinwalker had also killed two of the Indian-vet snipers before he attacked the house.

For some odd reason, the media never arrived before the survivors got shackled and bundled into the vehicles of the Albuquerque convoy, which had arrived at almost the same instant as the four FBI choppers. It took some soft words from Johnny to get Sallie to consent to be detached from his side and escorted into a sedan by a shocked-looking female assistant U.S. Attorney. Johnny himself as well as Snake and Angel went into ambulances to be taken under guard for treatment at University Hospital.

Annja's and Lonny's wounds were dressed by medics on the scene. They weren't serious, and aside from cleaning lacerations and applying some bandages there wasn't much to be done for them. They consisted mainly of massive bone-deep bruising and, at least in Annja's case, a crushing sadness compounded of adrenaline letdown and grief and trepidation for the fates of herself and her friends.

When she found herself ushered, not ungently, into a black SUV with dark-tinted windows, the first thing Annja saw was Edgar Martínez grinning at her. Rocendo and Frank were in there with him.

"Welcome, fellow jailbirds," he said. "We held 'em as long as we could. Hope it was enough."

"You were perfect," she said, with only a slight hitch in her voice.

Eventually they all wound up in the federal courthouse in Albuquerque. There they were subjected to what would later be termed extensive debriefing.

At the time it seemed to Annja a lot like plain old-fashioned interrogation. It went on for hours at a stretch. The only reason she wasn't subject to twelve-hour sessions was that they just didn't have enough personnel on hand to do that, especially given the gigantic investigation into the Dog Society and their now-infamous plot. Instead, between three- or four-hour grillings, Annja was left locked in the interrogation rooms to stew. Despite the fact she was deliberately not made comfortable she mostly slept.

They were clearly not happy, the Bureau agents and the U.S. attorneys. An edge actually came into Special Agent in Charge Lamont Young's bland voice as he told Annja in no uncertain terms how disappointed he was in her.

Annja had no way of knowing how long they kept her. She never wore a watch, and she'd left all her gear with the Indian good old boys staying behind at the vehicles in what proved the futile hope of avoiding detection by the tech-heavy Crazy Dogs. The sound of the door opening awakened her. A little trim Latino with a brush of dense, backswept steel-colored hair and a handlebar moustache, dressed in an immaculate dark blue suit and a bolo tie, was ushered in.

"Annja Creed?" he asked in one of those deep, mellifluous trial-lawyer voices. "My name is Reynaldo Montoya. I must say it's an honor and a privilege to meet you." He had a dark complexion obviously darkened further by long exposure to the Southwestern sun; it lent him craggy gravitas. Notwithstanding his lack of height he fairly radiated energy and sheer presence.

Annja stirred. She had been dead asleep, stacked in a corner with her Windbreaker huddled about her. It was colder in the interrogation room than it had been in the derelict ranch house out on the Great Plains.

"Thanks," she said. "I think. Are you the one playing good cop?"

He laughed. "Ms. Creed, I assure you, I'm not a cop at all."

He came to her side and helped her up. He got her settled into a chair at the obligatory interrogation-room table, then looked up at the blatantly obvious camera mounted in a corner of the ceiling.

"Get some hot coffee in here for this woman," he barked. "Now."

Montoya sat down across the table from her and smiled. "I'm eager to hear your story," he said. "But first there are some things I must tell you."

"Who are you?" she asked. Fatigue still weighed on her. "And, uh, what are you doing here?"

"Those are as good places to start as any. I am an attorney. I'm retired from paid practice. These days I devote my time and energy to fighting for the rights of those falsely accused, prosecuted or convicted. I am— I *was*—a friend of Tom Ten Bears. We met several years ago when he played a key role in helping us exonerate a young Acoma Pueblo man falsely charged with rape and murder in Lawton, Oklahoma."

That surprised Annja. She would've thought that, good man though she knew the lieutenant to be, his warrior ethos would dictate his putting cop solidarity above all. Instead, he seemed committed, as she herself was, to justice as an ideal. Not another empty promise chiseled into the wall of a government building.

She felt shame then at having underestimated the man, in even such a trivial way. It became easier likewise to understand how Johnny had misjudged him. He had grown up as the man's son, after all, ensuring that in ways he understood him less than anybody, for reasons of rivalry and adolescent rebellion.

As Tom, in fairness, had underestimated his son at least as badly.

"As to what I'm doing here," Montoya said, folding his hands on the desk before him after allowing her a moment to process his words, "I am assisting you and your comrades from the incident in Harding County. I might mention I am but one of a human wave of attorneys hurling themselves against the walls of this courthouse, by the way."

"Who's paying for all this?"

He laughed. "You've dealt with lawyers before, I take it? I donate my efforts. I have done well on investments made during a long and lucrative career, largely by ignoring the advice of pundits and advisers. As for the rest—some are likewise donating their time, as friends of Tom Ten Bears or simply of justice. And others constitute part of the truly imposing amounts of pressure being applied to the Federal Bureau of Investigation and the U.S. Attorneys' Office by the Oklahoma and New Mexico state governments, as well as half a dozen Indian tribes, to let you all go."

"Is there really even a chance of that?"

"Oh, yes, Ms. Creed. What I might term a very good chance. *If* you agree to certain terms, which, I admit, you might find unpalatable."

"Winding up in a federal penitentiary for the rest of my life would be pretty unpalatable, Mr. Montoya. But I have to warn you—I'm not going to sell my friends for my freedom."

"Fortunately, I don't believe it will come to that. Not if you agree to the terms I am about to convey to you. If not—" he shrugged "—then you may find yourself faced with such a dilemma."

"What's the deal?" Annja asked, as much out of curiosity as hope. Once law enforcement got their jaws in you, she had observed, they tended not to let go until they could shake you into pleading guilty to something.

"The Bureau and the Department of Justice find themselves in a most uncomfortable position," he said. "To be perfectly blunt, stumbling late onto a slaughter of unquestionable criminals does not provide nearly the media extravaganza as actually slaughtering the aforementioned criminals in a shootout, broadcast throughout the world in real time. Especially since the media, contrary to the evident expectations of Special Agent in Charge Lamont Young, who commanded the operation, never showed up until well after the action had ended and you and your associates were on your way here."

"That puzzled me, too. Especially since we heard before we went in that the FBI had leaked the operation to the media, and the U.S. Attorneys' Office—here, I guess—was hoping to avert a massacre that would play into the Crazy Dogs' hands. We, uh—we had contacts of our own in law enforcement, you see."

"Oh, yes," he said, and his dark eyes twinkled as he nodded. "I know that very well, believe me. It turns out that Tom's network has its tentacles in lots of unexpected places. A benefit of a culture that emphasizes strong bonds across extended families, I believe. It would appear that the media experienced certain technical difficulties. Including being mysteriously directed to the wrong location."

Annja laughed. It felt good to do that. Even if it made her feel as if she was being speared through the lungs.

"So here's what we find—fifteen more dead terrorists, nine dead civilians, a delightful and highly photogenic young Native American girl hostage released unharmed. And not a federal agent in sight until it was all over."

"And us no doubt facing a really remarkable array of federal charges," Annja said.

"Well, therein lies the rub. Technically, no doubt, laws were broken. Bent, at the very least. Now imagine, please, presenting defendants to a jury on the basis of crimes committed while combating terrorism, at substantial risk and cost to themselves and their accomplices, defeating those terrorists and returning young Allesandra Ten Bears safely to her mother. And you, as a prosecuting attorney, are asking these twelve good Americans to send those defendants to prison. Would *you* want to be that prosecutor, Ms. Creed?"

She thought about it. Then she laughed until the pain in her chest stole her breath.

"I don't think so."

"Indeed not. It's a truism that jury behavior is unpredictable. And I daresay their reaction would be unpredictable. For example, would they settle simply for acquitting on all charges after seconds of deliberation, or would they physically chase the U.S. Attorney out of the courtroom in an attempt to lynch him? Or her."

All Annja could muster this time was a pained chuckle.

"The Crazy Dogs Who Got Their Wishes to Die did a remarkably comprehensive job of fouling their own den," Montoya said. "Some of them were rogue law-enforcement agents, members in full standing of the national security network who themselves perpetrated some of the most heinous acts of domestic terrorism in America's history, and who came within a hair of taking top place almost within sight of the scene of the Oklahoma City bombing. There's no better way to forfeit the sympathies of an American public who, for better or worse, tend to harbor strong prejudices in favor of the police.

"Surviving members of the group have admitted to engaging in the abduction, torture and murder of various important personages with the Comanche Nation, not to mention a young female reporter and her African-American cameraman, which hasn't endeared them to the Numunu people, nor Oklahomans in general. They have even been accused of luring in a number of noted radicals—black, Latino and antiglobalist activists wanted for a whole spectrum of terrorist acts themselves—and murdering them in some abandoned training facility outside Lawton. That's turned the left and the radical community against them. At this point, the Dog Society could actively improve its image by enlisting Osama bin Laden."

Annja nodded. "I see. But what exactly are you offering me, Mr. Montoya?"

"The same thing all your associates are being offered. That includes the members of the Iron Horse

People Motorcycle Club, as well as a number of acquaintances of the late—and, might I add, highly decorated and widely respected—Oklahoma Highway Patrol officer and homicide investigator, Thomas Ten Bears."

"All right. I'm listening."

"You sign an agreement jointly presented by the Justice department and the Department of Homeland Security, undertaking never to speak, publicly or privately, about the events of the past few days or indeed anything concerning your interactions with the Dog Society, the late Dr. Michel and the kidnapping and rescue of Sallie Ten Bears. Should you all agree to and sign this document, the events will then be classified as secrets vital to national security. If subsequently you do speak of it, you will vanish from the face of the earth instantaneously. I cannot sufficiently emphasize that, regardless of the legalities involved, that *will* happen."

"I believe it," Annja said. "But what do we get?"

"Agreement not to prosecute you or your friends for any acts in any way connected with the events. Any acts, in any way connected. And please believe me, Ms. Creed, when I tell you that this is not an empty promise nor a trick, the way so many plea deals offered to accused persons turn out to be. Notwithstanding the enormous public and official support you and your associates enjoy, the blunt truth is that if the Bureau had not determined that this course was in its own best interests, it would never have assented."

"But that's a cover-up," she said, sitting up straighter. "Of fairly massive proportions."

"Yes to the first," he said. "The second—not so much."

She frowned and shook her head.

He laughed again. "From what I have been able to learn about you, Ms. Creed—and I am thoroughly impressed by it—you are far too intelligent a human being to be surprised by that."

She sighed. "Well. I can't argue with you in this case."

She sat for a moment without speaking. She would've liked to be able to say she was mulling his proposal over. The truth was she was nodding off to sleep.

She caught herself as her chin dropped toward her clavicle. "I suppose this includes anything pertaining to the skinwalker—to Dr. Michel?" she said.

"Yes."

"Doug Morrell will digest the lining of his own stomach. He's my producer on Chasing History's Monsters. But he can deal. Do you happen to know what's been learned about him, by the way? Uh, Dr. Michel, not Doug."

"I can tell you such of it as will eventually be released to the media by the Bureau. It seems agents have gotten their hands on Dr. Michel's journals. He describes everything in what I am told is blood-chilling detail. His sympathy for the plight of Native Americans, his hatred of U.S. cultural imperialism within its own borders as well as abroad, his growing fascination with the Navajo wolf life-way. Plus the horrid rituals, involving much torture, rape and murder whereby he made himself a witch and skinwalker."

Montoya shook his head. "He seems to have come to believe that a sufficient amount of killing would make him immortal."

"From the amount of gunfire he took before he went down," Annja said, "it almost seems he was on to something."

"The chief medical examiner who examined his body made a similar comment off the record, I'm given to understand. Here's an interesting detail. It turns out Dr. Michel was a veteran of the French paratroops, with a certain amount of combat experience, largely in Africa. He only entered medical school after his discharge. He was a skilled martial artist and a fitness fanatic."

"That would explain his strength and speed," she said. But not all of it. And far from everything. She shook her head to clear from behind her eyes the vision of slavering wide-open jaws with nothing remotely human about them. And those blue self-luminous eyes.

"The FBI claims the madman used a classified hallucinogenic military gas, akin to BZ, an agent whose use the U.S. abandoned years ago. He would open canisters upwind or throw grenades loaded with the gas to put his victims in a mild hallucinatory state. One in which they might be receptive to perceiving him as a man-wolf or an actual wolf."

"Huh," Annja said. That struck her as far-fetched. Yet she couldn't help recalling the recurrent sense of wooziness and light-headedness she'd experienced, near and inside the derelict ranch house.

And really, is it nearly as far-fetched as the alternative? she asked herself. Like, he really was a werewolf?

"Agents say they shot a large if scrubby wolf-dog hybrid near the ranch house. They had the impression it had been following Michel. It attacked as technicians were removing the body. They theorize he must've trained the animal to help in his murders."

He leaned back, clasping his hands and tapping the tips of his forefingers together.

"There remain a number of loose ends that I admit puzzle me. For instance, all the wounds inflicted by the skinwalker were consistent with canid teeth and natural claws, not just some. The late Dr. Michel displayed a fortitude worthy of Rasputin simply to survive as long as he did, much less inflict such frightful wounds as the ones he did on Mr. White Bird in that condition. Even extreme fitness and berserk fury can only account for so much. And Mr. White Bird's knife, with which you claim to have finally dispatched the murderer—a feat of truly epic courage, I have to say, Ms. Creed—fails to match the wound that took his life."

He drew a deep breath and sighed. "But these ends, I fear, must remain forever loose. They are the very sort of thing the Bureau has agreed it would be in the national interest to just forget about. *If* you sign the agreement, that is. Will you?"

"Answer me one more thing, if you will, Mr. Montoya."

"If it lies in my power and will not subject me to extraordinary rendition, of course."

"Just how on earth can they can possibly explain all this away?"

He smiled.

"The federal government employs a good many

public relations professionals tasked to provide just such explanations, Ms. Creed," he said. "Believe me, they have most extensive experience."

epilogue

The wind was rising as Annja walked out of a northern exit of the federal courthouse. Its cool caress was welcome on her face, and it felt good as she filled her lungs with it. It even smelled good to her, full as it was with the fumes of just-past-rush-hour exhausts. Because it smelled of freedom.

I didn't know if I'd ever breathe free air again, she thought.

With the muted growl of a powerful V-twin engine a big Indian motorcycle prowled around the corner of Third Street onto Marble, the back street onto which Annja had emerged. The sun, swelling and reddening as it sank behind the skyline of Albuquerque's modest downtown, gave glowing life to its red-and-cream paint job.

The motorcycle pulled to a stop at the curb in front of Annja. Illegally, on the wrong side of the street right behind the federal courthouse. Of course.

Johnny Ten Bears turned to look at Annja. Bending his head forward he pushed a pair of sunglasses down the narrow bridge of his nose.

"They just cutting you loose?" he asked.

"You mean they let you go before me?" she demanded, in partially mock outrage.

He shrugged. He wore a black leather jacket over his colors, she saw. "Hey, you're the famous media personality. You're a lot bigger threat to the FBI's rep than some Injun scooter-trash outlaw like me."

"You have an inflated estimate of my importance," she said with a laugh.

"Not for my family and me," he said seriously. "Either my blood family or the Iron Horse People."

"Thanks. And thank you for your help with…everything."

He looked at her. She looked at him. The sun continued to set.

"Why not climb on?" he asked, patting the leather-covered seat behind him.

"What happens then?"

"We ride away and live happily ever after."

She laughed. It still hurt.

"You think things can possibly go that simply for either one of us?"

"Hell, no. But a body can always hope. So how about it, Annja? Climb on behind me?"

She drew in a sharp breath.

"Thanks," she said, slowly shaking her head. "But I think not. I guess I'm not the kind to ride behind anyone."

He sighed and slumped slightly. George Abell had

given him a far more brutal battering than the false werewolf had given her. Yet he wore his hurts, physical and spiritual, even more lightly than she did. Even though she knew how deeply he grieved for his lost brothers and sisters. And for his father, lost, regained and lost again.

"You're right, I guess," he said. "Problem is, we're both pretty dominant type personalities, no?"

"Yes," she said, slumping with relief so dangerously that she had to snap herself back upright, almost to attention. One way or another she was going to collapse soon. She'd rather do it in the hotel room bed the U.S. government was buying her for the night than on the sidewalk outside the federal courthouse.

"It'd be great at first," she said. "I know that. But give us a few weeks—"

"Yes," he said. "We'd be all up in each other's faces."

"Six months for sure."

"If that."

"Scrapping."

"Fighting."

"Arguing about nothing."

"Right," she said. "You know how it goes."

"'Fraid that I do."

"So."

"So."

Someone walked past her with long confident strides. Mostly stifling an urge to jump, Annja looked around to see Snake heading toward Johnny and his vintage ride. The side of her exotically beautiful face was a big green bruise. Her colors were bulked out by the inflatable body cast that stabilized her broken ribs. Her left arm rode in a camouflage sling. Heaven knew how she'd gotten ahold of that. The skinwalker's assault had broken her ulna.

At the curb she stopped and looked back. "You're pretty good for a white girl, Creed," she said. "But one day you have to learn—sometimes even a warrior woman's gotta know when to ride behind her man."

She swung aboard the bike. Behind Johnny. She carefully wound her arms around his own bruised and battered torso. Johnny shrugged and gunned the engine.

"Happy trails, Annja," he said. "See you."

She raised a hand.

"Bye," she said in a small voice.

With a snarl of the powerful engine Johnny and his warrior woman rode off, into the wilds of downtown Albuquerque, and the red eye of the setting sun.

And Annja, bemused, was left alone.

Again.

TAKE 'EM FREE

2 action-packed novels plus a mystery bonus

NO RISK

NO OBLIGATION TO BUY

JAMES AXLER

DEATH LANDS®

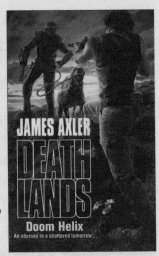

Doom Helix

A new battle for Deathlands has begun...

The Deathlands feudal system may be hell on earth but it must be protected from invaders from Shadow Earth, a parallel world stripped clean of its resources by the ruling conglomerate and its white coats. Ryan and his band had a near-fatal encounter with them once before and now these superhuman predators are back, ready to topple the hellscape's baronies one by one.

Available September wherever books are sold.

James Axler
Outlanders®

OBLIVION STONE

A shocking gambit by a lethal foe intensifies the war to claim planet Earth…

In the wilds of Saskatchewan, a genetically engineered Annunaki prince returns after 4,500 years in solitary confinement to seek vengeance against the father who betrayed him. And his personal mission to harness Earth's citizens to build his city and his army appears unstoppable.…

Available August wherever books are sold.